作者序
Preface

　　保持學習的習慣，自我進修已經成為現代生活的必修項目。其中提升外語能力更是無論幾歲，隨時隨地都可以做的頭腦體操，英文學習資源俯拾皆是，除了系統的訓練，每個人也能探索一些惠而不費的「旁門左道」。譬如提升英文文法的最容易方式，也許是將文法點融合在上下文背景中，透過對自己有意義的故事來做文法練習。

　　這本書摘取了八個重要的英文文法項目，融合在金庸武俠小說人物的描述裡，希望可以透過熟悉的武俠人物，使稍嫌枯燥的文法點變得比較活潑和易於理解。如果有人因為這本書得到些許裨益，作者真是感到萬分的榮幸。

武董

目　次
Contents

⟪ *Unit 1* ⟫

形容詞子句

〖天龍八部〗

文法主題介紹－形容詞子句

形容詞子句即是關係子句，是具有形容詞的功能的句中句，用來修飾前面的名詞或代名詞（稱為先行詞）。引導形容詞子句的主要有關係代名詞和關係副詞。

關係代名詞：兼具連接詞與代名詞的功能，所帶的子句，為形容詞作用，修飾前方的先行詞。

關代為主格(who which that)

🖋 The candidates **who** were late for the interview are not eligible for that position.

關代為受格 (whom which that)

一般情況下可以省略，但前有介系詞不可省。

🖋 Lancer Corporation is the company **which** we look forward to cooperating with.

關代為所有格 (whose)

🖋 Most of the clients whose data got hacked have suffered fraudulent charges.

關係代名詞 *that*

常用 that 作為關代之時機

🖋 先行詞前面有「最高級」

🖋 先行詞包括「人」與「非人」

🖋 先行詞前面有「序數」，如 the first、the last（最後）

- 先行詞前面有 all，no，every，any，the only，the same，the very（正是）
- 疑問句的開頭是 who，which，what 等，常用 that。避免重複

不能用 that 作為關代之時機

- 「介系詞」後面
- 「逗點」的後面
- 先行詞為 people, those（那些人），關係代名詞用 who

關係代名詞 what

- what 本身已含先行詞，句中無先行詞出現時用 what。
- what 之後的關係子句內，缺主詞或是受詞，是不完整的子句。
- what 所帶的句子，用法與名詞子句相同。

關係副詞 (where when why how)

- 關係副詞＝介系詞＋關係代名詞，具有副詞與連接詞的功用。
- 完整的子句：關係副詞後為完整的子句。
- 不應再有介系詞：其所帶的形容詞子句前不應再有介系詞。先行詞可以省略。

 ## 武俠人物 1 - Duan Yu (段譽)

MP3 01

Duan Yu (段譽) was born in the royal family of Dali. He was a kind-hearted person with a Buddhism belief. Meanwhile, Duan Yu avoided competition; he also disliked martial art and fighting. As a prince, he had many good qualities like well educated, knowledgeable, well mannered, honest, and considerate.

段譽出生於大理皇室。他篤信佛法，心地慈悲。段譽避免和人競爭，也不愛學武，反感打殺。作為大理皇世子，他受到了良好教育，知書達禮，誠實，並常替他人著想。

The process of Duan's martial arts learning was a serial of coincidences. He accidentally entered 'Langhuan Paradise' (瑯環福地) and learned two powerful kung fu from a jade statue: Magic Power of the Northern Sea (北冥神功) and Slide over the Water (凌波微步). Magic Power of the Northern Sea was a superior inner force that could absorb and convert opponents' power and use them freely. The power is described as the northern sea, which is broad and limitless. Duan has unintentionally absorbed power from several people; he also incautiously swallowed a venomous frog that made him free from all toxic elements.

段譽的武功學習過程都很偶然。他誤入「瑯環福地」，從一尊玉像習得逍遙派兩大神功：「北冥神功」和「凌波微步」。其中北冥神功是上乘內功，可以吸收化用他人的內力。這種力量被形容為寬廣無邊的北冥。段譽在不知情的狀況下用北冥神功吸納了很多人的功力。還意外吞食一隻劇毒青蛙令他變得百毒不侵。

Slide over the Water is a Ching Gung (輕功) acrobatics from the

Peripatetic Sect (逍遙派). The gait follows Yi-Jing Hexagram, which allows a person to dodge with unconstrained style. Duan flees with Slide over the Water whenever he encounters danger. Only when he has to protect others, Duan Yu could overcome his cowardice and engage in fighting.

凌波微步是逍遙派的輕功步法，依照周易六十四卦方位走步，使人可以自由閃躲。段譽遇到危險時常用凌波微步逃跑。只有在保護別人的時候他才會戰勝懦弱，與人交手。

The Six Pulse Sword (六脈神劍) is an unique skill in Duan's family; the skill transforms internal power to fingers that perform as a shapeless sword and harms enemies without contact. Duan Yu learned this in Tienlong Temple when conflicted with Tibetan Monk Jiu Mozhi (鳩摩智). Because of these skills, Duan Yu became the top martial arts master.

六脈神劍是大理段氏的獨特技藝，可以將內力運用到手指，猶如一把無形的劍隔空傷敵。天龍寺大戰鳩摩智時段譽學會了六脈神劍。段譽因為這三種神功成為頂尖高手。

 文法解析

 KEY 1

 The power is described as the northern sea, which is broad and limitless.

天龍八部
鹿鼎記
笑傲江湖
雪山飛狐
神鵰俠侶
射鵰英雄傳
連城訣 碧血劍
書劍恩仇錄

❌ The power is described as the northern sea, <u>that</u> is broad and limitless.

✦中譯✦ 這種力量被形容為寬廣無邊的北冥。

✦解析✦ 關係代名詞 **that** 不可以放在逗點後面。

 KEY 2

⭕ He also incautiously swallowed a venomous frog <u>that</u> made him free from all toxic elements.

❌ He also incautiously swallowed a venomous frog made him free from all toxic elements.

✦中譯✦ 他也意外吞食一隻劇毒青蛙令他變得百毒不侵。

✦解析✦ 關係代名詞 **that** 在形容詞子句中做主詞，不能省略。

 KEY 3

⭕ The gait follows Yi-Jing Hexagram, <u>which</u> allows person to dodge with unconstrained style.

❌ The gait follows Yi-Jing Hexagram, <u>who</u> allows person to dodge with unconstrained style.

✦中譯✦ 步法依照周易六十四卦，使人可以自由閃躲。

✦解析✦ 關係代名詞連接事物而不是人，所以用 **which**。

武俠人物 2 - Xiao Feng (蕭峰)

MP3
02

Xiao Feng (蕭峰) is a tall and strong man with heavy features. The hardship in his life gave him a rough look and dignified temperament. Xiao Feng's kung fu is the best of his time. He used to learn martial arts in Shaolin Temple, and then he joined the Beggars' Sect and became the leader. His predecessor had assigned him multiple tasks to verify his loyalty since Xiao Feng was ethnically from Khidan, which was the enemy of Han nationality by then. Xiao Feng made many achievements for the Sect and made himself a famous person in the martial arts world.

　　蕭峰身材魁偉，輪廓清晰，艱苦生活給了他飽經風霜的面容和威嚴的氣質。蕭峰在武功方面是當世絕頂高手之一。曾經在少林寺習武，後來加入丐幫並成為幫主。前代幫主因為蕭峰來自漢族當時的敵人契丹，所以指派他很多任務以考驗他的忠誠度。蕭峰不僅為丐幫立下許多功勞，也是領導中原武林的大人物。

Xiao Feng experienced many tragedies. His foster parents and master in Shaolin Temple were killed; then he was framed as the murderer and repelled by everyone. He was looking for the 'Big Brother' who set all the plots on him, but misled by someone and killed his Fiancée by accident. Xiao Feng became seriously traumatized after knowing the truth. He went to his hometown the Khitan Khanate and helped the king to cease a coup. <u>Eventually, he committed suicide in front of the Yanmen Pass (雁門關), which is the frontier between Song and Khitan.</u> He prayed the two countries could cease-fire and coexist in peace.

蕭峰經歷了許多悲劇。他的養父母和師父都被殺害，還被冤枉為兇手，受到所有人的排斥。在尋找陷害他的帶頭大哥時，蕭峰被人誤導失手殺害了未婚妻。他得知真相後精神受到打擊。蕭峰回到了他的家鄉遼國並幫助消弭了政變。蕭峰最後在宋遼邊界雁門關前自殺，他希望兩國可以和平相處，不再戰爭。

The heroic image of Xiaofeng seems rough, but he is actually meticulous and prudent. He had little ambition but dreamed to live a peaceful life with A'zhu as a flockmaster.

蕭峰外表看似粗獷，但心思縝密，做事穩重。他雖然身為豪傑卻沒有企圖心，希望能夠和阿朱過與世無爭的放牧生活。

Eighteen Dragon Subduing Palms(降龍十八掌) and Dog Beating Stick Technique (打狗棒法) are Xiaofeng's major kung fu skills. Dog Beating Stick Technique has a subtle variation of movements and hands down from each generation of the Beggars' Sect leader. Eighteen Dragon Subduing Palms is both rigid and soft; it has formidable power with simple movements.

蕭峰的武功絕學是降龍十八掌和打狗棒法。其中打狗棒法是丐幫幫主世代相傳的武功，變化精妙；降龍十八掌剛柔兼濟，招式簡單但功力深厚。

文法解析

 KEY 4

 His predecessor had assigned him multiple tasks to verify his loyalty since Xiao Feng was ethnically from Khidan, <u>which was</u> the enemy of Han nationality by then.

 His predecessor had assigned him multiple tasks to verify his loyalty since Xiao Feng was ethnically from Khidan, <u>which it was</u> the enemy of Han nationality by then.

✦中譯✦ 前代幫主因為蕭峰來自漢族當時的敵人契丹，所以指派他很多任務以考驗他的忠誠度。

✦解析✦ 關係代名詞本身兼具連接詞和代名詞功能，子句中不需要 it 做主詞。

 KEY 5

 He was looking for the 'Big Brother' <u>who</u> set all the plots on him; but misled by someone and killed his Fiancee.

天龍八部

鹿鼎記

笑傲江湖

雪山飛狐

神鵰俠侶

射鵰英雄傳

連城訣　碧血劍

書劍恩仇錄

He was looking for the 'Big Brother' <u>which</u> set all the plots on him; but misled by someone and killed his Fiancee.

◆中譯◆ 在尋找陷害他的帶頭大哥時，蕭峰被人誤導失手殺害了未婚妻。

◆解析◆ 先行詞為人，故關係代名詞要用 who。

KEY 6

○ Eventually, he committed suicide in front of the Yamen Pass, <u>which</u> is the frontier between Song and Khitan.

✕ Eventually, he committed suicide in front of the Yamen Pass which is the frontier between Song and Khitan.

◆中譯◆ 蕭峰最後在宋遼邊界雁門關前自殺。

◆解析◆ 當形容詞子句也是額外的補充說明，即使刪除子句也不影響主句的意思時，形容詞子句的前面要加上逗號，標示非限定子句。

 武俠人物 3 - Xu Zhu (虛竹) MP3 03

Xu Zhu (虛竹) is also a main character in "Demi-Gods and Semi-Devils". He is dull, honest, and ugly-looking guy with poor eloquence. Xu Zhu grew up at the Shaolin Temple as a little monk, and then was kidnapped by the Constellation Cult. He solved a complex tsumego and became apprentice of Wu Yazi (無崖子), who is the leader of Peripatetic Sect. He gained profound power from his mentor, including Magic Power of the Northern Sea and the Unseen Power (小無相功). Later in an icy cellar in Tungusen, he received the inner force from the Maiden of Mt. Heaven (天山童姥) and Lee Chiushui (李秋水). Two unique skills were passed to Xu Zhu: the Plum Strike (天山折梅手) and the Six-strength Slam (天山六陽掌).

虛竹也是《天龍八部》中的主要角色。他的性格木訥老實，相貌醜陋且不善言辭。虛竹自幼就是少林寺小僧，偶然被星宿派綁架。他破解了圍棋棋局，成為了逍遙派掌門人無崖子的徒弟。虛竹從老師那邊得到深厚功力，其中包含北冥神功以及小無相功。後來在西夏冰窖又因為天山童姥大戰李秋水而得到她們的內力。虛竹又因此得到兩大絕招天山折梅手和天山六陽掌。

Among Xu Zhu's kung fu skills: the Unseen Power can mimic movements from the opponents and fight back; the Plum Strike is a combination of palm method, joint locking, and flexibly using different weapons; the Six-strength Slam focuses on attacking enemy's Achilles heel; the Life-death Talisman is a grim concealed weapon which makes victims suffer from extreme pain and pruritus. Without an antidote, they would rather die. The Maiden of Mt. Heaven uses this to control her subordinates. Xu Zhu kindly broke the curse and saved

天龍八部

鹿鼎記

笑傲江湖

雪山飛狐

神鵰俠侶

射鵰英雄傳

碧血劍連城訣

書劍恩仇錄

everyone after he got power.

虛竹有幾項厲害的功夫：小無相功可以模仿別人的招式與對方較量；天山折梅手綜合了掌法、擒拿法以及活用刀劍等兵刃；天山六陽掌專攻要害；生死符是一種可怕的暗器，令中招者遭受劇痛和奇癢，如果沒有解藥寧願不要活。天山童姥以此挾持下屬聽命，虛竹在掌握權力後解除了這些人的符咒。

Xu Zhu has to do the very things that are against his will, such as breaking his religious taboos, learning martial arts, fighting and killing, and accepting power. His experience is full of adventures and contradictions.

虛竹不得不做那些違反他本性的事：包括放棄僧人的戒律、學習武功、打鬥殺人和接受權力。他的經歷可以說是奇遇不斷也充滿了矛盾。

 文法解析

 KEY 7

He solved a complex I-go puzzle and became an apprentice of Wu Yazi (無崖子), <u>who</u> is the leader of Peripatetic Sect.

He solved a complex I-go puzzle and became an apprentice of Wu Yazi (無崖子), <u>that</u> is the leader of Peripatetic Sect.

✦中譯✦ 他破解了圍棋棋局，成為了逍遙派掌門人無崖子的徒弟。

✦解析✦ 先行詞為人，關係代名詞要用 who。

 KEY 8

○ The Life-death Talisman is a grim concealed weapon <u>which</u> makes victims suffer from extreme pain and pruritus.

✗ The Life-death Talisman is a grim concealed weapon, <u>which</u> makes victims suffer from extreme pain and pruritus.

✦中譯✦ 生死符是一種可怕的暗器，令中招者遭受劇痛和奇癢。

✦解析✦ 先行詞 weapon＋which 引導的限定性形容詞子句，不應該加逗點。

 KEY 9

○ Xu Zhu has to do the very things <u>that</u> are against his will, such as breaking his religious taboos, learning martial arts, fighting and killing, and accepting power.

✗ Xu Zhu has to do the very things <u>which</u> are against his will, such as breaking his religious taboos, learning martial arts, fighting and killing, and accepting power.

天龍八部

鹿鼎記

笑傲江湖

雪山飛狐

神鵰俠侶

射鵰英雄傳

連城訣
碧血劍

書劍恩仇錄

✦中譯✦　虛竹不得不做與他本性正相反的事情：包括放棄僧人的戒
　　　　律，學習武功，打鬥殺人，和接受權力。

✦解析✦　先行詞前面有 all，no，every，any，the only，the
　　　　same，the very 時，關係代名詞用 that。

武俠人物 4 - Murong Fu (慕容復) MP3 04

Murong Fu (慕容復) is a reputed Kung fu master and nicknamed the "Southern Murong". He is equally respected as Xiao Feng the leader of Beggars' Sect. The fighting style of the Murong family is described as: returning back with your own way. He adopted the master skill of Star Orbit from his clan, which uses opponents' signature moves against themselves. No matter what movement the opponent used, the harm would reflect back to the opponent himself. He can brandish sword uninterrupted like drifting clouds. However, with a handsome look that covers his dark side, his personality shows malicious and treacherous side of him.

　　慕容復號稱「南慕容」，是和蕭峰齊名的武功高手。慕容家武功的風格被描述為：以彼之道，還施彼身。他繼承家傳絕招斗轉星移，用對手的典型招式回擊。不論對方施出何種功夫來，都能將力道反擊到對方自身。慕容劍法招式連綿不絕，行雲流水。然而，他帥氣的外表卻掩蓋了他性格中惡毒和奸詐的黑暗面。

Murong is a descendant of the royal family of the Yan states in the Sixteen Kingdoms era. He dreams to restore the Yan Kingdom. (In his name, "Fu" has the meaning of revival). To become the emperor, he learns different kinds of Kung fu. His cousin Wang Yuyan (王語嫣) who has a retentive memory adores him; she reads lots of kung fu notes to help him enhance his skills. Murong takes advantage of her to improve himself.

　　慕容復是十六國時期燕國皇室的後代，他心目中的宏大理想就是復興燕國（他的名字有復興的意思）。為了變成皇帝，他學習各門派的武功。他好記性的表妹王語嫣因為喜歡他，熟讀各路武功秘笈幫助他提高技藝。慕容復則利用了王語嫣的幫助自我提升。

Before his unscrupulous side had been revealed, he used to collaborate with people fighting the evils. However, he gradually became isolated. His reputation dented after fighting Duan Yu, whose kung fu skills were far superior. Duan had an upper hand on the situation and saved Murong's life, but when Murong seized the chance, he gave Duan Yu a fatal attack. To achieve the ultimate goal, Murong resorted to every method. He clung to those in power. He tried to become the Emperor's son-in-law in Tungusen and persuaded his cousin Wang to commit suicide because of that. He coveted the crown of Dali Emperor and killed his loyal followers. Eventually, all his plots failed and he became insane.

天龍八部

鹿鼎記

笑傲江湖

雪山飛狐

神鵰俠侶

射鵰英雄傳

連城訣

碧血劍

書劍恩仇錄

在他不道德的一面暴露之前，慕容復曾經與人合作共同對抗江湖上的邪惡勢力。但是他後來漸漸眾叛親離，尤其是被武功更強的段譽大戰後名聲掃地。段譽佔上風而手下留情，慕容復卻把握機會給段譽致命一擊。他為了復興事業不擇手段，千方百計依附權勢。為了成為西夏駙馬，王語嫣因此而自殺；覬覦大理王位而殺害忠心耿耿的下屬。最終他因為所有的計謀都未得逞而精神錯亂。

文法解析

KEY 10

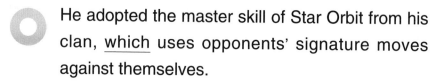

He adopted the master skill of Star Orbit from his clan, <u>which</u> uses opponents' signature moves against themselves.

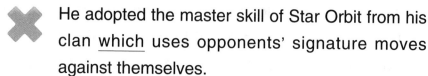

He adopted the master skill of Star Orbit from his clan <u>which</u> uses opponents' signature moves against themselves.

✦中譯✦ 他繼承家傳絕招斗轉星移，用對手的典型招式回擊。

✦解析✦ Which 引導了非限定性形容詞子句，先行詞是 the master skill of Star Orbit，不是 his clan。因而不可以刪除逗點。

KEY 11

His cousin Wang Yuyan <u>who</u> has a retentive memory adores him; she reads lots of kung fu notes to help him enhancing his skills.

His cousin Wang Yuyan <u>which</u> has a retentive memory adores him; she reads lots of kung fu notes to help him enhancing his skills.

✦中譯✦ 他好記性的表妹王語嫣因為喜歡他，熟讀各路武功秘笈幫助他提高技藝。

✦解析✦ 先行詞為人，關係代名詞要用 who。

 KEY 12

⭕ His reputation dented after fighting Duan Yu, <u>whose</u> kung fu skill is far superior.

❌ His reputation dented after fighting Duan Yu, <u>who</u> kung fu skill is far superior.

✦中譯✦ 他在與武功更強的段譽大戰後名聲掃地。

✦解析✦ 此處的關係代名詞要用所有格。

武俠人物 5 - Wang Yuyan (王語嫣) *MP3* *05*

Wang Yuyan (王語嫣) is a beautiful young maiden who grew up in Camellia Garden with her mother. She had a crush on her cousin Murong and tried to do everything that could possibly win his affection. Wang does not know any kung fu herself, but she memorized all kinds of martial arts esotericas in the hope of assisting her cousin to perfect his skills. Her comprehension and savvy for kung fu manuscripts are so excellent that she is

天龍八部

鹿鼎記

笑傲江湖

雪山飛狐

神鵰俠侶

射鵰英雄傳

連城訣 碧血劍

書劍恩仇錄

able to identify various types of martial arts by observation, and provide tips to Murong during the fight.

王語嫣是位漂亮的少女，一直與母親生活在曼陀山莊。她很喜歡表哥慕容復，為了獲得他的鍾愛她願意做任何事。王語嫣不諳功夫，但為了表哥可以增進武功，她記誦了各式武學秘笈。她對武學典籍有很好的記性和悟性，在許多場合看破各種武功招式，幫助慕容復克敵制勝。

<u>Wang lived in an enclosed environment where she did not have to deal with reality</u>. Therefore, she was naive and gentle, had a refined temperament, and was freed from vulgarity. Her adoration to Murong is sincere and persistent, even though he did not appreciate her help and treatd her coldly.

王語嫣成長在封閉的環境，從不接觸複雜的現實。所以她天真溫柔，氣質脫俗，不食人間煙火。她對表哥的感情非常真摯執著，雖然她的付出始終得不到回報。

Duan Yu fell in love with her at the first sight; he admires her as his fairy tale princess. But Wang tried to keep herself apart from Duan Yu because she loves Murong Fu. When she left the Camellia Garden to find her cousin; Duan Yu followed her everywhere and saved her life many times. Wang Yuyan finally realized Murong's only priority was his dream of restoring his kingdom. He pursued a political marriage to Princess Yin-Chuan and abandoned Wang without any hesitation. Wang was disappointed and attempted suicide. Fortunately, Duan Yu saved her again, eventually she was deeply touched and they lived happily ever after.

　　段譽對王語嫣一見鍾情並把她當作神仙姐姐。但是王語嫣因為心有所屬只好與他保持距離。王語嫣離開曼陀山莊出外尋找表哥，段譽一直跟著她並且多次救她。王語嫣最後明白了慕容復唯一考量是興復大燕，他追尋與銀川公主的政治婚姻毫不考慮的拋棄王語嫣。王感到失望且試圖自殺。幸而又得到段譽搭救，她終於深受感動和段譽之後過著幸福快樂的日子。

文法解析

KEY 13

 She has a crush on her cousin Murong and tries to do everything <u>that</u> could possibly win his affection.

 She has a crush on her cousin Murong and tries to do everything <u>which</u> could possibly win his affection.

 中譯 她很喜歡表哥慕容復，為了獲得他的鍾愛她願意做任何事。

◆解析◆ 先行詞時是 everything，關係代名詞用 that。

KEY 14

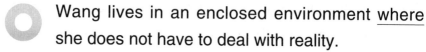

○ Wang lives in an enclosed environment <u>where</u> she does not have to deal with reality.

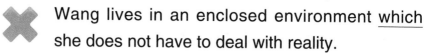

✗ Wang lives in an enclosed environment <u>which</u> she does not have to deal with reality.

◆中譯◆ 王語嫣成長在封閉的環境，從不接觸複雜的現實。

◆解析◆ 先行詞之後接表示地點的關係副詞，where＝in which。 Where 後面是一個完整的子句。

 武俠人物 6 - You Tanzhi (游坦之) MP3 *06*

You Tanzhi (游坦之) is a special master in "Demi-Gods and Semi-Devils". <u>He is the heir of the Heroes Gathering Manor that hosts a meeting against Xiao Feng after he was suspected of committing several murders.</u> You's father was defeated by Xiao Feng and committed suicide in shame, bringing about his ingrained hatred towards Xiao Feng. He attempted to kill Xiao Feng but was captured by A'zi (阿紫). During the period of imprisonment, he was tortured and disfigured. A'zi tormented him for her amusement; used him as the bait of poisonous bugs to practice her vicious skills. She left him to die after he was intoxicated and paralysed. <u>Luckily, he used techniques from Channel-changing Scripture which purged the poison from his body.</u> You Tanzhi was deeply in love with A'zi; he returned to her repeatedly but was always cruelly treated. He is still willingly to become her entertainment.

　　游坦之是天龍八部中的一位另類高手，他本是聚賢莊的少爺，聚賢莊在蕭峰被懷疑殺害多人後主辦了反蕭峰大會。他的父親被蕭峰打敗後羞愧自殺，因而他對蕭峰產生了仇恨。他曾為報仇去偷襲蕭峰，被阿紫捉住折磨並毀容。阿紫折磨他取樂，罔顧游坦之死活，練習邪門武功拿他當作毒蟲誘餌，還在他中毒癱瘓後拋棄他。幸得游坦之用了易筋經自行解毒。他對阿紫非常傾慕，他幾次三番回到阿紫身邊，卻總被殘忍對待，但他還是甘心取悅阿紫。

You Tanzhi was manipulated and became the new leader of the Beggars' Sect after Xiao Feng. His inability to perform Dragon-strike Palms and Dog-Beating Stick Techniques had aroused doubts of his leadership status. Seeing A'zi was threatened by villain Ding Chunqiu (丁春秋) of Constellation Sect, he kneeled down and called Ding 'master'. Therefore, he was denounced as a traitor of the Beggars' Sect. Although A'zi was blind (after being poisoned), You still followed her everywhere and took care of her. He offered his own eyes to help her regain sight. Sadly, he did not win any sympathy from her and was abandoned after she could see again. In the end, A'zi hugged Xiao Feng's body and jumped from the top of the cliff. Before that, she dug out her eyes and 'returned' them to You Tanzhi. You's infatuation led him to commit suicide after A'zi.

天龍八部

鹿鼎記

笑傲江湖

雪山飛狐

神鵰俠侶

射鵰英雄傳

碧血劍連城訣

書劍恩仇錄

游坦之在丐幫大會中被陰謀利用，並成為蕭峰的後任幫主。但他不會降龍十八掌和打狗棒法使得他幫主的領導地位受到質疑。又為了阿紫向星宿派惡人丁春秋下跪拜師，背叛丐幫被人鄙視。雖然阿紫雙眼被毒瞎，游坦之仍待在她身邊照顧，甚至為她犧牲自己雙眼，但阿紫雙眼復原後立刻棄他而去。最後阿紫抱著蕭峰的屍身跳下懸崖，自殺之前，她把雙目挖出來還給游坦之。游坦之癡情的追隨阿紫跳崖自殺。

 文法解析

 KEY 15

○ He is the heir of the Heroes Gathering Manor that hosts a meeting against Xiao Feng after he was suspected of committing murders.

✗ He is the heir of the Heroes Gathering Manor where hosts a meeting against Xiao Feng after he was suspected of committing murders.

✦中譯✦ 他是聚賢莊的少爺，聚賢莊在蕭峰被懷疑殺害多人後主辦了反蕭峰大會。

✦解析✦ 關係副詞 where 之後應該接一個完整的子句，所以此處的正確用法是關係代名詞 that。

 KEY 16

Luckily, he used techniques form Channel-changing Scripture which purged the poison from his body.

Luckily, he used techniques form Channel-changing Scripture <u>by which</u> purged the poison from his body.

◆中譯◆ 幸而游坦之用了易筋經自行解毒。

◆解析◆ **Which** 作為形容詞子句的主詞引導子句，**by which** 不能起名詞的作用當主詞。

 ## 武俠人物 7 - Jiumozhi (鳩摩智)

 MP3 *07*

Jiumozhi (鳩摩智) is a villain in the "Demi-Gods and Semi-Devils". He is also one of the top kung fu masters in the novel. He comes form Dalun Monastery in Tibet Snow Mountain. As a reputable monk, he is well-versed in both Dharma and martial arts; and serves as the advisor of the Tibetan monarchy. <u>Jiumozhi's unique skill is the Flame Blade, which condenses and discharges inner power through palms, making opponents unable to predict and react.</u>

　　鳩摩智是《天龍八部》中的反派人物，也是頂級高手之一。來自吐蕃大雪山大輪寺，精通佛法和武學，被吐蕃國國王冊封為國師。鳩摩智的絕招是「火燄刀」，能將內力凝結在手掌送出，使對手無法預測和反應。

He was obsessed with becoming the most powerful martial artist. He went to Dali, attempting to snatch the Six Pulse

Sword manual from the Heavenly Dragon Monastery. Six eminent monks in the temple used synergy skills to defeat him; but the sword manual was destroyed during the fight. He kidnapped Duan Yu who had practiced the script during the fight and forced him to write it down. But eventually, Duan successfully escaped.

他癡迷於稱霸武林。為了這個目的，他前往大理國搶奪「六脈神劍」的秘笈。天龍寺六大高僧合力將他打敗，導致劍譜被毀。他擄走了背下劍譜的段譽，強迫他默寫。但還是被段譽逃走。

Jiumozhi showed up in Shaolin Temple later and vanquished all monks by using seventy-two arts of Shaolin. He compelled Shaolin monks to surrender themselves to Tibet, but Xu Zhu found out the kung fu he used was actually the Unseen Power from Peripatetic Sect rather than Shaolin skills. Jiu Mozhi fought with Xu Zhu but did not win.

鳩摩智後來又出現於少林寺，他使出「少林七十二絕技」打敗了所有僧人，強迫少林眾僧臣服吐蕃。卻被虛竹識破鳩摩智使用的是逍遙派的「小無相功」，鳩摩智與虛竹大戰沒有取勝。

Jiumozhi was arrogant and cunning, always carrying out sneak attacks. He was too greedy to learn different skills and almost died from an inner energy imbalance from compulsive training. Duan Yu saved his life by draining out his energy that was out of control. Despite losing everything, Jiumozhi finally repented and returned to good; he went back to Buddhist practice.

鳩摩智高傲且心機深重，時常對人偷襲暗算。他貪婪學習太多武功，幾乎死於強練武功導致的內力失調。段譽吸走了他失控的內力救他一命。雖然武功盡失，鳩摩智因此徹悟，改邪歸正，回歸佛教。

 文法解析

 KEY 17

 Jiu Mozhi's unique skill is the Flame Blade, <u>which condenses and discharges</u> inner power through palms, making opponents unable to predict and react.

 Jiu Mozhi's unique skill is the Flame Blade, <u>which condense and discharge</u> inner power through palms, making opponents unable to predict and react.

✦中譯✦ 鳩摩智的絕招是「火燄刀」，能將內力凝結在手掌送出，使對手無法預測和反應。

✦解析✦ 先行詞是單數名詞，關係代名詞做主詞，形容詞子句中的動詞要和主詞一致，寫成第三人稱單數形式。

天龍八部

鹿鼎記

笑傲江湖

雪山飛狐

神鵰俠侶

射鵰英雄傳

連城訣 碧血劍

書劍恩仇錄

KEY 18

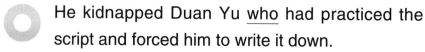

⭕ He kidnapped Duan Yu <u>who</u> had practiced the script and forced him to write it down.

❌ He kidnapped Duan Yu, <u>who</u> had practiced the script and forced him to write it down.

✦ 中譯 ✦ 他擄走了背下劍譜的段譽，強迫他默寫。

✦ 解析 ✦ 因為要強調段譽是背下來劍譜的那個人，所以是限定性形容詞子句，不能加逗點。

KEY 19

⭕ Duan Yu saved his life by draining out his energy <u>that</u> was out of control.

❌ Duan Yu saved his life by draining out his energy <u>what</u> was out of control.

✦ 中譯 ✦ 段譽吸走了他失控的內力救他一命。

✦ 解析 ✦ What 等於先行詞＋關係代名詞，後接不完整的句子。這個句子有先行詞 energy 所以不能用 what。

 武俠人物 8 - Ding Chunqiu (丁春秋) MP3 *08*

The old guy with white hair Ding Chunqiu (丁春秋) is a wicked character. His typical image is holding a goose feather fan and attired like a smart looking celestial. His followers flattered him as the Saint of Constellation Sect, while others are sicked of his shameless behaviors and nicknamed him "old freak".

　　白老翁丁春秋是一位惡質人物。他的典型形象是手持鵝毛扇，裝扮如同神仙。門下弟子吹捧他為「星宿老仙」，外人都鄙視他的無恥行徑，稱之為「老怪」。

He was a former apprentice of Peripatetic Sect leader Wuyazi (無崖子). He betrayed his master, poisoned him, and threw him off the cliff. Then he established his own cult the Constellation Sect, which is notorious for researching toxicology and poison-based martial arts. Ding Chunqiu practiced in the sorcery of dissolving power: implanting toxins that paralyze people and break their inner meridians. This evil kung fu is a variation from Peripatetic Sect's original Magic Power of the Northern Sea. His wicked deeds made himself and his group abhorred by the whole world.

　　丁春秋本是逍遙派掌門無崖子的弟子，他背叛師門，向老師下毒並將其打落懸崖。後來他自創了邪教星宿派，以研究毒物學和投毒的武功而臭名昭著。丁春秋專精於巫術化功大法：能向人體植入劇毒，令人手腳麻痺，經絡斷裂。是逍遙派北冥神功演化而來的邪功，武林人士無不深惡痛絕這一邪術。

Ding committed innumerable murders. He enjoyed being flattered; hence, all his followers are good at licking his shoes. Whenever he showed up, there would be victims. Ding used

天龍八部

鹿鼎記

笑傲江湖

雪山飛狐

神鵰俠侶

射鵰英雄傳

連城訣碧血劍

書劍恩仇錄

the 'Three Laughter Xiaoyao Powder' to poison his fellow apprentice and Shaolin abbot to death; he tried to intoxicate Murong Fu, but the poison was transferred to the bodies of his disciples instead because Murong used master skills to convert the poison back, he also blinded A'zi. Xu Zhu, who used the Plum Strike and the Six-strength Slam of the Peripatetic Sect, eventually defeated him. Ding was inferior and implanted with the Life-Death Talisman. The members of the Constellation Sect were imprisoned in Shaolin Temple and sorted for reforming.

丁春秋殺人如麻，且最愛聽人阿諛奉承，因此星宿派弟子都有拍馬屁的習慣。他一出現就會有人受害：他用「三笑逍遙散」毒死同門師兄和少林方丈；和慕容復對決時被對方使用「斗轉星移」，將毒害轉移回到了星宿派門徒身上；又毒瞎阿紫雙眼。丁春秋最後被同樣使用逍遙派天山折梅手和天山六陽掌的虛竹打敗。丁春秋武力不逮，被"生死符"降服。星宿派也被送入少林寺整合。

 文法解析

 KEY 20

 Then he established his own cult the Constellation Sect, which is notorious on researching toxicology and poison-based martial arts.

Then he established his own cult the Constellation Sect, <u>that</u> is notorious on researching toxicology and poison-based martial arts.

✦中譯✦　後來他自創了邪教星宿派，以研究毒物學和投毒的武功而臭名昭著。

✦解析✦　That 做關係代名詞，不能接在逗點後面。

KEY 21

○ Xu Zhu, who also used the Plum Strike and the Six-strength Slam of the Peripatetic Sect, eventually defeated him.

✕ Xu Zhu, whom also used the Plum Strike and the Six-strength Slam of the Peripatetic Sect, eventually defeated him.

✦中譯✦　他最後被同樣使用逍遙派天山折梅手和天山六陽掌的虛竹打敗。

✦解析✦　關係代名詞在形容詞子句中做主詞，所以用主格。

武俠人物 9 - The Maiden of Mt. Heaven (天山童姥)

MP3
09

The Maiden of Mt. Heaven (天山童姥) from the Peripatetic Sect is the ruler of Lingjiu Palace. She leads four attendants named Plum, Orchid, Chrysanthemum, and Bamboo. The Maiden has remarkable medical skills. <u>She practiced kung fu that leads to</u>

immortality since her childhood. Although her power increases gradually, the side effect was that her appearance remained as a six-year-old girl status. The Maiden practiced in the Plum Strike and the Six-strength Slam for self-defence purpose.

天山童姥是逍遙派弟子，靈鷲宮主人。下屬有梅、蘭、竹和菊四位仕女。童姥醫術高明。她自幼練習長生不老神功，雖然功力增長，但副作用是她的外貌停留在六歲女童的模樣。童姥專研天山折梅手和天山六陽掌作為防身神功。

The Maiden and her junior apprentice Lee Chiushui (李秋水) fell in love with the same person and hatred grew between them Lee set a plot while the Maiden was practicing at a very crucial moment, which made her unable to grow up forever. In return, the Maiden disfigured Lee. Animosity between the two lasted through their life.

天山童姥由於和師妹李秋水愛上了同一個人而成為宿敵。李秋水曾在童姥練功關鍵時刻設計陷害她，使她永遠無法長大作為報復，童姥也將李秋水毀容。兩人一生對彼此保持敵意。

The Maiden implanted the Lords of the 36 Caves and 72 Islands with the Life-death Talisman. The poisoned person relays on the Maiden's antidote which could temporarily ease their symptoms. These lords of caves and islands could not further tolerate her cruelty and decided to rebel; they kidnapped her when the Maiden was at her weakness. They forced her to release them from the Talisman. Xu Zhu as an innocent third party saved the Maiden and protected her from the rebels.

　　她為了控制靈鷲宮三十六洞主、七十二島主，為他們種下生死符，中毒的人仰賴童姥發放的緩解症狀的解藥。那些洞島主無法忍受童姥的殘忍行徑決定反抗，他們在童姥的虛弱時刻擒獲了她，迫使她解除生死符。不知情的虛竹把童姥從叛亂中解救了出來。

In the reward for his help, The Maiden taught Xu Zhu martial arts of Peripatetic Sect. Before the Maiden reached completeness of her practice, her old enemy Lee found her in the icy cellar. They had an intense fight and both were exhausted to death. Both of their life-long power was transferred to Xu Zhu.

　　作為感謝，童姥將逍遙派武功傳授給虛竹。在她自己練功即將圓滿之際，宿敵李秋水找到了她藏身的冰窖。二人打鬥到最後同歸於盡，她們的畢生功力全部傳到了虛竹身上。

文法解析

KEY 22

　　She practiced kung fu <u>that</u> leads to immortality since her youth.

She practiced kung fu leads to immortality since her youth.

✦中譯✦ 她自幼練習長生不老神功。

✦解析✦ 關係代名詞 that 做子句的主詞，不能省略。

KEY 23

⭕ The poisoned person relays on the Maiden's antidote which could temporarily ease their symptoms.

❌ The poisoned person relays on the Maiden's antidote temporarily ease their symptoms.

✦中譯✦ 中毒的人仰賴童姥發放的緩解症狀的解藥。

✦解析✦ 錯誤的例句是有兩個動詞的並列句，不是主句和子句的關係。

 武俠人物 10 - A'zhu (阿朱) MP3 10

A'zhu is the elder daughter of the Dali Prince Duan Zhengchun (段正淳) and one of his lovers Ruan Xingzhu (阮星竹). Duan has romantic relationships with many partners, and A'zhu was abandoned by her mother. She initially served in the Murong family, where she developed her talent of disguise.

阿朱是大理皇儲段正淳與阮星竹的長女。段正淳女友很多，而阿朱

從小就被母親棄養。她原本是在慕容家服務，在那裡她開發了易容術的才能。

A'zhu's story in the novel is mainly a romantic affair with Xiao Feng. To assist Murong Fu in learning different kung fu skills, she disguised herself as a monk and infiltrated into Shaolin Temple to steal martial arts manuals. Xiao Feng went to Shaolin at the same time to seek for the truth of his parents' death. They were both discovered and besieged. A'zhu was seriously injured during the fight, and Xiao Feng took her to escape. He used inner energy to preserve her life and brought her to the best doctor to heal her wounds. This was risky because Xiao Feng was a hatred target at the time. A'zhu recovered later and waited five days at the Yanmen Pass for Xiao Feng to tell him that she would like to accompany him forever. They were touched by each other and developed romantic feelings.

　　阿朱在小說中的經歷主要是和蕭峰的愛情故事。她假扮成少林僧人，潛入少林寺為慕容復盜取武功典籍；恰好蕭峰也在少林寺打探自己養父母被害真相。他們都被發現且被圍攻，在打鬥中阿朱身受重傷，蕭峰帶她逃跑並決意將她治好。他用內力幫助阿朱續命，身為武林的眾矢之的，他冒著危險帶阿朱找神醫治療。康復後的阿朱在雁門關等了蕭峰五天，表明她願意一生追隨蕭峰，兩人都被彼此感動並產生愛意。

They decided to settle down after Xiao Feng found out the

天龍八部

鹿鼎記

笑傲江湖

雪山飛狐

神鵰俠侶

射鵰英雄傳

連城訣碧血劍

書劍恩仇錄

identity of the Big Brother, who had killed his parents and master in Shaolin. But Kang Min, one of Duan Zhengchun's lovers who intended to use Xiao Feng's hand to kill Duan as revenge, misled them. A'zhu tried to prevent a fight between Xiao and her father, so she disguised as Duan Zhengchun and went to the duel. It was too late when Xiao Feng realized he had killed A'zhu. He would never forgive himself, and their love story ended with sorrow.

他們決心在找到殺害蕭峰養父母和少林師父的帶頭大哥後就回歸平凡的生活。但是被段正淳的其中一個女友康敏誤導，她計畫借蕭峰之手殺害段正淳。阿朱想要阻止蕭峰與父親的衝突，她假扮成段正淳模樣參加決鬥。蕭峰發現自己親手害死阿朱時為時已晚，他永遠不能原諒自己，他們的愛情故事也以悲劇結束。

 文法解析

 KEY 24

 She initially served in the Murong family, <u>where</u> she developed her talent of disguise.

 She initially served in the Murong family, <u>which</u> she developed her talent of disguise.

✦中譯✦ 她原本在慕容家服務，在那裡她開發了易容術的才能。

✦解析✦ 先行詞後接關係副詞，where＝in which。

KEY 25

⭕ They decided to settle down after Xiao finds out the identity of the Big Brother, who had killed his parents and master in Shaolin.

❌ They decided to settle down after Xiao finds out the identity of the Big Brother who had killed his parents and master in Shaolin.

◆中譯◆ 他們決心在找到殺害蕭峰養父母和少林師父的帶頭大哥後就回歸平凡的生活。

◆解析◆ 這是一個非限定性形容詞子句，刪除對 **Big Brother** 解釋的子句部分，對整個句子意思沒有影響，所以要有逗點。

Glossary 字彙一覽表

abbot *n.* 方丈	abhor *vt.* 痛恨，憎惡
acrobatics *n.* 雜技，巧妙手法	adoration *n.* 崇拜，敬愛
animosity *n.* 敵意	antidote *n.* 解藥
besiege *vt.* 圍攻，圍困	celestial *n.* 天上
completeness *n.* 完整性	chrysanthemum *n.* 菊花
constellation *n.* 星座	coincidence *n.* 巧合
cowardice *n.* 怯懦，懦弱	covet *vt.* 垂涎
denounce *vt* 聲討，指責，譴責	crucial *adj.* 關鍵的
disguise *vt.* 偽裝	eminent *adj.* 傑出的

天龍八部

鹿鼎記

笑傲江湖

雪山飛狐

神鵰俠侶

射鵰英雄傳

連城訣　碧血劍

書劍恩仇錄

ethnically *n.* 種族	impassive *adj.* 冷漠的，無情的
grim *adj.* 嚴峻的	infatuation *n.* 癡情
incautiously *adv.* 魯莽地	malicious *adj.* 惡毒的
infiltrate *vt.* 滲透	misapprehend *vt.* 誤解
pruritus *n.* 瘙癢	peripatetic *n. adj.* 逍遙
repel *vt.* 擊退	purge *vt.* 清洗
sorcery *n.* 巫術	repent *vt. vi.* 懺悔
talisman *n.* 護符	retentive *adj.* 保持的
torment *vt.* 煎熬	snatch *vt.* 搶奪
unintentionally *adv.* 無意地	synergy *n.* 協同
vulgarity *n.* 俗氣	treacherous *adj.* 奸詐的
unscrupulous *adj.* 不擇手段的	venomous *adj.* 有毒的

筆記欄

Unit 2

名詞子句

《 鹿鼎記 》

文法主題介紹－名詞子句

　　名詞子句本身是完整獨立的簡單句，子句的語序是先主詞，後動詞。典型的名詞子句是前面加上連接詞 that，that 是只有文法功能的無意義的連接詞，標示後面跟著一個名詞子句。

名詞子句的主要型態有：
- That+S+V
- 疑問詞+S+V
- Whether/if+S+V

名詞子句可以放在名詞的位置，作主句的主詞，受詞，補語，或同位語。

名詞子句在主詞的位置：

That he didn't come is abnormal.

這個句子可以改寫為：

It is abnormal **that** he didn't come.

用 it 這個虛詞填入主語位置，讓名詞子句移到句子後面。**That** 是不能省略的從屬連接詞。**That** 放在句首也不能省略，後面須接單數動詞。

名詞子句在受詞的位置：

Tom said (**that**) he had lunch with Mike.

名詞子句放在及物動詞 said 後面，that 可以省略。

I know who you are.

Who 作為連接詞引導名詞子句，改寫成非倒裝的順序。

名詞子句在補語位置：

The important thing is **that** everyone is safe.

補語和主詞是對等關係。

名詞子句在同位語位置：

I'm afraid **that** you must do it yourself.

Whether 引導名詞子句時有幾種情況不能被 if 替代：

當主詞或 be 動詞的補語時：

Whether our company will embark on a new business depends on the President.The problem is **whether** Mr. Johnson is authorized to act for the President or not.

當名詞的同位語時：

It's your decision **whether** you stay or job-hop.

放在介系詞後：

What we will invest depends on **whether** we can maximize our earning from it or not.

介系詞之後必須接名詞或名詞短語，不適合跟著連接詞引導的名詞子句，只有 whether 引導的名詞子句是例外，可以跟在介系詞後（whether＝which＋either）。

名詞子句作為建議性動詞之受詞: S + 此類 V + that + S + (should) + 原形 V

The other party suggested that a new clause (should) be annexed to the treaty.

此類動詞有：ask, require, demand, request, command, order, advise, propose, suggest, recommend, insist, urge, maintain

名詞子句作為建議、懇求理性判斷形容詞之補語：It is + 此類 adj + that + S + (should) + 原形 V

It is necessary that a parent company (should) provide

sufficient support for its subsidiary.

此類形容詞有：important, vital, necessary, essential, imperative, proper, advisable, urgent.

武俠人物 11 - Wei Xiaobao Yu (韋小寶) MP3 11

The Deer and the Cauldron is the last work of Jin Yong (金庸). In the epilogue, the author said: the Deer and the Cauldron is not so much a historical novel as a typical martial arts novel. The author believed that the protagonist Wei Xiaobao's (韋小寶) behavior was sometimes against the social values. The character of a novel is not necessarily a 'good person'.

《鹿鼎記》是金庸的最後一部作品，作者在《鹿鼎記》後記中說，這部小說不太像武俠小說，毋寧說是歷史小說。作者認為主角韋小寶的行為有時違反了一般的社會價值觀，但小說的主角不一定都是「好人」。

Jin Yong is of paramount importance in the creation of the New Style Martial Art Novels. He gradually built up the martial arts world and the swordsmanship, but he deconstructed them in his last masterpiece. The Deer and the Cauldron is an amusing and spectacular story. Unlike the author's other works, readers will find that there is no emphasis on Buddhism, politics, or nationalism in this novel.

　　金庸是「新派武俠」小說中的翹楚，他之前創造的江湖和武林神話，於自己最後一部作品中解構他們。鹿鼎記是一個包羅萬象的有趣故事。不同於作者的其他小說，讀者會發現這部作品裡沒有強調佛法、政治或民族主義。

Wei Xiaobao is neither an idealist nor a pursuer for anything that has a noble cause. He has no intention of becoming a hero or carrying any hatred. The typical protagonist in Jin Yong's novels is generally a person with excellent characteristics and preeminent kung fu skills. However, what Wei Xiaobao does is the opposite. Especially, he does not know any martial arts. He starts from a teenage scamp, and relies on wit and cunning to get rid of troubles. In the end, he does not become a swordsman. Oppositely, he has an illustrious political career with great fortune rolling in, and a big shot who had a pleasant life.

　　韋小寶完全不是理想主義者，也沒有價值追求。既不想做英雄，也沒有背負國仇家恨。金庸小說的典型主角都是人品一流，武功卓越；但是韋小寶做的正相反，尤其是不會武功。他起步於一個小混混，一路靠小聰明蒙混過關，最後沒有變成大俠。而是成了一個官運亨通、財源滾滾、人生順利的大人物。

天龍八部

鹿鼎記

笑傲江湖

雪山飛狐

神鵰俠侶

射鵰英雄傳

連城訣 碧血劍

書劍恩仇錄

文法解析

KEY 26

⭕ The author believes <u>that</u> the protagonist Wei Xiaobao's (韋小寶) behaviors are against the social values.

❌ The author believes that the protagonist Wei Xiaobao's (韋小寶) behaviors are sometimes against social values.

✦中譯✦ 作者認為主角韋小寶的行為有時違反了一般的價值觀。

✦解析✦ 在 that 名詞子句中，that 後面的句子須為一個完整的句子，錯誤的例句中省略了動詞。

KEY 27

⭕ Unlike the author's other works, readers find out <u>that there is</u> no emphasis on Buddhism, politics, or nationalism in this novel.

❌ Unlike the author's other works, readers find out <u>that</u> no emphasis on Buddhism, politics, or nationalism in this novel.

✦中譯✦ 不同於作者的其他小說，讀者會發現這部作品裏沒有強調佛法、政治或民族主義。

✦解析✦ 名詞子句做動詞 find out 的受詞，that 為連接詞作用，後接完整的句子。

KEY 28

○ <u>What</u> Wei Xiaobao does is the opposite.

✗ <u>That</u> Wei Xiaobao does is the opposite.

✦中譯✦ 韋小寶做的正相反。

✦解析✦ **That** 名詞子句之後所接子句是完整的句子，而關係代名詞 **what** 後面接不完整的句子。Wei Xiaobao dose 是 S+V 後面沒有受詞或補語。

 武俠人物 12 - Wei Xiaobao Yu (韋小寶) MP3 *12*

Wei Xiaobao in the Deer and the Cauldron is an illiterate man with neither martial art skills nor remarkable morality. He is crafted to live in the early Qing dynasty. Faithfulness to friends and quick wit are his significant advantages. Meanwhile, <u>it is believed that Wei Xiaobao has much more shortcomings compared to his merits.</u> He is addicted to gambling and very greedy, and he is used to telling lies and acting shamelessly. He flatters the bigwigs and bullies the unprivileged, and he sometimes feigns ostensibly to obey and acts sneakily in his own interest.

　　《鹿鼎記》的主角韋小寶是一個生活在清朝早期的架空人物。是個既沒有武功和文化，又品行一般的人。他的顯著優點是講義氣和頭腦靈

活。同時，人們認為韋小寶的缺點比優點多，譬如貪財好賭、耍賴說謊、溜鬚拍馬、欺軟怕硬、兩面三刀、陽奉陰違等等。

Wei Xiaobao's story is a series of astonishing adventures. He was kidnapped to the imperial palace and became close friends with the Emperor Kangxi (康熙皇帝). Then he assisted the emperor to purge Aobai (鰲拜) from autocracy. At the moment that Xiaobao assassinated Aobai, a group of swordsmen from the Heaven and Earth Society took him out of the palace and endorsed him as a branch leader in the anti-government group. The leader of the Heaven and Earth Society Chen Jinnan (陳近南) decided that Xiaobao should become his apprentice and stay in the palace as their spy. During that time, Xiaobao pretended he was a little eunuch serving in the palace, he found out the Empress Dowager was disguised by a member from the Mystic Dragon Cult. Luckily, he had connection with the sinister cult leader Hong Antong (洪安通). Xiaobao flattered the leader and saved him from a rebellion. Thus, he earned the title, White Dragon Marshal, and was under the protection of the cult, this prevented him from the fake Empress Dowager's assassination.

韋小寶的經歷令人驚嘆。他被綁架進皇宮並且成為了康熙皇帝的好友。之後他協助康熙把專權的鰲拜趕下台。小寶刺殺鰲拜的時候被一群天地會的英雄劫出皇宮，他因為殺鰲拜有功被推舉為反清組織天地會的香主，會長陳近南決定收小寶為徒，並派他待在皇宮做內應。韋小寶裝

作小太監在皇宮服務期間，發現太后是邪教組織神龍教成員假扮的。幸好韋小寶識得神龍教教主洪安通，他不僅奉承教主，還在洪安通被部下叛亂時救他一命。因而成為了白龍使受到神龍教庇護，免於被假太后暗殺。

 文法解析

 KEY 29

 It is believed <u>that</u> Wei Xiaobao has much more shortcomings compared with his merits.

 It is believed Wei Xiaobao has much more shortcomings compared with his merits.

✦中譯✦ 人們認為韋小寶的缺點比優點多。

✦解析✦ It 是虛詞填入主詞的位置，名詞子句後移。這種情況下 that 不能省去，因為省略之後句子就沒有了從屬連接詞。

 KEY 30

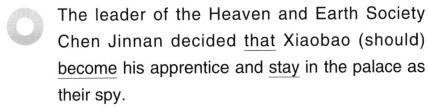 The leader of the Heaven and Earth Society Chen Jinnan decided <u>that</u> Xiaobao (should) <u>become</u> his apprentice and <u>stay</u> in the palace as their spy.

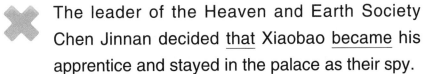 The leader of the Heaven and Earth Society Chen Jinnan decided <u>that</u> Xiaobao <u>became</u> his apprentice and <u>stayed</u> in the palace as their spy.

✦中譯✦ 天地會會長陳近南決定收小寶為徒並待在皇宮做內應。

✦解析✦ Decide 後接名詞子句構成 S+V+that+S+(should)+V 原型子句的動詞用原形，因為子句中實際上省略了 should。

KEY 31

○ He found out (that) the Empress Dowager was disguised by a member from the Mystic Dragon Cult.

✗ He found out that the Empress Dowager was disguised by a member from the Mystic Dragon Cult.

✦中譯✦ 他發現太后是神龍教成員假扮的。

✦解析✦ That 引導的名詞子句在主句中做受詞，此時 that 可以省略。

 武俠人物 13 - Wei Xiaobao (韋小寶) MP3 13

After surviving from several precipices, Wei Xiaobao then went to the Mount Wutai (五臺山) and found out (that) the ex-emperor Shunzhi (順治皇帝) was still alive. The old ex-emperor gave Xiaobao one of the eight books of the Sutra of Forty-two Chapters (四十二章經) that concealed the map indicating the location of the Qing Dynasty's precious deposits. Wei Xiaobao collected all the books and discovered the treasure of the empire, but he did not seize it for himself or disclose the information to anyone.

　　經歷過多次僥倖脫險後，韋小寶去了五台山並發現順治皇帝仍然健在。老皇帝送給韋小寶《四十二章經》中的一本，滿清帝國將至關重要的藏寶圖分別藏在八本經書裏。後來韋小寶收集到了所有經書，發現了帝國寶藏的秘密。但是他沒有把秘密洩露給任何人，也沒有把寶藏據為己有。

Wei Xiaobao was fit into several real historical events. In the novel, the author makes an arrangment for him to assist Emperor Kangxi to suppress the revolt of the Three Feudatories (三藩之亂). Xiaobao bribed Wu Sangui's (吳三桂) allies and alienated the anti-central government alliance, which accelerated the crush of the rebels. He helped the Qing Empire to reach the agreement of boundary delimitation with Russia and assisted the Russian Princess Sophia to consolidate her control as well. Wei Xiaobao also met Shi Lang (施琅) and spent sometime as a local governor in Taiwan.

　　韋小寶被作者寫入很多真實歷史事件中。小說裡面作者安排他協助康熙皇帝平定三藩之亂。小寶賄賂並離間了吳三桂的同盟，使得反清聯盟分化，加速了政府軍清剿叛軍。他幫助清帝國和俄羅斯簽訂了邊境協議，也協助俄國的索非亞公主鞏固權力。韋小寶並且結識了施琅，並且在台灣做官一段時間。

Many achievements of Wei Xiaobao are attributable to

天龍八部

鹿鼎記

笑傲江湖

雪山飛狐

神鵰俠侶

射鵰英雄傳

連城訣 碧血劍

書劍恩仇錄

cheating and good luck. He destroyed the Mystic Dragon Cult by causing an internal conflict. He protected the Emperor Kangxi from assassins. Meanwhile, he also facilitated people in the Heaven and Earth Society to escape from the government troop's sieges. <u>People from the anti-Qing groups were grateful that Wei risked his own life to save them.</u> At the same time, Wei Xiaobao also earned trust from the emperor. He collected huge wealth and gained the title of 'Duke of Mount Deer'.

韋小寶的很多成就都要歸功於他擅長欺騙和運氣好。他挑起神龍教的內部分裂瓦解了神龍教。他一方面保護康熙皇帝不被反清團體刺殺，另一方面又協助天地會眾人從官軍的圍攻中脫困。反清聯盟的人們感激韋小寶捨身營救他們；同時他還贏得了皇帝的信任。韋小寶積累了很多財富並且被封為「鹿鼎公」。

 文法解析

 KEY 32

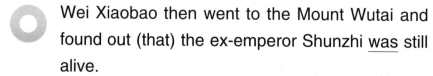
Wei Xiaobao then went to the Mount Wutai and found out (that) the ex-emperor Shunzhi <u>was</u> still alive.

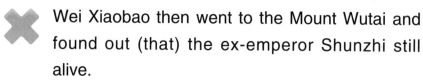
Wei Xiaobao then went to the Mount Wutai and found out (that) the ex-emperor Shunzhi still alive.

◆中譯◆ 韋小寶去了五台山並發現順治皇帝仍然健在。

◆解析◆ 在 that 名詞子句中，that 後面的句子須為一個完整的句子，
錯誤的例句中省略了動詞。

KEY 33

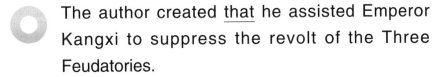

The author created <u>that</u> he assisted Emperor
Kangxi to suppress the revolt of the Three
Feudatories.

The author created he assisted Emperor Kangxi
to suppress the revolt of the Three Feudatories.

◆中譯◆ 作者安排他協助康熙皇帝平定三藩之亂。

◆解析◆ 子句在受詞的位置時，**that** 只有標誌子句的文法功能，可以
省略。

KEY 34

People from the anti-Qing groups were grateful
that <u>Wei risked his own life to save them.</u>

People from the anti-Qing groups were grateful
that <u>risked his own life Wei to save them.</u>

◆中譯◆ 反清聯盟的人們感激韋小寶捨身營救他們。

◆解析◆ That 引導的名詞子句的一種用法是 be+表示知覺的
adj+that+S+V. That 名詞子句做補語。表示感情的形容詞
還有 pleased, glad, happy, delighted, regretful 等。錯

誤例句用了倒裝結構，**that** 引導的名詞子句必須是先主詞而後動詞的語序。

武俠人物 14 - Mao Shiba (茅十八)

Mao Shiba (茅十八) is Wei Xiaobao's first friend. He only possessed normal kung fu skill; however, Mao is a slapdash hero and faithful to friends. He hated the Qing Empire and adored the leader of the Heaven and Earth Society Chen Jinnan. Mao valued rules in the martial arts world; <u>his righteousness can be seen from that he became excessively angry seeing Wei Xiaobao throwing lime powder into rival's eyes during the fighting.</u> Mao Shiba tried to challenge Obio — the bravest warrior in Manchuria. Wei Xiaobao was glad that he could take the chance and followed Mao to the capital city.

茅十八是韋小寶的第一個朋友。他的武功一般，講義氣，是個粗線條的草莽英雄。他痛恨清帝國，最佩服天地會的領袖陳近南。茅十八重視江湖規矩，他的正直可以從有一次韋小寶在打鬥時向對手眼睛撒石灰讓他非常氣憤看出來。當茅十八去找滿州第一勇士鰲拜比武，韋小寶很高興他可以因為這次機會跟著茅十八進北京。

Mao Shiba is a short-tempered and always stands out defending people against injustice. He is conservative and sometimes unaware of his limitation. Mao Shiba was experienced in fighting and brave enough to challenge much stronger rivals.

茅十八個性暴躁，喜歡打抱不平，理念保守，自不量力。不過他有豐富的實戰經驗，並且有勇氣挑戰比自己更強大的對手。

After Mao Shiba brought Wei Xiaobao to Beijing, they were both kidnapped by the leader eunuch Hai Dafu (海大富). Only Mao escaped and Wei Xiaobao started his dramatic journey. Mao is only a minor role in this novel. His next scene is at the end of the novel when he was captured and sentenced to death. Emperor Kangxi forced Wei Xiaobao to supervise the execution of the Heaven and Earth Society members. Mao accused Wei of becoming a betrayer of the anti-Qing dynasty group. It was dangerous to save Mao shiba under close surveillance; Wei managed to substitute him with someone else before the execution. Regardless of Wei Xiaobao's drawbacks, his faithfulness to friends is consistent.

茅十八把韋小寶帶到北京後，他們倆都被太監首領海大富綁架。茅十八獨自逃脫，韋小寶則開始了他的傳奇經歷。茅十八是個小說中的過場人物。他下一次露面是在小說末尾。茅十八被捕而且判死刑。康熙皇帝強迫韋小寶做天地會眾人的監斬官。茅十八大罵韋小寶背叛天地會。在嚴密監控下營救茅十八是十分危險的，韋小寶用掉包方式在處決前救了他。從茅十八身上可以看出，雖然有很多缺點，韋小寶不辜負朋友的特質是貫徹始終的。

天龍八部

鹿鼎記

笑傲江湖

雪山飛狐

神鵰俠侶

射鵰英雄傳

連城訣碧血劍

書劍恩仇錄

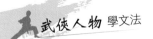
文法解析

KEY 35

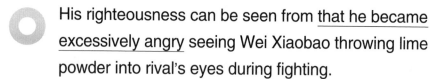

His righteousness can be seen from <u>that he became excessively angry</u> seeing Wei Xiaobao throwing lime powder into rival's eyes during fighting.

His righteousness can be seen <u>that he excessively angry</u> seeing Wei Xiaobao throwing lime powder into rival's eyes during fighting.

✦中譯✦ 他的正直之處在於韋小寶在打鬥時向對手眼睛撒石灰讓他非常氣憤。

✦解析✦ 這個例句是名詞子句當主詞的補語。主詞補語和主詞是對等關係。子句需要遵循 that 名詞子句的規則,是一個主詞和動詞完整的句子。

KEY 36

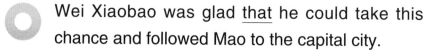

Wei Xiaobao was glad <u>that</u> he could take this chance and followed Mao to the capital city.

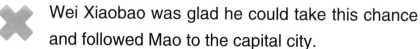

Wei Xiaobao was glad he could take this chance and followed Mao to the capital city.

✦中譯✦ 韋小寶很高興他因為這次機會跟著茅十八進了北京。

✦解析✦ 這個例句是名詞子句當作形容詞的補語。形容詞是表示感情的 glad。be+表示知覺的 adj+that+S+V 是習慣用法,that 不能省去。

KEY 37

○ it was dangerous to save Mao Shiba under close surveillance

✕ It was dangerously to save Mao Shiba under close surveillance.

✦中譯✦ 在緊密監控下營救茅十八是十分危險的。

✦解析✦ 此處為 It is adj to V... 的句型，也可以改用名詞子句表示建議的句型：it+adj+that+S+(should)+原 V 的句型，類似形容詞有 vital, advisable 等等。

 武俠人物 15 - Chen Jinnan (陳近南) MP3 *15*

Chen Jinnan (陳近南) is the leader of the Heaven and Earth Society. Wei Xiaobao is Chen's apprentice, although he is not keen to learn any martial arts. Chen Jinnan is based on a real person in history.

　　陳近南是天地會總舵主。韋小寶是天地會總舵主陳近南的學徒，只是他不熱心練習武藝。陳近南是根據真實歷史人物創造的角色。

Chen is a special character. In the Deer and the Cauldron, there are various characters that are selfish and greedy. Chen, on the other hand, treasures chivalrous spirits and holds the righteous virtue. He knows from the very beginning that Wei Xiaobao does not possess the quality of being his successor.

天龍八部

笑傲江湖

雪山飛狐

神鵰俠侶

射鵰英雄傳

連城訣 碧血劍

書劍恩仇錄

Xiaobao does not possess the quality of being his successor. However, he still accepts Wei as the group leader of the Heaven and Earth Society since there is a promise that the person who killed Aobai will become the leader of the Green Wood branch.

陳近南是一個特別的人物。在《鹿鼎記》裡有各種貪圖私慾的角色，而陳近南和他們完全相反，他重視俠義精神且保持正義美德。從一開始，他就明白韋小寶並不具有自己繼任者的資質，但他還是接受韋小寶為徒，還遵守了「殺鰲拜者，將被奉為青木堂堂主」的約定，讓他做了天地會的青木堂堂主。

In Jin Yong's last novel, Chen Jinnan is the only swordsman in the traditional sense. He seems incompatible with everyone else sacrificing himself in rescuing others, and persisting in doing correct things. The problem is Chen always feels powerless. It was not the era of swordsmanship. He was killed by Zheng Keshaung's (鄭克塽), the person he served for his whole life. It was an unworthy death, indicating a real swordsman is not fitting to the realistic world anymore. Ironically, Wei Xiaobao is the only one who held true sentiments to Chen and cherished the memories as if they were father and son. Whether Wei Xiaobao's flexibility triumphs Chen Jinnan's rigidness has developed a significant influence; the successfulness of Wei Xiaobao deepened the tragic feature of a real hero.

在金庸的最後一部小說中，陳近南是唯一的一位傳統意義上的俠客。他看起來和所有人格格不入，總是捨己救人，堅持原則。問題是陳近南經常覺得無能為力。他為鄭家鞠躬盡瘁卻死在鄭克塽手上，死得非常不值，也證明了他的時代已經不適合真的俠客生存了。更諷刺的是，最後只有韋小寶對陳近南深切緬懷而且把他當作父親來敬重。韋小寶的靈活能否勝過了陳近南的古板有重要的影響，韋小寶的成功也深化了一個真正英雄的悲哀。

 文法解析

 KEY 38

⭕ He knows from the very beginning <u>that Wei Xiaobao does</u> not possess the quality as his successor.

❌ He knows from the very beginning Wei Xiaobao not possess the quality as his successor.

✦中譯✦ 從一開始，他就明白韋小寶並不具有自己繼任者的資質。

✦解析✦ 錯誤例句中，**that** 可以省略，因為 **that** 引導的子句是主句的受詞。但 **does** 不可以省略，因為 **that** 後的名詞子句須為完整句子。

 KEY 39

⭕ The problem is Chen often <u>feels</u> powerless.

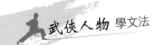

 The problem is Chen often <u>feel</u> powerless.

◆中譯◆ 問題是陳近南經常覺得無能為力。

◆解析◆ 這個例句是名詞子句當主詞補語。錯誤例句是子句中的主詞和動詞沒有一致。

 KEY 40

 <u>Whether</u> Wei Xiaobao's flexibility triumphs Chen Jinnan's rigidness has a significant influence.

 <u>If</u> Wei Xiaobao's flexibility triumphs Chen Jinnan's rigidness has a significant influence.

◆中譯◆ 韋小寶的靈活能否勝過了陳近南的古板有重要的影響。

◆解析◆ **Whether** 引導的名詞子句，如果 **whether** 在句首，則不能被 **if** 取代。因為句首位置的 **if** 子句會被以為是表示"如果"的副詞子句。

 武俠人物 16 - Hong Antong (洪安通) *MP3* *16*

Hong Antong (洪安通) is the hierarch of the Mystic Dragon Cult. Although he has the best kung fu skill, Hong is a typical vicious person. He is ambitious to collect all the Sutra of Forty-two Chapters and seizes the national treasure of the Qing Dynasty. His preference is to be flattered by others; he enjoys followers to bless him with a long life.

洪安通是神龍教教主。他雖然武功高強，但是是一個邪惡的人。洪安通野心勃勃想收集所有的《四十二章經》奪取清國的國家寶藏。他的愛好是被人奉承，最喜歡教徒祝福他壽與天齊。

Hong is a paranoid and overconfident person. Due to distrust in people, he uses drugs to control his followers. His beautiful young wife Su Quan (蘇荃) ruthlessly killed hundreds of Hong's old mates. In fact, Su is only the executor. Whether those victims will be eliminated or not depends on Hong Antong; since he is constantly in fear of losing power, Hong trained young followers to challenge and torture the old founders of the cult.

洪安通多疑且自負。因為他對人缺乏信任，所以下藥控制別人。他年輕貌美的妻子蘇荃殘忍的殺害了數百位老兄弟。事實上蘇荃只是個執行者，是否剷除這些受害人是洪安通決定的，因為他太害怕失去權力。他還訓練年輕的信眾挑戰和折磨神龍教的眾多老創始人。

The Mystic Dragon Cult is a heresy that aims to unify and consolidate the whole martial arts world. Furthermore, the cult has bigger aspirations in politics. A fake Empress Dowager was sent into the imperial palace; Hong also colluded with Wu Sangui (吳三桂) and Russia. Hong Antong's misfortune started from Wei Xiaobao's arrival on Mystic Dragon Island. Wei Xiaobao then became the White Dragon Marshal and after escaping from Mystic Dragon Island, he brought back with the

天龍八部

鹿鼎記

笑傲江湖

雪山飛狐

神鵰俠侶

射鵰英雄傳

連城訣碧血劍

書劍恩仇錄

government troops bombarding the island. Most cult members died in this attack; Hong Antong managed to escape but an internal rebel costs his life. Su Quan then became one of Wei Xiaobao's wives. It is believed that Hong Antong is based on Mao Zedong (毛澤東) and the chaos in Mystic Dragon Island implies the Cultural Revolution since this novel was written during 1960's -1970's.

神龍教是一個志在統一武林的邪教，不僅如此，神龍教還有更大的政治野心。他們派了假太后在宮中潛伏，洪安通自己也和吳三桂以及俄國暗中勾結。洪安通的厄運從韋小寶來到神龍島開始。韋小寶做了白龍使，逃出後帶領官兵砲轟神龍島。洪安通沒有像大多數人一樣死於砲轟，他最後因為教徒反叛死於神龍島。蘇荃後來成了韋小寶的妻子之一。洪安通被認為是以毛澤東為人物原型，神龍島上的混亂狀況則暗指文化革命，因為小說創作於一九六零至七零年代。

 文法解析

 KEY 41

 Whether those victims will be eliminated or not depends on Hong Antong.

 If those victims will be eliminated or not depends on Hong Antong.

◆中譯◆ 是否剷除這些受害人是洪安通決定的。

✦解析✦ **Whether** 引導的名詞子句做主詞，**whether** 不可以被 **if** 替代。

KEY 42

○ It is believed that Hong Antong is based on Mao Zedong and the chaos in Mystic Dragon Island implies the Cultural Revolution since this novel was written during 1960's -1970's.

✕ It is believed Hong Antong is based on Mao Zedong and the chaos in Mystic Dragon Island implies the Cultural Revolution since this novel was written during 1960's -1970's.

✦中譯✦ 洪安通被認為是以毛澤東為人物原型，神龍島上的混亂狀況則暗指文化革命，因為小說創作於一九六零至七零年代。

✦解析✦ 名詞子句放在主詞的位置，用 **it** 這個虛詞填入主詞的位置，名詞子句後移。這種情況下 **that** 不能省略，如果省去就沒有了從屬連接詞。

 武俠人物 17 - Jiunan (九難) *MP3* *17*

Jiunan (九難) is a Buddhist nun. Her other identity is Princess Changping (長平公主). She is the daughter of Ming Dynasty's last emperor Chongzhen (崇禎皇帝). When the capital was conquered, her father decided the whole families sacrifice for the fallen Ming Empire. She survived but lost one arm. Jiunan

天龍八部

鹿鼎記

笑傲江湖

雪山飛狐

神鵰俠侶

射鵰英雄傳

連城血訣劍

書劍恩仇錄

then became a nun and practiced martial arts. She gained the reputation as one-armed Magic Nun (獨臂神尼) after initiating anti-Qing activities. (In the real history, Princess Changping deceased at her young age).

　　九難是一位出家師父，她的另一個身分是明朝的長平公主。因為她是末代崇禎皇帝的女兒。九難失去了一隻手臂。當首都被攻破時候，崇禎帝決定他們全家要自殺殉國。九難沒有死但只剩下一條胳膊。她後來出家為尼並且練習武藝開展反清活動，贏得了獨臂神尼的綽號。在真實歷史上，長平公主很年輕就去世了。

Jiunan stole baby A'ke (阿珂) from her mother Chen Yuanyuan (陳圓圓) and raised A'ke She believes A'ke is the daughter of Wu Sangui, and Wu is the one who opened Shan-Hai-Kuan (山海關) so that the Manchus were able to conquer Ming Empire. Jiunan has a complex emotion towards A'ke; she intends to train her into an assassin and kills Wu Sangui for revenge.

　　九難從陳圓圓那裡擄走了她的女兒阿珂，並且撫養阿珂長大成人。她相信阿珂應該是吳三桂的女兒，吳三桂曾經打開山海關放清兵入關打敗了明朝。九難對阿珂感情複雜，她計畫訓練阿珂刺殺吳三桂協助自己的復仇行動。

Jiunan showed up in Mount Wutai (五臺山) and failed to kill emperor Kangxi because Wei Xiaobao saved the emperor.

She kidnapped Wei Xiaobao but then was persuaded by his eloquence and accepted him as her martial arts apprentice. Xiaobao gained trust from Juinan, but his real intention of following Jiunan was to chase A'ke. When several Tibetan monks injured Jiunan, Xiaobao saved her and later she taught him a special escaping skill. In the end, Jiunan gave up her plan of revenge after A'ke failed to assassinate Wu Sangui.

　　九難在五臺山刺殺康熙不成，因為韋小寶出手搭救。她將韋小寶劫走後被小寶的好口才說服，反倒收他為徒。小寶取得九難的信任，但其實他追隨九難的真正目的是追求阿珂。九難被眾喇嘛圍攻受傷，得到小寶救助，她傳授逃跑術給韋小寶。到最後，阿珂刺殺吳三桂失手，九難師太也放棄了她的復仇計畫。

文法解析

KEY 43

 When the capital was conquered, her father decided the whole families (should) <u>sacrifice</u> for the fallen Ming Empire.

 When the capital was conquered, her father decided the whole families <u>sacrificed</u> for the fallen Ming Empire.

✦中譯✦ 當首都被攻破時候，崇禎帝決定他們全家要自殺殉國。

✦解析✦ 名詞子句做 decide 的受詞，子句裡有一個被省略的情態動詞 should，所以子句中的動詞要用原形。

KEY 44

⭕ She believes A'ke is the daughter of Wu Sangui, and Wu is the one who opened Shan-Hai-Kuan (山海關) so that the Manchus is able to conquer Ming Empire.

❌ She believes that A'ke is the daughter of Wu Sangui, and Wu is the one who opened Shan-Hai-Kuan (山海關) so that the Manchus is able to conquer Ming Empire.

✦中譯✦ 她相信阿珂應該是吳三桂的女兒，吳三桂曾經打開山海關放清兵入關打敗了明朝。

✦解析✦ 這是一個形容詞子句在名詞子句內，引導名詞子句的 that 只有標示子句的文法功能，可以省略。整個名詞子句作 believe 的受詞。

武俠人物 18 - Hai Dafu (海大富)

MP3
18

Hai Dafu (海大富) is an old eunuch who appears sick and weak. However, he is a top martial artist. He kidnapped Wei Xiaobao and brought him into the palace. He was aware that Wei Xiaobao pretended to be Xiao Guizi (小桂子). Hai Dafu trained Wei Xiaobao with Shaolin kung fu and sent him to fight with the younger Emperor Kangxi. That everything he did has an investigation purpose. Hai previously served the ex-Emperor Shunzhi who felt disappointed after his favourite concubine died and turned himself into a monk. Shunzhi suspected the concubine was poisoned by someone and secretly tasked Hai Dafu to find out the truth of her death.

海大富是個看似病弱的老太監。但他實際上是功夫高手。他綁架了韋小寶把他帶進宮。海大富知道韋小寶在冒充小桂子。他教給韋小寶少林功夫並派遣他去和年輕的康熙皇帝比武。海大富所做的每一件事都有調查的目的。他曾經為順治皇帝服務,順治帝因為寵妃過世而心灰意冷出家為僧。但他懷疑妃子是被人所害所以派海大富調查真相。

The mission became Hai Dafu's life focus. Realizing the rival utilized 'exploding palm'(化骨綿掌) to kill the victim; he risked his life to practice the kung fu which counters that vicious skills. He did not disclose Wei Xiaobao's true identity but used him to confuse the murderer. Through meticulous reasoning, Hai Dafu found out from Xiaobao and Emperor Kangxi's fighting practice that the Empress Dowager, who taught the Emperor kung fu skills, is the person who committed the crimes.

這個任務成為海大富的生活重心。他發現被害人身中"化骨綿掌"而亡,不惜身體受傷練習了對付化骨綿掌的武功。他沒有揭穿韋小寶的真實身分而是利用他來迷惑兇手。透過精密的推理,海大富從小寶和康熙的比武中發現教給皇帝武功的太后是殺人真兇。

During the final fight with the fake Empress Dowager Mao

Dongzhu (毛冬珠), he provoked and disturbed Mao and attacked her weak point; then prevailed fake Empress Dowager and prepared for a deadly strike. However, Wei Xiaobao snooped the scene and gave Mao a hand to kill Hai Dafu. This surreptitious old eunuch disappeared by the cooperation of his two adversaries.

在和假太后毛冬珠的最後一場打鬥中，海大富先是激怒和擾亂對方暴露弱點實施攻擊，佔上風後準備致命一擊。可惜韋小寶窺探到了這一幕並協助假太后殺了海大富。這個詭異的老太監終於死在韋小寶與假太后聯手合作之下。

文法解析

KEY 45

 <u>That</u> everything he did has an investigation purpose.

 Everything he did has an investigation purpose.

✦中譯✦ 他所做的每一件事都有調查的目的。

✦解析✦ **That** 名詞子句放在句首做主詞時，that 不可以省略。

KEY 46

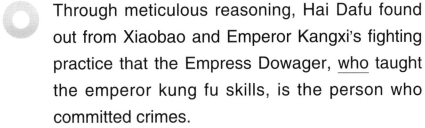

○ Through meticulous reasoning, Hai Dafu found out from Xiaobao and Emperor Kangxi's fighting practice that the Empress Dowager, <u>who</u> taught the emperor kung fu skills, is the person who committed crimes.

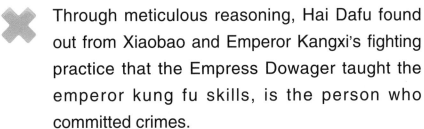

✕ Through meticulous reasoning, Hai Dafu found out from Xiaobao and Emperor Kangxi's fighting practice that the Empress Dowager taught the emperor kung fu skills, is the person who committed crimes.

✦中譯✦ 透過精密的推理，海大富從小寶和康熙的比武中發現教給皇帝武功的太后是殺人真兇。

✦解析✦ 形容詞子句在名詞子句中，**who** 引導一個句子修飾 the dowager，不可以省略。

武俠人物 19 - Su Quan (蘇荃)、Fang Yi (方怡)、Mu Jianping (沐劍屏)

MP3
19

Wei Xiaobao married seven wives through his amazing adventures. Su Quan (蘇荃) used to be the lady of Mystic Dragon Island. She was beautiful and confident. Su acted as the leader of Wei Xiaobao's family since she was the most experienced and competent one in the ladies group. Her martial arts skill was also the best among the seven. Her beauty amazed Xiaobao when they first met and <u>he would</u>

never expect he could finally marry her. Su decided to follow Wei Xiaobao after the Mystic Dragon Cult fell.

　　韋小寶的神奇經歷讓他收獲七個太太。蘇荃曾經是神龍島的女主人，非常美麗自信。因為蘇荃最有能力並且見多識廣，所以她是太太團和韋小寶全家的領頭人。她的武功也是七人中最高強的。韋小寶初見蘇荃就被她的美貌折服，並且從沒想到自己會和她結婚。蘇荃在神龍教倒台後決定追隨韋小寶。

Fang Yi (方怡) is an intelligent girl from the House of Prince Mu (沐王府). She used to pretend as Wu Sangui's subordinate and attempted to assassinate the Emperor Kangxi. She failed the task and got injured. Wei Xiaobao protected her and forced Fang to promise to marry him if he could save her boyfriend Liu Yizhou (劉一舟) from capture. She was then controlled by the Mystic Dragon Cult and had trapped Wei Xiaobao in the island. Wei Xiaobao managed to save them again. It was Fang Yi's decision to decide whether she should stay with Liu Yizhou or accept Wei Xiaobao; she finally gave up Liu after realizing he acted cowardly and betrayed friends.

　　方怡是來自沐王府的聰明女生。她曾經假扮吳三桂手下行刺康熙皇帝未果，受傷後被韋小寶救下。方怡被迫向韋小寶承諾，如果他可以從牢裡救出方的男友劉一舟，她就要嫁給韋小寶。方怡後來被神龍教控制，把韋小寶騙到島上抓了起來。後來韋小寶又一次救大家脫身。方怡要在繼續和劉一舟在一起或者是接受韋小寶之間作出選擇，最後在發現

劉的懦弱和背叛朋友後放棄了他。

Mu Jianping (沐劍屏) is also from the House of Prince Mu. She is an innocent and naive princess. Mu was the first young lady came into Wei Xiaobao's life. The Heaven and Earth Society kidnapped her and sent her into the palace as hostage. Wei Xiaobao as the Heaven and Earth Society undercover associate guarded her during her capture. She gradually relied on Wei Xiaobao's protection. She was also controlled by the Mystic Dragon Cult and forced to join Fang Yi to deceive Wei Xiaobao into the island.

　　沐劍屏也來自沐王府，是個天真無邪的小郡主。她是第一個進入韋小寶生活的年輕女生。沐劍屏被天地會綁架送入宮中作人質，韋小寶作為天地會臥底負責看管她，她也漸漸對韋小寶的保護產生依賴。沐劍屏後來也被神龍教控制，和方怡一道騙韋小寶到神龍島。

文法解析

KEY 47

 He would never expect he could finally marry her.

 He would never expect he finally marries her.

✦中譯✦ 他從沒想到自己會和她結婚。

✦解析✦ 名詞子句的主要動詞要用動詞原形，來強調動詞。

天龍八部

鹿鼎記

笑傲江湖

雪山飛狐

神鵰俠侶

射鵰英雄傳

連城訣

碧血劍

書劍恩仇錄

KEY 48

⭕ It is Fang Yi's decision to decide <u>whether</u> she should stay with Liu Yizhou or accept Wei Xiaobao.

❌ It is Fang Yi's decision to decide <u>if</u> she should stay with Liu Yizhou or accept Wei Xiaobao.

✦中譯✦ 方怡要在繼續和劉一舟在一起或者是接受韋小寶之間作出選擇。

✦解析✦ Whether 不能作為疑問詞來引導一個帶問號的疑問句，但可以引導名詞子句。Whether 有時可以用 if 來替代，這個例句中 whether 引導的子句做名詞 decision 的同位語，這種情況不能用 if 代替 whether。

武俠人物 20 - Princess Jianning (建寧公主)、Zeng Rou's (曾柔)、Shuang'er (雙兒)、A'ke (阿珂)

MP3 20

Princess Jianning (建寧公主) is the Emperor's younger sister; in fact, she is the daughter of the fake Empress Dowager and the Thin Monk (瘦頭陀). Princess Jianning is spoiled and violent. She has sadistic hobbies and enjoys whipping Wei Xiaobao as well as threats to burn his hair. Jianning was not happy that the Emperor Kangxi assigned her a political marriage with Wu Sangui's son; she opposed this arrangement and eloped with Wei Xiaobao. Among Wei's seven wives, Princess Jianning is the only one who chases after him. She set a plot and got pregnant with Wei Xiaobao. In the end, the Emperor accepted their relationship.

建寧公主是皇帝的妹妹，但實際上她是假太后和瘦頭陀的女兒。建寧公主非常驕縱暴力，她還有施虐的嗜好，時常鞭打韋小寶並威脅火燒他的頭髮。建寧對於康熙皇帝安排她嫁給吳三桂兒子的政治婚姻很不高興，她反對這椿婚事並且和韋小寶私奔。在韋小寶的七個老婆中，建寧公主是唯一一個主動追求韋小寶的。她設局讓自己懷了韋小寶的小孩，皇帝最後也接納了他們的關係。

Zeng Rou's (曾柔) ancestor was a military officer in the Ming Dynasty. She joined the anti-Qing force in Mountain Wangwu while she was quite polite and well educated. Zeng Rou's love towards Wei Xiaobao came from gratitude. Wei Xiaobao was ordered to wipe out Wangwu Sect; instead, he merged the Sect with the Heaven and Earth Society. He also revenged for Zeng Rou's master. This shy and charming girl then followed Wei Xiaobao after she was impressed by his kind behaviors. Shuang'er (雙兒) was a servant of the Zhuang family. To appreciate Xiaobao who has killed the family enemy Obio, the matriarch of Zhuang sent Shuang'er to serve Wei Xiaobao and act as his bodyguard. Shuang'er is the most faithful among Wei's seven wives. She took care of Wei and cherished him as the center of her life.

曾柔是明朝軍官的後代，她是反清組織王屋派中知書達禮的一員。

曾柔對韋小寶的愛來自於感激之情。韋小寶奉命剿滅王屋派，但他實際上卻將王屋派收歸到同是反清組織的天地會。他也幫曾柔的師傅報了仇。因為被韋小寶的行為打動，這位害羞而有魅力女生也開始追隨韋小寶。

雙兒是莊家的丫鬟，為了感謝韋小寶殺了莊家仇人鰲拜，女主人派雙兒照顧韋小寶並做他的保鑣。雙兒是七個老婆中對韋小寶最為死心塌地的一個，她把韋小當作自己的生活重心，悉心照顧他。

A'ke (阿珂) is Jiunan's apprentice and Chen Yuanyuan's daughter. She is mysterious and extremely beautiful. Wei Xiaobao loved her at the first sight, but A'ke had previously had affection to Zheng Keshuang. A'ke's decision to choose depends on whether Wei Xiaobao is persistent or not. She was eventually moved by Wei Xiaobao and also became one of his wives.

阿珂是九難師太的弟子、陳圓圓的女兒。她充滿神秘感並且美貌非常。韋小寶對她一見鍾情，但阿珂本來喜歡的是鄭克塽。阿珂的選擇端視韋小寶是否鍥而不捨。她最終被韋小寶打動成了他的七個妻子之一。

 文法解析

 KEY 49

 Jianning was not happy that Emperor Kangxi assigned her a political marriage with Wu Sangui's son.

Jianning was not happy Emperor Kangxi assigned her a political marriage with Wu Sangui's son.

✦中譯✦ 建寧對於康熙皇帝安排她嫁給吳三桂兒子的政治婚姻很不高興。

✦解析✦ Be+表示感情的 adj+that+S+V 的習慣用法。That 名詞子句做主句的補語。That 不能省去。

 KEY 50

 A'ke's decision to choose <u>depends on whether</u> Wei Xiaobao is persistent or not.

 A'ke's decision to choose <u>depends on if</u> Wei Xiaobao is persistent or not.

✦中譯✦ 阿珂的選擇端視韋小寶是否鍥而不捨。

✦解析✦ Whether 引導的名詞子句放在介系詞後，這種情況不能用 if 替換 whether。

 Glossary 字彙一覽表

adversary *n.* 對手，敵人	alliance *n.* 聯盟
apprentice *n.* 學徒	aspiration *n.* 心願
autocracy *n.* 專制	betrayer *n.* 背叛者，叛國賊
cauldron *n.* 釜，大鍋	collude *vt.* 勾結，串通

天龍八部
鹿鼎記
笑傲江湖
雪山飛狐
神鵰俠侶
射鵰英雄傳
連城訣碧血劍
書劍恩仇錄

competent *adj.* 勝任，有能力的	conceal *vt.* 隱藏，隱瞞
concubine *n.* 妾	conservative *adj.* 保守的
consolidate *vt.* 鞏固，合併	cowardly *adv.* 懦弱地
decease *n.vi.* 死亡，亡故	deceive *vt.vi.* 欺騙，欺詐
delimitation *n.* 劃界	disclose *vt.* 洩露
dowager *n.* 貴婦，太后	elope *vi.* 私奔，潛逃
eloquence *n.* 口才，雄辯	endorse *vt.* 擁護，背書
epilogue *n.* 結語，後記	eunuch *n.* 太監
excessively *adv.* 過分地	feign *vt.vi.* 假裝，捏造
heresy *n.* 異端	hierarch *n.* 教主，掌權者
hostage *n.* 人質	illustrious *adj.* 傑出的
immortality *n.* 不朽	incompatible *adj.* 不相容的
lime *n.* 石灰	Manchu *n.adj.* 滿族的，滿族人
marshal *n.* 元帥	matriarch *n.* 女族長，女家長
master *n.* 大師	morality *n.* 道德
nun *n.* 修女	ostensible *adj.* 表面的
paranoid *adj.* 偏執	persistent *adj.* 堅持不懈的
precipice *n.* 懸崖，絕境	preeminent *adj.* 傑出的
prevail *vi.* 勝過，獲勝	protagonist *n.* 主角
revolt *vi.n.* 起義，反叛	ruthlessly *adv.* 無情地
sadistic *adj.* 虐待狂的	scamp *n.* 惡棍
sentiment *n.* 情緒，心情	slapdash *adj.* 草率的，粗心的

snoop *vt.* 窺探	spectacular *adj.* 壯觀的
subordinate *n.* 下屬	successor *n.* 繼任者
surreptitious *adj.* 偷偷摸摸的	sutra *n.* 佛經
whip *n.vt.* 鞭子，鞭打	

筆記欄

天龍八部

鹿鼎記

笑傲江湖

雪山飛狐

神鵰俠侶

射鵰英雄傳

連城訣 碧血劍

書劍恩仇錄

Unit 3

副詞子句

‖笑傲江湖‖

文法主題介紹－副詞子句

　　副詞子句是具有副詞的功能的句中句，是結構體較大的副詞，功能為修飾主要子句，用於表示主要子句發生的原因、時間、條件、讓步、目的等。

　　副詞子句的位置彈性，可放主要子句後（無需逗號），或放主要子句前（需逗號）。

🗡 表「時間」的從屬連接詞: 時間副詞子句要用現在式代替未來式

when, whenever, while, before, after, since, until, once, as soon as

🗡 表「條件」的從屬連接詞: 條件副詞子句要用現在式代替未來式

if, once, unless, as long as, in case (that), providing that, provided that

🗡 表「原因」的從屬連接詞: 不可與對等連接詞 so 一起使用 because, since, as, in that, now that

🗡 表「目的」的從屬連接詞:

so (that), in order that

🗡 表「讓步」的從屬連接詞: 不可與對等連接詞 but 一起使用

although, though, even if, even though, while, whereas, whether... or not

🗡 表「結果」的從屬連接詞:

so + adj /adv + that 與 such + N + that

武俠人物 21 - Linghu Chong (令狐沖) *MP3* *21*

The Smiling, Proud Wanderer (笑傲江湖) is a martial arts novel by Jin Yong. On the surface, The title literally means to live a carefree life under any circumstances. The author aims to craft human nature through the story. Jin Yong says The Smiling, Proud Wanderer expressed a philosophy which is indifferent and non-competitive. In the intellectual world throughout history, there is always a tendency of keeping distance from power competition; however, in reality people still chase after fame and wealth. <u>Because of the depiction of the human nature in the novel transcends time constraints, The Smiling, Proud Wanderer does not have the exact historical period.</u>

　　笑傲江湖是金庸創作的武俠小説。從表面來看，書名表示的意思是無論在何種境遇下都能過著不羈的生活。作者試圖透過這個故事刻畫人性。金庸曾説《笑傲江湖》是想表達一種沖淡、不太注重爭權奪利的人生觀。傳統的知識分子一直有種淡泊名利的傾向，但是現實社會裡人們難免追名逐利。因為這部小説描寫的人性穿越了時間限制，所以《笑傲江湖》並沒有確切的時代背景。

The protagonist Linghu Chong (令狐沖) is the senior apprentice of Yue Buqun (岳不群) from the Huashan Sect (華山派). The mentor Yue Buqun is famous for his righteous conduct and behavior. Surprisingly, he later turns out to be a real hypocrite. In contrast to Yue, Linghu Chong is scruffy and waggish; he makes friends with people from the 'deviated cult'. Although Linghu Chong sometimes behaves loosely, he is the one who possesses kind nature and heroic property. Even after he was expelled from the Huashan Sect, Linghu Chong still remains respectful and loyal towards his Master and fellow apprentices. Linghu Chong and Yue Buqun both had a dramatic change in their life; the 'Gentleman Sword' is a villain while the inconspicuous man is a real hero.

　　小説的主人公令狐沖是華山派岳不群的大弟子。他的老師岳不群因正直的行為操守而聞名。意外的是，他最後成了徹底的偽君子。和岳不群相反，令狐沖有點邋遢又愛開玩笑，又結交邪派朋友。雖然令狐沖有時行為不受拘束，但他才是擁有善良本性和英雄氣概的人。就算在他被華山派掃地出門之後，他對待他的老師仍是尊重且忠誠。令狐沖和岳不群的生活都有戲劇化的轉變，「君子劍」是大惡人，而不起眼的小子是真英雄。

Linghu Chong is not ambitious to seek supremacy in a power-driven world. In a sense, he is lonely. Nevertheless, he is the one who enjoys life as a proud wanderer.

　　令狐沖並沒有企圖心在這個被權力主導的世界裡追求至高地位，從某種意義上說他是孤獨的，但是他才是個笑傲江湖的人。

文法解析

KEY 51

○ Because the depiction of the human nature in the novel transcends time constraints, The Smiling, Proud Wanderer does not fit into any specific historical period.

✕ Because the depiction of the human nature in the novel transcends time constraints, so The Smiling, Proud Wanderer does not fit into any specific historical period.

✦中譯✦ 因為這部小說描寫的人性穿越了時間限制，所以《笑傲江湖》並沒有確切的時代背景。

✦解析✦ Because 與 So 不能同時出現在一個句子中，且依句意要用 because of。

KEY 52

○ Although Linghu Chong sometimes behaves loosely, he is the one who possesses kind nature and heroic property.

✕ Although Linghu Chong sometimes behaves loosely, but he is the one who possesses kind nature and heroic property.

天龍八部
鹿鼎記
笑傲江湖
雪山飛狐
神鵰俠侶
射鵰英雄傳
連城訣 碧血劍
書劍恩仇錄

✦中譯✦ 雖然令狐沖有時行為不受拘束，但他才是擁有善良本性和英雄氣概的人。

✦解析✦ 表讓步的從屬連接詞 although 不能和 but 一起使用。

KEY 53

⭕ Even after he was expelled from the Huashan Sect, Linghu Chong still remains respectful and loyal towards his mentor and fellow apprentices.

❌ Even after he was expelled from the Huashan Sect; Linghu Chong still remains respectful and loyal towards his mentor and fellow apprentices.

✦中譯✦ 就算在他被華山派掃地出門之後，他還是尊重和忠誠於他的老師和同門。

✦解析✦ 副詞子句修飾主句動詞，與主句不是對等關係，所以用逗點。

武俠人物 22 - Linghu Chong (令狐沖) MP3 22

Linghu Chong is the senior disciple in the Huashan Sect. He is sanguine and optimistic. In addition to practising swords skills, he also enjoys drinking. He was once punished for his unconstrained behaviors and was locked in a cave where he met the reclusive Kungfu Master Feng Qingyang (風清揚). Feng Qingyang taught him the skills of 'Nine Swords Of Dugu' (獨孤九劍), and trained him to use merely the swords techniques without any internal energy. His Kungfu skills had a significant improvement after learning the 'Nine Swords Of Dugu'. <u>Since then Linghu Chong became a formidable swordsman, and he could defeat opponents without much effort.</u>

令狐沖是華山派的大師兄，個性樂觀開朗。他熱愛劍術和飲酒。因為行為不羈，他被罰在崖洞中思過，在那裡他遇到了隱居的武術大師風清揚。風清揚教授他獨孤九劍，並訓練他完全運用劍術而不使用內力。練習獨孤九劍後，令狐沖的功夫突飛猛進，他變成了令人景仰的劍客，可以輕鬆戰勝敵人。

Soon after his horizon of swordsmanship was opened, his tremendous improvement had drawn suspicion from his Master Yue Buqun, who doubted that Linghu Chong possessed the Bixie Manual (辟邪劍法) and personally linked with the Sun Moon Holy Cult (日月神教). <u>LingHu Chong did not defend himself as he had promised not to reveal the fact that Feng Qingyang was still alive.</u> Due to the accumulation of misunderstandings, Linghu Chong was expelled from the Hushan Sect.

就在令狐沖劍術飛躍進步後不久，他的師傅岳不群對他極大的進步產生了懷疑，岳不群覺得令狐沖可能偷練了辟邪劍法並且和日月神教的人有聯繫。因為已經承諾絕不向外透露風清揚還健在，令狐沖沒有為自己辯解。由於日積月累的誤會逐漸加深，令狐沖被逐出華山派。

天龍八部

鹿鼎記

笑傲江湖

雪山飛狐

神鵰俠侶

射鵰英雄傳

連城訣・碧血劍

書劍恩仇錄

While he was still faithful to the Huashan Sect, all his previous fellows considered him a betrayer. His connection with the Jianghu heretics made himself away from the orthodox sects. Another heart-broken incidence in his life was Linghu Chong's junior sister apprentice Yue Lingshan (岳靈珊)，who fell in love with the new apprentice Lin Pingzhi (林平之) and married Lin later. Linghu Chong became an outlier from the world he used to belong , but he started new adventures in broader Jianghu.

他仍然對華山派忠心耿耿，但他的師兄弟都把他當做背叛師門的人。和邪派人士的交往讓他與名門正派漸行漸遠。另外一件傷心事就是他的小師妹岳靈珊愛上了新的師弟林平之並且嫁給了林。令狐沖成了自己本來世界的局外人，但是他在更廣闊的江湖開始了新的探險。

 文法解析

 KEY 54

○ Since then Linghu Chong became a formidable swordsman, and he could defeat opponents without much effort.

✗ Since then Linghu Chong became a formidable swordsman, and he could defeat opponents without much effort.

◆中譯◆ 那之後他變成了令人景仰的劍客，可以輕鬆戰勝敵人。

天龍八部

鹿鼎記

笑傲江湖

雪山飛狐

神鵰俠侶

射鵰英雄傳

連城訣碧血劍

書劍恩仇錄

✦ 解析 ✦ 副詞子句放在主要子句前面時候需要加逗點。放在主句後則不需要加逗點。

 KEY 55

◯ Linghu Chong did not defend himself <u>as</u> he had promised not to reveal that Feng Qingyang was still alive.

✗ Linghu Chong did not defend himself he had promised not to reveal that Feng Qingyang was still alive.

✦ 中譯 ✦ 因為已經承諾絕不向外透露風清揚還健在,令狐沖沒有為自己辯解。

✦ 解析 ✦ 副詞子句前須加上表原因的從屬連接詞。

 KEY 56

◯ <u>While</u> he was still faithful to the Huashan Sect, all his previous fellows considered him a betrayer.

✗ <u>While</u> he was still faithful to the Huashan Sect, <u>but</u> all his previous fellows considered him a betrayer.

✦ 中譯 ✦ 他仍然對華山派忠心耿耿,但他的師兄弟都把他當做背叛師門的人。

✦ 解析 ✦ While 在這裡是表示讓步的從屬連接詞(不是表時間),不可以與 but 同時使用。

武俠人物 23 - Linghu Chong (令狐沖) *MP3* *23*

After he left the Huashan Sect, Linghu Chong met Ren Yingying (任盈盈), a lady in veil. Linghu Chong considered her a respectable grandma; he shared his story and sadness with her. In fact, she was young, and having Linghu Chong around led to the development of the affection towards him. He did not find out her true identity until quite late. During the time when Linghu Chong searched for treatment of his internal injury, he got acquaintaned with many friends, including Xiang Wentian (向問天), an outcast form the Sun Moon Holy Cult. They became sworn brothers and Xiang took him to a dungeon under the West Lake where Ren Woxing (任我行) was locked. Linghu Chong assisted Ren Woxing for prison break; he substituted Ren and practised the 'Star Sucking Skill' (吸星法) following the notes Ren Woxing inscribed in the dungeon .

　　離開華山派之後，令狐沖遇見了任盈盈，一位戴頭巾的女士。令狐沖覺得她是位年事已高的婆婆，和她分享了自己的故事和感傷情緒。實際上她很年輕，與令狐沖的相處中對他產生了好感，他在很久後才知道她的真實身分。令狐沖在為自己內傷求醫途中結識了許多朋友，包括被日月神教拋棄的向問天。他們成了結義兄弟，向問天帶他去了西湖底的地牢，在那裡囚禁著任我行。令狐沖協助了任我行越獄，他代替任我行被關並依據任我行刻在地牢的筆記，練習了「吸星大法」。

Linghu Chong later helped Ren Woxing defeat Dongfang

Bubai (東方不敗) and regain power in the Sun Moon Holy Cult. He refused to join the cult, but as the head of the Hengshan Sect, he was involved in the chaos of the combination of Five Mountains Sword Sects Alliance. After the cruel fighting, Yue Buqun became the leader of the new alliance.

令狐沖後來幫助任我行戰勝了東方不敗，重新奪回了日月神教的控制權。令狐沖回絕了加入日月神教的邀請，但是作為恆山派掌門，他捲入了五岳劍派合併的紛爭。在經歷殘酷的爭鬥後，岳不群成為了新聯盟的領袖。

A slaughter started inside the 'orthodox' sects, because most people were intoxicated by power, and they killed each other for mutual distrust. Meanwhile, Ren Woxing became greedy after seizing power; he was triggered by megalomania and planned to attack those sects at their weak time. Linghu Chong refused to collude. Ren Woxing later died from losing control of his inner power. His daughter Ren Yingying ceased the conflict between the orthodox sects and the cult.

正統門派之間開始了相互殘殺，因為大多數人醉心於權力，互相猜忌而展開殺戮。同時，重掌權利的任我行也變得貪婪自大，策劃在正統門派虛弱時候將他們一網打盡，令狐沖拒絕與他合謀。任我行後來死於內力失控，他的女兒任盈盈平息了正邪之爭。

天龍八部
鹿鼎記
笑傲江湖
雪山飛狐
神鵰俠侶
射鵰英雄傳
連碧城血訣劍
書劍恩仇錄

文法解析

KEY 57

○ After he left Huashan Sect, Linghu Chong met Ren Yingying.

✗ After he leaving Huashan Sect, Linghu Chong met Ren Yingying.

✦中譯✦ 離開華山派之後，令狐沖遇見了任盈盈。

✦解析✦ **After** 作表示時間的從屬連接詞，**after** 後的句子作為副詞子句，要和主句時態保持一致。如果 **after** 作為介系詞，則不能引導一個句子，應當去掉主詞 **he**，並把動詞改為動名詞型態。

 ### KEY 58

○ During the time Linghu Chong searched for treatment of his internal injury, he <u>got</u> acquainted with friends, including Xiang Wentian, an outcast form the Sun Moon Holy Cult.

✗ During the time Linghu Chong searched for treatment of his internal injury, he <u>get</u> acquainted with friends, including Xiang Wentian, an outcast form the Sun Moon Holy Cult.

✦中譯✦ 令狐沖在為自己內傷求醫途中結識了許多朋友，包括被日月神教拋棄的向問天。

✦解析✦ 時間副詞子句中，如果主句是未來時，子句要用一般現在時。而主句是過去時的情況子句不需要變成一般現在時。

 KEY 59

○ A slaughter started inside the 'orthodox' sects, because most people were intoxicated by power and they <u>killed</u> each other for mutual distrust.

✗ A slaughter started inside the 'orthodox' sects, because most people were intoxicated by power and they <u>kill</u> each other for mutual distrust.

✦中譯✦ 正統門派之間開始了自相殘殺，因為大多數人利慾薰心，互相猜忌而展開殺戮。

✦解析✦ 整個句子的時態應該保持一致，所以 kill 的現在時用法不正確。

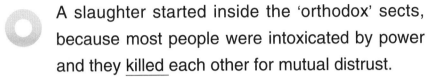 武俠人物 24 - Ren Yingying (任盈盈) **MP3 24**

Ren Yingying (任盈盈) is the daughter of Ren Woxing. Dongfang Bubai imprisoned her father and raised her Although she is one of the top leaders in the Sun Moon Holy Cult, Ren Yingying is not keen on seizing power. She lives in seclusion and seldom reveals her appearance whenever she goes out. Besides martial arts, Ren Yingying was also skilled in playing instruments. She managed to play the abstruse melody of < The Smiling, Proud Wanderer >.

天龍八部
鹿鼎記
笑傲江湖
雪山飛狐
神鵰俠侶
射鵰英雄傳
連城訣
碧血劍
書劍恩仇錄

任盈盈是任我行的女兒。東方不敗囚禁了她父親並把她養大。雖然任盈盈在日月神教地位甚高，但她並不熱心於掌權。她離群獨居，外出時很少以真面目示人。除了武藝之外，任盈盈也精通樂器，她能夠演奏艱深的笑傲江湖曲。

Ren Yingying's personality is complex. She is magnanimous and considerate, but she also has a facet of cruelness. When she met Linghu Chong, she dressed like an old lady and listened to his story behind her veil. Linghu Chong's chivalrous personality attracted her. She carried severely wounded Linghu Chong to the Shaolin Temple and fought desperately for a cure for him.

任盈盈有複雜的個性，她對人寬宏體貼，但也有殘忍的一面。她遇到令狐沖的時候扮成老嫗模樣，在面紗後面聽了很多他的故事。令狐沖的俠義個性吸引了她，她背著受重傷的令狐沖上少林寺，拼死求得救他一命。

Her calmness and wisdom saved her father and Linghu Chong's life. During the fight between Ren Woxing and Dongfang Bubai, Ren Yingying distracted Dongfang Bubai by attacking his lover; otherwise, Dongfang Bubai would never be defeated. Linghu Chong and Ren Yingying have undergone many challenges together; his affection to Ren Yingying has gradually overcome sadness from the previous relationship with Yue Lingshan. After Ren Woxing died, Ren Yingying succeeded her father as the leader of the Sun Moon Holy Cult. She negotiated with the people in the orthodox sects and reached an agreement of ceasing fire between the 'right' and the 'evil' groups. She eventually retired and started a reclusive happy life with Linghu Chong.

　　她的智慧和冷靜也曾挽救她父親和令狐沖的性命。在任我行和東方不敗的大戰中，任盈盈攻擊了東方不敗的情人使他分心，不然沒有人能勝過東方不敗。令狐沖和任盈盈一起經歷了許多挑戰，他對任盈盈的愛意也漸漸讓他忘卻之前與岳靈珊的失敗感情。任我行死後，任盈盈繼承了日月神教的教主。她與正派人士談判，達成了正邪門派間對休戰的協議。她最後退隱江湖，和令狐沖過著快樂的隱居生活。

 ## 文法解析

 ### KEY 60

 Although she is one of the top leaders in the Sun Moon Holy Cult, Ren Yingying is not keen on seizing power.

 Although she is one of the top leaders in the Sun Moon Holy Cult, but Ren Yingying is not keen on seizing power.

✦中譯✦ 雖然任盈盈在日月神教地位甚高，但她並不熱心於掌權。

✦解析✦ 表示讓步的從屬連接詞 although 不能與對等連接詞 but 同時使用。

KEY 61

⭕ She lives in seclusion and seldom reveals her appearance when <u>goes</u> out.

❌ She lives in seclusion and seldom reveals her appearance when <u>go</u> out.

✦中譯✦ 她離群獨居，外出時很少以真面目示人。

✦解析✦ 副詞子句的主詞 she 被省略，因為與主句主詞一致。根據時態一致的原則，子句動詞也要配合主詞 she，用第三人稱單數。

KEY 62

⭕ Ren Yingying distracted Dongfang Bubai by attacking his lover; otherwise, Dongfang Bubai <u>would</u> never be defeated.

❌ Ren Yingying distracted Dongfang Bubai by attacking his lover; otherwise, Dongfang Bubai <u>will</u> never be defeated.

✦中譯✦ 任盈盈攻擊了東方不敗的情人使他分心，不然沒有人能勝過東方不敗。

✦解析✦ 因為整個句子都是過去時，所以表讓步的副詞子句中動詞 will 要寫作過去時態 would。

武俠人物 25 - Yue Buqun (岳不群) *MP3* *25*

Yue Buqun (岳不群) is the leader of the Huashan Sect. He is nicknamed The Gentleman Sword for his upright conduct and behavior. His decent and humble act makes him the role model of many Huashan apprentices, including Linghu Chong. Yue Buqun is a powerful martial arts expert. He leads the Qi Fiction (氣宗) of Huashan Sect which focuses on utilizing the internal energy. The 'Violet Mist Divine Skill'(紫霞神功) is Yue's master skill. Feng Qingyang, who always knows about Yue's hypocrisy, commented him with contempt and mocked him as a dogmatic fool, since he teaches his apprentices in a rigid way that wastes students' talent.

岳不群是華山派掌門人。他因為正直的操守行為得到了君子劍的綽號。岳不群得體謙遜的作為讓他成為包括令狐沖在內的眾華山派弟子的道德楷模。岳不群是一位武功大師,他領導華山派的氣宗,氣宗重在運用內力,他的看家功夫是紫霞神功。一直知曉岳不群虛偽本性的風清揚輕蔑的評價他是一個守教條的笨蛋,因為他用死板的方式培養弟子,浪費他們的才能。

Because there were not many people know about Yue Buqun's true personality, he has always been trusted and respected. However, he gradually reveals his selfishness and greed. Unlike Ren Woxing's frankness to his hunger towards power, Yue plots sneakily and conspires to annex the whole martial arts world under the cover of his scholarly and righteous behavior.

由於明白岳不群真正個性的人並不多，所以他一直受到尊敬信任。不過他還是逐漸顯露出自私貪婪的一面。與任我行不掩蓋自己對權力的企圖相反，岳不群在大師風度和正直行為的掩護下暗中策劃，陰謀吞併武林。

He pretended to save Lin Pingzhi from the deadly family tragedy so that he could steal Lin's Bixie Sword Manual. To master the skill in the manual, Yue Buqun castrated himself. He schemed an elaborate plan and seized the top position of the Five Mountains Sword Sects Alliance. He deceived all members in the Alliance by luring them into a cave and triggered a slaughter among one another. His wife committed suicide in shame after finding out Yue Buqun's true nature; however, he was not imprevious to that. Finally, Yilin, the little nun in Hengshan Sect, accidentally killed Yue Buqun in the chaos of the Alliance internal strife.

為了偷林家的辟邪劍譜，他假意解救了慘遭滅門之災的林平之。岳不群揮刀自宮練習辟邪劍譜，他策劃了精密的陰謀，取得了五岳劍派的掌門人位置。他把所有五岳劍派的人們騙到山洞裡，挑起了大家互相殘殺。他的妻子因為發現岳不群的本性羞憤自殺，但岳不群並不為之所動。最後他在五岳劍派內鬨的混亂中碰巧死在了恆山派的小尼姑儀琳手下。

文法解析

KEY 63

○ Feng Qingyang, who always knows about Yue's hypocrisy, comments him with contempt and mocks him as a dogmatic fool, <u>since</u> he teaches his apprentices in a rigid way that wastes the students' talent.

✕ Feng Qingyang, who always knows about Yue's hypocrisy, comments him with contempt and mocks him as a dogmatic fool, <u>so</u> he teaches his apprentices in a rigid way that wastes the students' talent.

──────────────────────────

✦中譯✦ 一直知曉岳不群虛偽本性的風清揚輕蔑的評價他是一個守教條的笨蛋，因為他用死板的方式培養弟子，浪費他們的才能。

✦解析✦ 子句解釋了風清揚嘲笑岳不群的原因，所以要用表原因的從屬連接詞。

KEY 64

○ <u>Because</u> there was not many people know about Yue Buqun's true personality, he was always trusted and respected.

❌ <u>Because</u> there was not many people know about Yue Buqun's true personality, <u>therefore</u>, he was always trusted and respected.

✦中譯✦ 由於明白岳不群真正個性的人並不多,所以他一直受到尊敬信任。

✦解析✦ 從屬連接詞 because 不與對等連接詞 therefore 用在同一句子中。

 KEY 65

⭕ He pretended to save Lin Pingzhi from the deadly family tragedy <u>so that</u> he could steal Lin's Bixie Sword Manual.

❌ He pretended to save Lin Pingzhi from the deadly family tragedy <u>that</u> he could steal Lin's Bixie Sword Manual.

✦中譯✦ 為了偷林家的辟邪劍譜,他假意解救了慘遭滅門之災的林平之。

✦解析✦ So that 為表目的地從屬連接詞,引導副詞子句。That 是關係代名詞不能引導副詞子句。

武俠人物 26 - Zuo Lengchan (左冷禪) MP3 *26*

Zuo Lengchan (左冷禪) is the leader of the Songshan Sect (嵩山派). Relative to Yue Buqun's hypocrisy, Zuo Lengchen represents the characteristic of despicable. <u>Zuo Lengchan self-proclaimed as the leader of the alliance since Songshan is located in the middle of the five mountains.</u>

左冷禪是嵩山派掌門人。與偽君子岳不群相對，左冷禪是真小人的代表。因為嵩山座落於五岳的中心，所以左冷禪也自封為五岳劍派盟主。

Zuo Lengchan is a formidable Kungfu master. He practises the 'Freezing Inner Energy' (寒冰真氣), a powerful skill that allows him to increase his inner force tremendously. He is ambitious to dominate the martial arts world. To achieve this target, whoever blocks his way will be ruthlessly killed. Zuo Lengchan sent Lao Denuo (勞德諾) to join the Huashan Sect as an undercover agent and drew Taishan Sect over his side by bribing their leader. He feigned as a member from the Sun Moon Holy Cult and killed the chief of the Hengshan Sect.

左冷禪是一位強大的功夫高手，他的厲害功夫"寒冰真氣"讓他可以極大的提高內力。他野心勃勃想要一統江湖。為了達成這個目標，所有阻擋他的人都會被無情殺害。左冷禪派勞德諾去華山派臥底並且收買拉攏了泰山派，還扮作日月神教的人殺死了恆山派掌門人。

Even with a meticulous plot, Zuo Lengchan was eventually defeated by Yue Buqun. Lao Denuo stole the Bixie Sword Manual for Zuo Lengchan; so he practised accordingly. <u>As

天龍八部

鹿鼎記

笑傲江湖

雪山飛狐

神鵰俠侶

射鵰英雄傳

連城訣血劍

書劍恩仇錄

Yue Buqun had falsified the Manual, Zuo Lengchan exercised a wrong version with incorrect techniques.

　　即使左冷禪有周密計畫，他最終還是敗給了岳不群。左冷禪練習了勞德諾為他偷來的辟邪劍譜。因為劍譜被岳不群竄改過，所以左冷禪依照錯誤版本練習了錯誤的技術。

Zuo assembled the alliance and tried to intimidate them. Yue Buqun defeated and blinded him by using the real Bixie Swordplay. Zuo pretended that he sucuumbed to Yue Buqun on the surface but later was planning on having a revenge with his followers. Yue Buqun saw through his plan and trapped them inside the cave in Huashan. In the end, Zuo Lengchan was killed by Linghu Chong.

　　左冷禪聚集了五岳劍派所有門人，試圖威嚇他們。岳不群使出真正的辟邪劍法擊敗了左冷禪並且刺瞎他的雙眼。左冷禪佯裝屈服於岳不群，然後引領自己的追隨者去華山報仇。岳不群看透了他的計畫，把他們誘入洞穴裡。最後左冷禪死於令狐沖劍下。

 文法解析

 KEY 66

 Zuo Lengchan self-proclaimed as the leader of the alliance since Songshan locates in the middle of the five mountains.

Zuo Lengchan self-proclaimed as the leader of the alliance <u>since Songshan located</u> in the middle of the five mountains.

+中譯+ 因為嵩山座落於五岳的中心，所以左冷禪也自封為五岳劍派盟主。

+解析+ 因為嵩山的位置是一個固定的事實，所以不需要配合主句用過去式。

KEY 67

○ As Yue Buqun had falsified the Manual, Zuo Lengchan exercised a wrong version with incorrect techniques.

 As Yue Buqun had falsified the Manual, <u>so</u> Zuo Lengchan exercised a wrong version with incorrect techniques.

+中譯+ 因為劍譜被岳不群竄改過，所以左冷禪依照錯誤版本練習了錯誤的技術。

+解析+ 對等連接詞 so 不與表原因的從屬連接詞 as 合用在一句中。

 武俠人物 27 - Dongfang Bubai (東方不敗) *MP3* **27**

Dongfang Bubai (東方不敗) is the leader of the Sun Moon Holy Cult. His name indicates that he is invincible. To obtain perfect martial arts skills, he castrated himself to practise the

天龍八部

鹿鼎記

笑傲江湖

雪山飛狐

神鵰俠侶

射鵰英雄傳

連城訣 碧血劍

書劍恩仇錄

Sunflower Manual (葵花寶典). The Manual has such an evil nature that whoever touches it will become addicted and obsessed with the dangerous practice. <u>After mastering the Sunflower Manual, Dongfang Bubai's Kungfu became extremely superior.</u> His weapon was tiny swift needles, making his opponents unable to instantly react.

　　東方不敗是日月神教的教主。他的名字表示了他是不可戰勝的。為了讓武功臻於完美，他閹割了自己以練習葵花寶典。葵花寶典的邪惡本質讓所有接觸到它的人都深陷其中並且沈迷於危險的練習。在掌握葵花寶典後，東方不敗的武功變得極為強大。他的武器是微小迅捷的繡花針，使對手根本無法立即地反應。

The Sunflower Manual corrupts one's will as well. Dongfang Bubai became very cruel. He imprisoned the previous leader of the Sun Moon Holy Cult Ren Woxing and replaced this position. He controlled people by poisoning them; all his subordinates need his antidotes to relieve symptoms. In addition, Dongfang Bubai developed feminine personality and engaged in an intimate relationship with a male lover Yang Lianting (楊蓮亭). He was deeply involved in the relationship and ignored affairs in the cult; the power had transferred to his lover.

　　葵花寶典也腐蝕人的意志。東方不敗變得非常殘暴。他把日月神教的前任教主任我行囚禁起來，自己取代了他的位置。他控制別人的方法

是下毒，所有他的下屬都要仰賴他的解藥緩解中毒症狀。另外東方不敗變得女性化並愛上了男性情人楊蓮亭。他深陷感情中，忽略教派事務，權力被轉移到他的情人手裡。

Ren Woxing escaped from the dungeon and regathered his former followers; he led Linghu Chong, Xiang Wentian and Ren Yingying to challenge Dongfang Bubai. <u>Ren Woxing's side is outnumbered; but Dongfang Bubai was so powerful that the joint effort from these top martial artists could only reach a draw with him.</u> Ren Yingying attacked Yang Lianting to make Dongfang Bubai lose his focus. Other three took advantage of the distraction and stroke Dongfang Bubai devastatingly. Before his death, Dongfang Bubai blinded Ren Woxing with his needle.

　　任我行從地牢脫身後結集了他的舊部屬，並與令狐沖、向問天和任盈盈一道挑戰東方不敗。任我行一邊人數占優，但東方不敗太過強大，幾個功夫頂尖高手合力也只能和他打成平手。任盈盈攻擊楊蓮亭，分散了東方不敗的注意力。其他三人趁東方不敗精神不集中給他致命一擊。東方不敗在死前還是用他的繡花針射瞎任我行的眼睛。

  文法解析

 KEY 68

After <u>mastering</u> the Sunflower Manual, Dongfang Bubai's Kungfu became extremely superior.

After <u>master</u> the Sunflower Manual, Dongfang Bubai's Kungfu became extremely superior.

✦中譯✦ 在掌握葵花寶典後，東方不敗的武功變得極為強大。

✦解析✦ After 用作引導副詞子句的從屬連接詞時，主句和子句時態需要一致。或者視 after 為介系詞，將 master 改寫成動名詞 mastering。

KEY 69

⭘ Ren Woxing's side is outnumbered, but Dongfang Bubai was <u>so powerful that</u> the the joint effort from these top martial artists could only reach a draw with him.

✗ Ren Woxing's side is outnumbered, but Dongfang Bubai was <u>so powerful</u> the the joint effort from these top martial artists could only reach a draw with him.

✦中譯✦ 任我行這邊人數占優，但東方不敗太過強大，幾個功夫頂尖高手合力也只能和他打成平手。

✦解析✦ So＋adj＋that 為表結果的從屬連接詞，that 後面的子句表示主句的結果。That 不能省略。

 武俠人物 28 - Lin Pingzhi's (林平之) MP3 28

Lin Pingzhi (林平之) character experienced a dramatic change

in the novel. His family operated a security escort business; Lin Pingzhi is well-protected and lighthearted. He always stands up against injustice disregarding how powerful the rival is whereas Lin only practises normal kungfu skills. The Bixie Sword Manual that handed down in Lin's family attracted lots of greedy eyes. Yu Canghai (余滄海) from the Qingcheng Sect (青城派) plotted a deadly massacre and Lin Pingzhi suddenly became the only survivor in his clan.

林平之的個性在小説中有戲劇化的轉變。林家經營鏢局,林平之被保護的很好,性格無憂無慮。雖然他功夫平凡,卻時常不管對手有多強都出頭主持公道。林家家傳的辟邪劍譜吸引來覬覦的目光。青城派的余滄海血腥屠殺了林家,林平之成了他們家唯一的倖存者。

After losing everything, Lin Pingzhi made himself an apprentice of Yue Buqun, who showed sympathy towards him. Yue Buqun treated Lin affably and arranged marriage between him and Yue Lingshan. The family tragedy made Lin Pingzhi indulge in resentment. Furthermore, when he eventually realized that Yue Buqun's ulterior target was also the Bixie Sword Manual, all his faith and trust collapsed. Lin was driven by hatred and became a vicious villain.

在失去一切之後,林平之拜師岳不群門下。岳不群對林平之展現出同情之意,他親切對待林平之,並安排了林平之和岳靈珊的婚事。家庭悲劇已經使林平之沈浸在仇恨當中。更嚴重的是,當他終於發現岳不群

天龍八部

鹿鼎記

笑傲江湖

雪山飛狐

神鵰俠侶

射鵰英雄傳

連城訣碧血劍

書劍恩仇錄

的隱密目標也是辟邪劍譜後，他的信念倒塌了。林平之變成了被仇恨驅使的惡人。

Lin Pingzhi found out only formidable kungfu power could make him survive. He utilized Yue Lingshan as a shield and practised the Bixie Swordplay. When he had mastered the Manual, he killed all his family enemies brutally. His wife Yue Lingshan also died in his hand. Lin's successful revenge activity made himself known as an alive Bixei Sword Manual. He joined Zuo Lengchan to carry out an ambush towards Yue Buqun; but during the fight, Linghu Chong overtrumped him. Lin Pingzhi was finally locked in the dungeon where Ren Woxing used to be imprisoned; this is because Linghu Chong promised Yue Lingshan to protect Lin from other people's assassins.

林平之發現只有自己掌握蓋世武功才能生存。他利用岳靈珊做幌子練習辟邪劍法。掌握劍法之後，他殘忍的殺害了林家的仇人們，也殺死了自己的妻子。林平之報仇成功讓人們知道他是一個活劍譜。他與左冷禪一道策劃伏擊岳不群，在打鬥中輸給了令狐沖。林平之最後被囚禁在曾經關著任我行的地牢裡，因為令狐沖答應岳靈珊要保護他不要被人暗殺。

文法解析

KEY 70

○ He always stands up against injustice disregarding how powerful the rival is, <u>whereas</u> Lin only practises normal kungfu skills.

✗ He always stands up against injustice disregarding how powerful the rival is <u>as</u> Lin only practises normal kungfu skills.

✦中譯✦ 雖然他功夫平凡，卻時常不管對手有多強都出頭主持公道。

✦解析✦ **Whereas** 是表讓步的從屬連接詞而 **as** 表原因。此處應當是 whereas。

KEY 71

○ Furthermore, <u>when</u> he eventually realized that Yue Buqun's ulterior target was also the Bixie Sword Manual, all his faith and trust <u>collapsed</u>.

✗ Furthermore, when he eventually realized that Yue Buqun's ulterior target was also the Bixie Sword Manual, all his faith and trust <u>collapse</u>.

✦中譯✦ 更嚴重的是，當他終於發現岳不群的隱密目標也是辟邪劍譜後，他的信念倒塌了。

✦解析✦ 時間副詞子句應當與主句的時態一致。

天龍八部

鹿鼎記

笑傲江湖

雪山飛狐

神鵰俠侶

射鵰英雄傳

連城訣 碧血劍

書劍恩仇錄

武俠人物 29 - Ren Woxing (任我行) *MP3* *29*

Ren Woxing (任我行) is Ren Yingying's father. He used to be the leader of the Sun Moon Holy Cult. Dongfang Bubai's betrayal made him imprisoned and out of power for twelve years. He was one of the top martial artists in the novel. Ren Woxing mastered the 'Star Sucking Skill', which can drain and absorb other people's inner energy.

任我行是任盈盈的父親。他曾是日月神教的教主，東方不敗背叛了他並把他囚禁了十二年，使他失去了權力。任我行是小說中的頂尖高手，他的吸星大法能夠吸收他人的內力。

Ren Woxing is imperious and arrogant; on the other hand, he is a shrewd expert in politics and manipulation. He gave the Sunflower Manual to Dongfang Bubai as a gift, even though he knew about the wicked nature of the Manual. Ren Woxing gathered several people's joint effort to defeat Dongfang Bubai and restored his leadership.

任我行傲慢自大，另一方面他也是個精明有手腕的政治家。儘管他知曉葵花寶典的邪惡本質仍然將之送給東方不敗作為禮物。任我行集結了多人的力量打敗了東方不敗，重掌大權。

When Dongfang Bubai was the hierarch, he established the power order in the cult. Everyone must eulogize him as the brilliant supreme leader who will eventually unify the whole martial arts world. Ren Woxing was initially sick of the flattery but gradually accustomed to the praise and started believing and enjoying the blandishment.

東方不敗做教主的時候在教內建立了權力法則，每個人必須讚頌他是至高無上的英明教主，必將一統江湖。任我行一開始覺得這種奉承非常噁心，但他也漸漸習慣了，並且相信和享受這些稱讚。

The craving of power engulfed Ren Woxing. He determined to consolidate his control in the cult and eliminate all the orthodox sects. After the Sun Moon Holy Cult made it clear that they will slaughter the Hengshan Sect, people decided to boom him to death. They planned to trick Ren Woxing to sit on an armchair that was decorated with worshipful slogans and bombs, since nobody was able to physically defeat him. Ren Woxing finally died from a stroke at the moment of reaching ultimate power.

對權力的渴望吞噬了任我行。他決定鞏固自己在神教的地位並剷除所有名門正派。日月神教宣布要屠殺恆山派之後，人們決定炸死任我行。他們計劃把任我行騙到裝了奉承標語和炸彈的太師椅上，因為沒有人的武功能夠勝過他。任我行在登上權力巔峰的時刻中風而死。

天龍八部

鹿鼎記

笑傲江湖

雪山飛狐

神鵰俠侶

射鵰英雄傳

連城訣 碧血劍

書劍恩仇錄

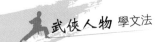

 文法解析

 KEY 72

○ He gave the Sunflower Manual to Dongfang Bubai as a gift <u>even though</u> he knew about the wicked nature of the Manual.

✕ He gave the Sunflower Manual to Dongfang Bubai as a gift <u>even</u> he knew about the wicked nature of the Manual.

✦中譯✦ 儘管他知曉葵花寶典的邪惡本質仍然將之送給東方不敗作為禮物。

✦解析✦ Even 為副詞,而 even though 引導副詞子句。

 KEY 73

○ They planned to trick Ren Woxing to sit on an armchair that was decorated with worshipful slogans and bombs, <u>since</u> nobody was able to physically defeat him.

✕ They planned to trick Ren Woxing to sit on an armchair that was decorated with worshipful slogans and bombs, <u>so</u> nobody was able to physically defeat him.

✦中譯✦ 他們計劃把任我行騙到裝了奉承標語和炸彈的太師椅上,因為沒有人的武功能夠勝過他。

✦ 解析 ✦ 沒有人可以戰勝任我行是主句的原因而不是結果，所以連接
詞要用表原因的 since。

 ## 武俠人物 30 - Yilin (儀琳)

 MP3 30

Yilin (儀琳) is a nun in the Hengshan Sect; her teacher is one of the 'Three Elder Nuns' Dingyi. Yilin is the daughter of Monk Bujie (不戒和尚) and Mute Granny in Hengshan. Tian Boguang once kidnapped Yilin and Linghu Chong rescued her. She fell in love with Linghu Chong since then, but she had to suppress her feelings because of her religious discipline.

　　儀琳是恆山派的尼姑，她的師傅是恆山三定中的定逸師太。儀琳的父母是不戒和尚和恆山的啞婆婆。儀琳曾被田伯光擄走又被令狐沖解救，那之後她就愛上了令狐沖，可是由於宗教的戒律不得不壓抑自己的感情。

Yilin is innocent and kind-hearted. She firmly upheld the Buddhist precepts. Linghu Chong was seriously injured and desperately need to be hydrated. Yilin struggled; and then decided to break her commandment and steal a watermelon for him. She confided her secret to the Mute Granny who was actually her mother. Granny promised to help her marry Linghu Chong, but Yilin selected to follow her vow of celibacy and continue her unrequited love. While Linghu Chong was in love with Yue Lingshan, Yilin prayed for them; later his romance with Ren Yingying also received Yilin's sincere blessing.

儀琳善良無邪，嚴格遵守佛教清規。令狐沖有一次嚴重受傷需要喝水，儀琳經過內心掙扎，破戒幫他偷顆西瓜解渴。她曾向她的母親啞婆婆傾訴自己心裡的秘密，啞婆婆承諾要幫助她嫁給令狐沖，但是儀琳還是決定繼續保持獨身和單戀。當令狐沖苦戀岳靈珊時，儀琳曾幫他們祈福；後來令狐沖和任盈盈的感情也受到儀琳的祝福。

The second time Yilin broke her conduct was in Huashan. Yue Buqun set a snare and trapped Linghu Chong into a net. <u>Just before Yue Buqun was going to kill Linghu Chong, Yilin stabbed Yue Buqun on his back.</u> By killing Yue Buqun, Yilin saved Linghu Chong's life as well as revenged for her masters. The author says Yilin is the one who understands Linghu Chong the most. As a happy go lucky person, Linghu Chong pursuits freedom. His love towards Yue lingshan and Ren Yingying both made him constrained; only in Yilin's one-sided love, Linghu Chong keeps his carefree nature.

儀琳第二次破戒是在華山，當時岳不群設下陷阱將令狐沖捉進網裏。就在岳不群要殺害令狐沖之前，儀琳從背後刺死了岳不群。這不但救了令狐沖還為她的師傅報了仇。作者說儀琳最了解令狐沖，他是個無憂無慮追求自由的人。他在對岳靈珊和任盈盈的愛情裡都受到約束，只有在儀琳的單戀中保持了自由天性。

文法解析

KEY 74

○ While Linghu Chong was in love with Yue Lingshan, Yilin prayed for them.

✗ While Linghu Chong was in love with Yue Lingshan Yilin prayed for them.

✦中譯✦ 當令狐沖苦戀岳靈珊時，儀琳曾幫他們祈福。

✦解析✦ 表時間的副詞子句放在主要子句前，逗點不能省略。

KEY 75

○ Just before Yue Buqun <u>slaughtered</u> Linghu Chong, Yilin stabbed Yue Buqun on his back.

✗ Just before Yue Buqun <u>slaughters</u> Linghu Chong, Yilin stabbed Yue Buqun on his back.

✦中譯✦ 就在岳不群要殺害令狐沖之前，儀琳從背後刺死了岳不群。

✦解析✦ 時間副詞子句中，主句是將來時，子句才需要改用一般現在時。

Glossary 字彙一覽表

abstruse *adj.* 深奧難懂的	affably *adj.* 和顏悅色的
blandishment *n.* 奉承，諂媚	carefree *adj.* 暢快的
celibacy *n.* 獨身	collude *vt.* 串通
commandment *n.* 戒律	confide *vt.vi.* 吐露，信任
conspire *vt.* 合謀	contempt *n.* 鄙視
despicable *adj.* 卑鄙的	devastatingly *adj.* 毀滅性的
disciple *n.* 弟子	dogmatic *adj.* 獨斷的
dungeon *n.* 地牢	eulogize *n.* 頌揚，讚揚
facet *n.* 面，方面	feminine *adj.* 女性的，陰性的
heretic *n.* 異教徒	humble *adj.* 謙遜的
hypocrite *n.* 偽君子	imperious *adj.* 專橫的，傲慢的
invincible *adj.* 不可戰勝的	inconspicuous *adj.* 不起眼的，不顯眼的
indifferent *adj.* 無所謂的	inscribe *vt.* 題寫，雕刻
intimate *adj.* 親密的	intimidate *vt.* 恐嚇，威脅
lighthearted *adj.* 輕鬆的	magnanimous *adj.* 坦蕩的，有雅量的
manipulation *n.* 操作，控制	massacre *n.* 大屠殺
megalomania *adj.* 狂妄自大的	outcast *n.adj.* 棄兒，流浪者，被遺棄的
precept *n.* 箴言，訓誡，格言	reclusive *adj.* 深居簡出的

resentment *n.* 怨恨	rigid *adj.* 死板的，嚴格的，精確的
sanguine *adj.* 樂觀的	scruffy *adj.* 邋遢的
seclusion *n.* 隱居	shield *n.vt.vi.* 盾，遮蔽，防禦
shrewd *adj.* 精明的	strife *n.* 衝突，爭吵，不和
supremacy *n.* 霸權，主權，至高地位	tremendous *adj.* 巨大的
ulterior *adj.* 別有用心的	unrequited *adj.* 單相思的
veil *n.* 面紗	waggish *adj.* 滑稽的

筆記欄

天龍八部

鹿鼎記

笑傲江湖

雪山飛狐

神鵰俠侶

射鵰英雄傳

連城訣碧血劍

書劍恩仇錄

Unit 4

主詞與動詞的一致性
〖雪山飛狐〗

文法主題介紹－主詞與動詞的一致性

英文句子中的動詞變化，除了時態外，便取決於主詞的人稱和單複數。

主詞為單數，動詞則用單數形；若主詞為第三人稱、現在式時，動詞字尾加-s / -es 或去 y 加-ies。主詞為複數，動詞則搭配複數。

達成主詞與動詞的一致性的三步驟：

(1) 判斷真正的主詞

(2) 判斷主詞的單複數

(3) 判斷時態與主被動

以下幾種狀況要特別判斷主詞：

1. 主詞和動詞分開

主詞後帶有修飾的介系詞片語/不定詞片語/分詞片語

EX: The result *of the previous year's training surveys* is available online.

主詞後帶有修飾的子句

EX: Initial reports *which were collected by the institute* show that cancer is a leading *cause of death in the world.*

2. 主詞部分呈現

all, some, most, part, the rest, half, fraction, percent/percentage＋單數名詞

單數動詞

all, some, most, part, the rest, half, fraction, percent/

percentage+ 複數名詞

✒ 複數動詞

表示一部分時，動詞的單、複數形由 of 後面的名詞來決定

3. 連接詞片語連接兩主詞

(Either) A or B, Neither A nor B, Not only A but also B, Not A but B, B as well as A, B along with A, B together with A + 動詞單複數看 B

Both A and B 則+複數動詞

4. 其他

✒ 動名詞或不定詞當主詞時，動詞要用單數型。

✒ There is + 單數名詞

There are + 複數名詞

✒ Each/Every +單數名詞 + 單數動詞

Each of the + 複數名詞 + 單數動詞

✒ a number of + 複數名詞 + 複數動詞

the number of + 複數名詞 + 單數動詞

✒ 關係子句中動詞的單複數

單數名詞 +【who/which +單數動詞】

複數名詞 +【who/which +複數動詞】

武俠人物 31 - Overview(概要)

MP3
31

Fox Volant of the Snowy Mountain (雪山飛狐) is one of Jin Yong's shortest novels. This story is unique in structure. It

天龍八部

鹿鼎記

笑傲江湖

雪山飛狐

神鵰俠侶

射鵰英雄傳

連城訣

碧血劍

書劍恩仇錄

employs storytelling flashbacks which is quite rare in martial arts literature. In this novel, Narration based on several people's memory dates back decades ago, while the actual time frame only lasts for one day.

《雪山飛狐》是金庸的最短篇小說之一。這個故事結構特別。採取了武俠文學中罕見的倒敘式。在小說中，幾個人回憶敘述了幾十年前的往事，而小說本身的故事在一天內完成。

The story happened in Manchuria during the Qianlong Emperor's (乾隆皇帝) time in the Qing Dynasty. Some pugilists unearthed a treasure chest on the Snowy Mountain. They started to fight for it. During the fight, a highly skilled monk Baoshu (寶樹和尚) trumped all other opponents and forced people to make their way to a manor in Jade Brush Peak (玉筆峰). The owner of the manor was waiting for a mysterious swordsman's challenge. This swordsman is Hu Fei (胡斐), nicknamed the fox volant of the snowy mountain.

這個故事發生在清朝乾隆年間的滿州。幾個拳師在雪山挖出一個寶盒並開始搶奪，在爭鬥中，武功高強的寶樹和尚戰勝了所有對手並強迫人們去了玉筆峰的山莊。莊園主人正在等候一位神秘劍客的挑戰，這位劍客就是綽號雪山飛狐的胡斐。

While waiting for Hu Fei, people opened the treasure chest and found a precious sword inside. They started to exchange stories about the sword and lots of secrets revealed via story telling. Monk Baoshu narrated the origin of the sword. It used to belong to Li Zicheng (李自成) who led a riot against the previous Ming Dynasty. Among Li's four body guards, the one surnamed Hu (Hu Fei's ancestor) stayed with Li Zicheng when Li died in a siege. Other three body guards misunderstood Hu as a betrayer and the feud lasted for generations. The Hu clan became the public enemy while descendants from the other three families gathered an ally.

在等待胡斐期間，人們打開了寶盒發現裡面的寶刀。他們開始交換自己所知的寶刀的秘密。寶樹和尚講了刀的來源：它曾經屬於反明起義領袖李自成。在李自成的四個侍衛中，胡姓侍衛（胡斐的祖先）在李自成死於圍困時待在李的身邊，其他三位侍衛誤以為胡姓侍衛背叛了闖王，仇恨持續了幾代人。胡家子弟成了其餘三姓後代的公敵。

文法解析

KEY 76

⭕ It employs <u>storytelling flashbacks</u> which <u>is</u> quite rare in martial arts literature.

❌ It employs a <u>storytelling flashback</u> which <u>is</u> quite rare in martial arts literature.

✦中譯✦ 它採取了武俠文學中罕有的倒敘式。

✦解析✦ 關係子句中的 which 後的動詞要和 which 之前的主詞相匹配，此處的 flashbacks 意思是倒敘式，不是一個複數名詞。

 KEY 77

⭕ In this novel, Narration based on several people's memory dates back decades ago, while the actual time frame only lasts for one day.

❌ In this novel, Narration based on several people's memory dates back decades ago, while the actual time frame only last for one day.

✦中譯✦ 在小說中，幾個人回憶敘述了幾十年前的往事，而小說本身的故事在一天內完成的。

✦解析✦ 前句主詞為 Narration 主要動詞為第三人稱單數須加 s 故為 dates，主詞 the actual time frame 是第三人稱單數現在式，動詞字尾加 s。

 KEY 78

⭕ This swordsman is Hu Fei, nicknamed the fox volant of the snowy mountain.

❌ This swordsman are Hu Fei, nicknamed the fox volant of the snowy mountain.

✦中譯✦ 這位劍客就是綽號雪山飛狐的胡斐。

✦解析✦ 主詞為單數，動詞應當用 is。

武俠人物 32 - Overview(概要) MP3 *32*

The hatred continued throughout several generations until Hu Fei's father Hu Yidao (胡一刀) met Miao Ruolan's (苗若蘭) father Miao Renfeng (苗人鳳). Both Hu Yidao and Miao Renfeng were skillful martial artists, and they fought a duel for five days and neither of them could defeat the other. On the contrary, they started to treat each other with respect and developed a special friendship.

世仇持續了幾代，一直到胡斐的父親胡一刀遇到苗若蘭的父親苗人鳳。胡一刀和苗人鳳都是功夫高手，他們決鬥了五天而不能戰勝對方，反倒變得敬重彼此並發展出特別的友情。

Tian Guinong (田歸農), another descendant from one of the three body guards, had a bad intention and his malicious plan of smearing their weapons with poison was triggered by jealousy, but both Hu Yidao and Miao Renfeng were unaware of this; Hu was accidentally injured by Miao's weapon containing poison, costing his life.

另一個侍衛的後人田歸農卻懷謀不軌，而出於妒忌，將二人的武器上抹了毒藥，但胡苗對此均不知情。胡不小心被苗的武器刺傷而毒發身亡。

Hu Yidao's wife committed suicide after Miao Renfeng

promised to raise up their infant son Hu Fei. Miao Renfeng soon became deeply remorseful for not only the manslaughter of Hu Yidao, but also the lost of Hu Fei. Luckily, Hu Fei was rescued by Hu Yidao's servent Ping A'si (平阿四) and grew up to be a powerful martial artist. Back to the actual time in the novel, Hu Fei is coming to finalize the long-lasting vendetta.

胡夫人在苗人鳳承諾會好好照顧他們的幼子胡斐後也自殺追隨丈夫。苗人鳳不久後陷入深切的愧悔中，因為他不但誤殺胡一刀，而且還丟掉了胡斐。幸運的是胡斐被胡一刀的僕從平阿四救走，並成長為一位強大的劍俠。回到小説本身的時間點，胡斐正準備了結這持續已久的世仇。

As the narrate continues, another story teller revealed an ultimate secret with the sword. People could find out the national treasure of the Ming Dynasty by matching the sword with a special map. The map was handed down in Miao's family, and the sword is in Monk Baoshu's hand. The group of swordsmen robbed the map from Miao Ruolan and started to search for the national treasure together. Finally, all these greedy people were locked with treasures forever.

隨著講故事持續下去，另一個人講出了寶刀蘊含的極大秘密。如果把刀和一份特別的地圖相匹配，人們就可以找到明朝的國家寶藏。地圖在苗家世代相傳，而寶刀正在寶樹和尚手中。這群劍客從苗若蘭手中搶了地圖開始一同尋寶。到最後這些貪婪的人和寶藏被永遠鎖在了一起。

文法解析

KEY 79

○ Both Hu Yidao and Miao Renfeng were skillful martial artists, and they fought a duel for five days and neither of them could defeat the other.

✕ Both Hu Yidao and Miao Renfeng was skillful martial artists, and they fought a duel for five days and neither of them could defeat the other.

✦中譯✦ 胡一刀和苗人鳳都是功夫高手，他們決鬥了五天而不能戰勝對方。

✦解析✦ Both A and B ＋複數動詞。

KEY 80

○ Tian Guinong, another descendant from one of the three body guards, had a bad intention and his malicious plan of smearing their weapons with poison was triggered by jealousy.

✕ Tian Guinong, another descendant from one of the three body guards, had a bad intention and his malicious plan of smearing their weapons with poison were triggered by jealousy.

✦中譯✦ 另一個侍衛的後人田歸農懷謀不軌而出於妒忌，將二人的武器上抹了毒藥。

天龍八部

鹿鼎記

笑傲江湖

雪山飛狐

神鵰俠侶

射鵰英雄傳

連城訣碧血劍

書劍恩仇錄

✦ 解析 ✦ 第一句主詞是 Tian Guinong，而第二句的主詞為 plan 故動詞要用 was。

KEY 81

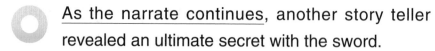

⭕ <u>As the narrate continues</u>, another story teller revealed an ultimate secret with the sword.

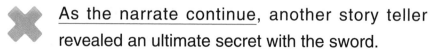

❌ <u>As the narrate continue</u>, another story teller revealed an ultimate secret with the sword.

✦ 中譯 ✦ 隨著講故事持續下去，另一個人講出了寶刀蘊含的極大秘密。

✦ 解析 ✦ 主詞 narrate 是一個單數名詞，因而動詞 continue 要配合第三人稱單數現在式，詞尾加 s。

 ## 武俠人物 33 - Overview(概要) MP3 *33*

<u>The Young Flying Fox (飛狐外傳) is a prequel of the Fox Volant of the Snowy Mountain.</u> The novel focuses on Hu Fei's story before he appears in the Fox Volant of the Snowy Mountain.

《飛狐外傳》是《雪山飛狐》的前傳。小說講了胡斐出現在《雪山飛狐》之前的故事。

The protagonist, Hu Fei is a chivalrous young swordsman experiencing various adventures, while in the Fox Volant of the Snowy Mountain, he is more mysterious and mature.

When Hu Fei was an infant, his father Hu Yidao died in a duel. Hu Fei was raised up by his farther's servant. He took over the family skills and became a powerful martial artist. <u>As a young swordsman, Hu Fei traveled around searching for adventures.</u> He met Zhao Banshan (趙半山), a hero from the Red Flower Society. They admired each other's generous personality and became sworn brothers.

作為小說主角，胡斐是一個深具俠義精神的年輕劍客，他經歷了一系列冒險；而《雪山飛狐》中的胡斐則更加神秘且成熟。胡斐的父親死於決鬥時他還是個嬰兒，他被父親的僕人養大。胡斐承襲了胡家武功絕學，功夫強大。作為年輕的劍俠，胡斐在各處雲遊探險。他認識了紅花會的英雄趙半山並仰慕彼此的慷慨個性而成為結義兄弟。

Hu Fei traveled to the south; there he met a villain Feng Tiannan (鳳天南) who ruthlessly bullied innocent people. Hu was furious about this wicked behavior and planned to kill Feng Tiannan to deliver justice. <u>However, his action of cracking down the evildoer was interfered by a young maiden Yuan Ziyi (袁紫衣).</u> She stopped Hu Fei from killing Feng Tiannan. On the way of chasing Feng Tiannan, Hu Fei met Yuan Ziyi several times and they became friends. Yuan promised that she would only save Feng Tiannan's life for three times as he is her biological father. Later, she kept her words and assisted Hu to put down Feng. In spite of her deep affection to him, Yuan Ziyi had to leave Hu Fei since she was

天龍八部

鹿鼎記

笑傲江湖

雪山飛狐

神鵰俠侶

射鵰英雄傳

連城訣碧血劍

書劍恩仇錄

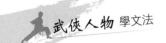

a Buddhist nun.

　　胡斐遊歷到南方，遇到了惡霸鳳天南殘暴地欺凌無辜。胡斐被這種惡劣行為觸怒，他決定殺掉惡人主持正義。可是他的除惡行動被少女袁紫衣干擾，她阻止了胡斐狙殺鳳天南。在追殺鳳天南的路上，胡斐多次遇到袁紫衣並成為她的朋友。袁紫衣承諾她只會救鳳天南三次，因為他其實是袁的父親。後來袁紫衣果然協助胡斐殺死了鳳天南。由於是出家人的身分，袁紫衣儘管深愛胡斐，也不得不離開了他。

 文法解析

 KEY 82

　○　The Young Flying Fox is a prequel of the Fox Volant of the Snowy Mountain.

　✕　The Young Flying Fox are a prequel of the Fox Volant of the Snowy Mountain.

✦中譯✦　《飛狐外傳》是《雪山飛狐》的前傳。

✦解析✦　書名《飛狐外傳》是作為單數名詞來做主詞，動詞用 is。

 KEY 83

　○　As a young swordsman, Hu Fei traveld around searching for adventures.

　✕　As a young swordsman, Hu Fei travels around searching for adventures.

✦中譯✦ 作為年輕的劍俠，胡斐在各處雲遊探險。

✦解析✦ 此處要用過去式詞。

KEY 84

⭕ However, <u>his action of cracking down the evildoer was</u> interfered by a young maiden Yuan Ziyi.

❌ However, <u>his action of cracking down the evildoer were</u> interfered by a young maiden Yuan Ziyi.

✦中譯✦ 可是他的除惡行動被少女袁紫衣干擾。

✦解析✦ 主詞是單數名詞 **his action**，動詞應當是單數動詞。

 武俠人物 34 - Hu Fei (胡斐) *MP3*
34

Hu Fei (胡斐) had a mission of finding out the murderer of his father, Hu Yidao. <u>He was told that Miao Renfeng should be responsible for Hu Yidao's death.</u> During the time of seeking Miao Renfeng and preparing for revenge, Hu Fei found out that Miao Renfeng is a highly respectable person. He started to suspect the story he had already known about his father's death and secretly protected Miao Renfeng.

　　胡斐以找到殺害父親胡一刀的兇手為使命。他被告知苗人鳳要對胡一刀的死負責。在尋找苗人鳳報仇的過程中，他發現苗人鳳是個非常值得尊敬的人物。胡斐開始懷疑他所知的關於父親之死的說詞，並暗中保護苗人鳳。

After Miao Renfeng was poisoned to blind, Tian Guinong gathered several Miao's enemies and planned to take this chance to kill him. Impressed by Miao Renfeng's chivalry, Hu Fei decided to find a cure for Miao Renfeng's eyes. The deceased 'King of Venoms' (毒手藥王) was famous for curing different diseases; Hu Fei found Cheng Lingsu (程靈素), the youngest apprentice of the pharmaceutic master, and took her to heal Miao Renfeng's eyes.

苗人鳳中毒失明後，田歸農集結了一些苗人鳳的仇家，策劃趁這個機會殺害苗人鳳。深受苗人鳳豪俠精神的感染，胡斐決定為他尋求治療眼睛的藥物。已故的毒手藥王由於擅長治療各種疾患而知名，胡斐找到了藥王的最年輕弟子程靈素，帶她去治療苗人鳳的雙眼。

Miao Renfeng regained sight after Cheng Lingsu's treatment. He admitted to Hu Fei that he had accidentally killed Hu Yidao years ago. Knowing the truth, Hu Fei was deeply in sorrow. He left with Cheng Lingsu and they made each other sworn siblings. During a fight with several enemies, Hu Fei's back hand was hit by poisoned hidden weapon. He was unaware of the poisonousness while Cheng Lingsu knew how severe the consequence would be. She sucked out the venom from Hu Fei's hand and lost her life from this. Cheng Lingsu confessed her admiration to Hu Fei before her death, leaving Hu Fei with a long lasting regret.

　　程靈素幫助苗人鳳恢復視力後，苗人鳳向胡斐坦承他曾經誤殺胡一刀。得知真相的胡斐萬分難過，他與程靈素一起離開並成為結義兄妹。在與敵人打鬥中，胡斐的手背被有毒暗器所傷，胡斐對毒藥一無所知而程靈素知道中毒的嚴重性。她捨命用嘴巴吸出了胡斐手背的毒液。程靈素在死前向胡斐坦白了自己的傾慕，使胡斐陷入了長期的悔恨中。

 文法解析

 KEY 85

 He was told that Miao Renfeng should be responsible to Hu Yidao's death.

 He was tell that Miao Renfeng should responsible to Hu Yidao's death.

✦中譯✦ 他被告知苗人鳳要對胡一刀的死負責。

✦解析✦ 被動語態 be 動詞後應當為動詞的過去分詞，情態動詞 should 後要加動詞原形。

 KEY 86

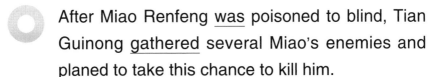 After Miao Renfeng was poisoned to blind, Tian Guinong gathered several Miao's enemies and planed to take this chance to kill him.

 After Miao Renfeng was poisoned to blind, Tian Guinong gathers several Miao's enemies and plans to take this chance to kill him.

天龍八部

鹿鼎記

笑傲江湖

雪山飛狐

神鵰俠侶

射鵰英雄傳

連城訣血劍

書劍恩仇錄

✦中譯✦ 苗人鳳中毒失明後，田歸農集結了一些苗人鳳的仇家，策劃趁這個機會殺害苗人鳳。

✦解析✦ 一個句子中時態應當保持一致，幾個並列關係的分句裡前半句為過去式，其他分句也應為過去式。

KEY 87

⭕ He was unaware of the poisonousness while Cheng Lingsu knew how severe the consequence would be.

❌ He was unaware of the poisonousness while Cheng Lingsu knows how severe the consequence would be.

✦中譯✦ 胡斐對毒藥一無所知而程靈素知道中毒的嚴重性。

✦解析✦ 主詞 Cheng Lingsu 後面接單數動詞，由於整個句子是過去式，動詞 know 也應當用過去式。

武俠人物 35 - Cheng Lingsu (程靈素) MP3 35

Cheng Lingsu (程靈素) is the most prominent apprentice of the 'King of Venoms'. She was named after two medical classics and skilled in both medicine and toxicity. Cheng Lingsu inherited her master's lifelong achievements; she had further developed the 'King of Venoms' skill by cultivating a virulent poison which was colorless and odorless.

程靈素是毒手藥王最卓越的弟子，她精通藥學和毒物學，名字也是由兩本藥學經典而來。程靈素繼承了她師傅的畢生所學，還更進一步發展毒手藥王的技藝，調配出無色無味的劇毒。

Cheng Lingsu is witty and intelligent. Her instinct with wiseness helps her always make correct predictions. In addition to her shinny bright eyes, she has an unattractive appearance, looking younger than her real age, like a skinny girl.

However, this little girl is a medical expert as well as a disguise master. She used to decorate herself as a granny and dressed Hu Fei up to a beard guy; they interfered Fukang'an's (福康安) plot of controlling the martial arts world.

程靈素非常聰明機智，強大的洞察力和智慧令她料事如神。除了靈動的雙眼，她外表並不出眾，看起來像個比實際年齡更小的瘦弱農家女。然而這個小女孩卻是醫學專家和喬裝大師。她曾喬裝成老婆婆並把胡斐易容成鬍鬚男，攪亂了福康安控制武林的陰謀。

Hu Fei met Cheng Lingsu when searching for a cure for Miao Renfeng's eyes. He witnessed that she calmly defeated three evil seniors apprentices and was astonished by her intelligence. At the same time, Cheng Lingsu fell in love with Hu Fei at the first sight. She cured Miao Renfeng and followed Hu Fei for many adventures. Cheng Lingsu found out that Hu Fei was attracted by beautiful Yuan Ziyi; so she hid her

天龍八部 鹿鼎記 笑傲江湖 雪山飛狐 神鵰俠侶 射鵰英雄傳 連城訣碧血劍 書劍恩仇錄

emotions and became Hu Fei's sworn sister.

胡斐在為苗人鳳求醫過程中認識了程靈素，他目睹了程靈素打敗三位邪惡的師姐，被她的聰慧折服。同時程靈素對胡斐一見鍾情，她醫好了苗人鳳並追隨胡斐闖蕩天下。程靈素發現了胡斐鍾情於美麗的袁紫衣，所以她隱藏自己的情感做了胡斐的義妹。

Cheng Lingsu is a kind-hearted girl. <u>She obtains superior poison skills but never abuses her ability.</u> She always helps unprivileged people fighting for justice and kindly treats people who abused her. She gave up her life for the person she loves.

程靈素非常善良，她擁有高超的下毒技藝但從不濫用她的能力。她時常扶助弱小，為正義而戰，對傷害過她的人以德報怨。她為了自己所愛的人犧牲了生命。

 文法解析

 KEY 88

 <u>She was named</u> after two medical classics and <u>skilled</u> in both medicine and toxicity.

 <u>She was named</u> after two medical classics and <u>skills</u> in both medicine and toxicity.

✦中譯✦ 她精通藥學和毒物學，名字也是由兩本藥學經典而來。

✦解析✦ was skilled 是 skill 的被動語態，和 was named 並列做主詞 she 的動詞。

 **KEY 89**

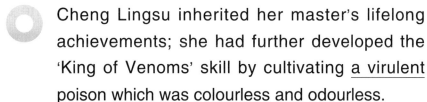

○ Cheng Lingsu inherited her master's lifelong achievements; she had further developed the 'King of Venoms' skill by cultivating <u>a virulent poison which was</u> colourless and odourless.

✗ Cheng Lingsu inherited her master's lifelong achievements; she had further developed the 'King of Venoms' skill by cultivating <u>a virulent poison which were</u> colourless and odourless.

✦中譯✦ 程靈素繼承了她師傅的畢生所學，還更進一步發展毒手藥王的技藝，調配出無色無味的劇毒。

✦解析✦ 「一種劇毒」是單數名詞，因而後接單數動詞 was。

 KEY 90

○ <u>She obtains</u> superior poison skills but never <u>abuses</u> her ability.

✗ <u>She obtain</u> superior poison skills but never <u>abuse</u> her ability.

✦中譯✦ 她擁有高超的下毒技藝但從不濫用她的能力。

✦解析✦ 主詞為第三人稱單數現在式，動詞詞尾要加 s。

天龍八部

鹿鼎記

笑傲江湖

雪山飛狐

神鵰俠侶

射鵰英雄傳

連城訣碧血劍

書劍恩仇錄

武俠人物 36 - Miao Renfeng (苗人鳳) *MP3* *36*

Miao Renfeng (苗人鳳) is a top martial artist nicknamed 'Golden Faced Buddha' (金面佛). He is famous for his undefeated quality. Miao Renfeng is skilled in using swords; he used to fight with another powerful swordsman Hu Yidao for five days. Impressed by each other's kungfu skills and chivalry, the two swordsmen decided to cease the enmity that lasted for generations from their ancestors and become friends. Miao Renfeng was bitterly remorseful after he unintentionally killed Hu Yidao; he decided not to teach his daughter any martial arts in order to prevent further tragedies.

　　苗人鳳是頂尖功夫高手，綽號金面佛，因打遍天下無敵手而知名。苗人鳳劍術極高，曾與另一位強大劍客胡一刀大戰五天。兩位劍客被彼此的功夫和義氣打動，決定化敵為友，結束持續了幾代人的仇恨。苗人鳳在失手誤殺胡一刀後無限懊悔，為了讓悲劇不再發生，他決定不傳授自己的女兒任何武功。

Miao Renfeng is very talented in martial arts but not good at expressing himself. He is taciturn and conservative. He once saved a beautiful maiden Nan Lan's (南蘭) life and she married Miao out of gratitude. Miao devoted all his passion to martial arts practise and neglected his effeminate and sensitive wife. The relationship was deviated by their different personalities. Tian Guinong the villain coveted for the map of national treasure that inherited in Miao family; he lured Nan Lan and made her elope with him. Miao Renfeng did not seek for vengeance to Tian Guinong as his generosity prevented him from hurting others. He shifted his life focus on raising his daughter Miao Ruolan.

　　苗人鳳武功高超但是拙於言辭。他寡言且保守。美麗的少女南蘭因為曾被苗人鳳所救，出於感激嫁給了他。苗人鳳醉心於武術練習，忽略了他柔弱敏感的妻子。不同的個性影響了他們的感情。惡人田歸農覬覦苗家藏寶圖，引誘了南蘭和他私奔。苗人鳳沒有找田歸農報仇，善良的本性阻止了他去傷害別人。他把生活的焦點轉移到了對女兒苗若蘭的培育之上。

At the end of the Fox Volant of the Snowy Mountain, Miao Renfeng and Hu Fei went to a cliff for a duel. Miao Renfeng misunderstood that Hu Fei harassed his daughter. The novel ended at Hu Fei's decision. He had a chance to kill Miao Renfeng, but a hesitation would cost his life. The author left an open-ended conclusion for the novel.

　　在《雪山飛狐》最後，苗人鳳和胡斐在懸崖邊決鬥。苗人鳳誤會胡斐冒犯了苗若蘭。小說停筆在胡斐的決定關頭。他有機會殺死苗人鳳，但錯過機會就會被苗人鳳所殺。作者為故事留下了這個開放式結局。

天龍八部

鹿鼎記

笑傲江湖

雪山飛狐

神鵰俠侶

射鵰英雄傳

連城訣 碧血劍

書劍恩仇錄

文法解析

KEY 91

○ Impressed by each other's kungfu skills and chivalry, <u>the two swordsmen decided</u> to cease the enmity that lasted for generations from their ancestors <u>and become</u> friends.

✕ Impressed by each other's kungfu skills and chivalry, <u>the two swordsmen decided to cease</u> the enmity that lasted for generations from their ancestors <u>and become</u> friends.

✦中譯✦ 兩位劍客被彼此的功夫和義氣打動，決定化敵為友，結束持續了幾代人的仇恨。

✦解析✦ cease 和 become 都是 decide to 後接的動詞，所以都用動詞原形。

KEY 92

○ <u>Tian Guinong the villain coveted</u> for the map of national treasure that inherited in Miao family; <u>he lured Nan Lan and made</u> her elope with him.

✕ <u>Tian Guinong the villain coveted</u> for the map of national treasure that inherited in Miao family; <u>he lured Nan Lan and makes</u> her elope with him.

✦中譯✦ 惡人田歸農覬覦苗家藏寶圖，引誘了南蘭和他私奔。

✦解析✦ lure 和 make 都的主詞都是 he，要時態一致。

 ## 武俠人物 37 - Hu Yidao (胡一刀) *MP3* *37*

Hu Yidao (胡一刀) is a forthright hero from Manchuria. He is highly renowned of his upright conduct and gregarious property. He makes friends with the Liaodong local tribes as well as his foes, including Miao Renfeng. Hu Yidao has legendary martial arts skills with considerable character. He is a respectable swordsman.

　　胡一刀是出身關外的直率英雄。胡一刀由於正直豪邁廣為人知。他交友廣泛，朋友裡既有遼東在地部落的人，也有包括苗人鳳在內的他的敵人。胡一刀功夫高超，舉足輕重，是一位備受尊敬的大俠。

Hu Yidao and his wife were ambushed by the villain Tian Guinong. However, the sudden attack posed no threat to Hu Yidao since his prowess skill overwhelmingly exceeded his opponents'. After Miao Renfeng showed up, Hu Yidao was involved into a fight with him. The fight made them admire each other's kung fu and personal charisma. Hu Yidao decided to solve the feud with Miao Renfeng peacefully but obstructed by Tian Guinong.

　　胡一刀和妻子曾被壞人田歸農伏擊，但是突襲完全沒有威脅到胡一

刀，因為他的高超武功遠非對手可及。苗人鳳出現後，胡一刀向他發起決鬥，兩個人被彼此的功夫和個人魅力折服，相互敬佩。胡一刀決定與苗人鳳和平化解世仇，但是被田歸農阻撓。

The night before the duel, Hu Yidao admitted to his wife that he was afraid of this formidable rival. He concerned about the future of his infant baby boy Hu Fei if he lost his life. Hu Yidao traveled three hundred miles and killed one of Miao Renfeng's enemy. He did this not for bribing Miao Renfeng but for completing his friend's wish; since Hu Yidao had already considered Miao Renfeng as a trustworthy friend. During the fight, Hu Yidao took the lead several times but he never used any chance to kill Miao Renfeng. He died from a tiny cut because Miao Renfeng's sword was secretly smeared with poison. Hu Yidao kept righteous and benevolent all his life.

決戰前夕，胡一刀向妻子承認他懼怕這個可畏的對手。因為他擔心自己一旦死去，小嬰兒胡斐前途堪憂。胡一刀奔波三百哩殺死一名苗人鳳的仇敵，他這樣做並非意在討好對手，而是幫助朋友了結心願，因為胡一刀已經把苗人鳳當作可信的友人。在決鬥中，胡一刀幾次佔上風但從不下手置對方於死地。胡一刀死於小傷，因為苗人鳳的武器被偷偷塗上了毒藥。胡一刀的一生都保持了正直仁義。

文法解析

 KEY 93

○ Hu Yidao decided to solve the feud with Miao Renfeng peacefully but obstructed by Tian Guinong.

✕ Hu Yidao decided to solve the feud with Miao Renfeng peacefully but obstruct by Tian Guinong.

✦中譯✦ 胡一刀決定與苗人鳳和平化解世仇,但是被田歸農阻撓。

✦解析✦ decide to 後接動詞原形,決定的內容是解決世仇,因而 solve 被 decide to 涵蓋而 obstruct 並不被涵蓋。所以 solve 用動詞原形,obstruct 符合整個句子的時態用過去式。

 KEY 94

○ The night before the duel, Hu Yidao admitted to his wife that he was afraid of this formidable rival.

✕ The night before the duel, Hu Yidao admit to his wife that he was afraid of this formidable rival.

✦中譯✦ 決戰前夕,胡一刀向妻子承認他懼怕這個可畏的對手。

✦解析✦ 因為整個句子是過去式,動詞 admit 也應當是過去式。

天龍八部

鹿鼎記

笑傲江湖

雪山飛狐

神鵰俠侶

射鵰英雄傳

連城訣碧血劍

書劍恩仇錄

143

武俠人物 38 - Tian Guinong (田歸農) MP3 **38**

Tian Guinong (田歸農) is an antagonist in the Fox Volant of the Snowy Mountain. His ancestor is also one of Li Zicheng's four body guards. Tian Guinong is an incompetent leader of the Tianlong Sect (天龍門). He is ambitious to pursuit wealth and fame disregarding the limitation of his personal abilities. Tian Guinong would wipe out obstacles on his way unscrupulously. He smeared poison on Miao Renfeng's sword, causing Hu Yidao's death.

田歸農是《雪山飛狐》中的大反派，他的祖先也是李自成的四位侍衛之一。田歸農是天龍門不合格的掌門人。他不顧自己能力的侷限，野心勃勃的追尋財富和名利，不擇手段的掃除自己成功路上的障礙。田歸農在苗人鳳劍上塗毒，導致了胡一刀的死亡。

Tian Guinong is handsome and eloquent. He uses his personal traits to seduce innocent girls, including Miao Renfeng's wife. Nan Lan abandoned her husband and daughter to elope with Tian Guinong. She did not realize that Tian Guinong deceived her, and his real target was the precious map in Miao family. <u>Nan Lan suffered bitter regret after finding out Tian Guinong was a despicable person.</u> Hence, Tian Guinong did not get the map; he was even tricked by Nan Lan and returned the map back to Miao Renfeng by his own hands.

田歸農英俊瀟灑，口才過人。他利用自己的優勢引誘無知女孩，包括苗人鳳的妻子。南蘭拋夫棄女，和田歸農私奔。她不知道自己被田歸農所騙，他的真正目標是苗家的藏寶圖。南蘭發現田歸農是無恥小人後甚為後悔痛苦，所以田歸農從未得到過地圖，他甚至被南蘭用計引導，親手把地圖還給了苗人鳳。

Tian Guinong's <u>kung fu skills were</u> immeasurably poor compared with Hu Yidao and Miao Renfeng, but he was unwilling to accept this reality. He used plots to get rid of them and succeeded in killing Hu Yidao without being noticed. To chase a higher social status, Tian Guinong pledged loyalty to Fu Kang'an, another vicious person from government who planned to manipulate the whole martial arts world. Fu Kang'an promised to assign Tian Guinong as the chief of Wulin after he gets everyone under control. Fu Kang'an's conspiracy was disturbed by Hu Fei and Cheng Lingsu, so did Tian Guinong's.

田歸農的功夫與胡一刀和苗人鳳根本無法相比，但他不願接受現實。他設計除掉了胡一刀而沒有被人察覺。為了追求更高的地位，田歸農向朝廷鷹犬福康安宣誓效忠。福康安陰謀要操控武林，他承諾會讓田歸農成為武林盟主。胡斐和程靈素攪亂了福康安的陰謀也粉碎了田歸農的美夢。

天龍八部

鹿鼎記

笑傲江湖

雪山飛狐

神鵰俠侶

射鵰英雄傳

連城訣碧血劍

書劍恩仇錄

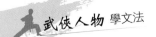

 文法解析

 KEY 95

〇 Nan Lan suffered bitterly regret after finding out Tian Guinong was a despicable person.

✗ Nan Lan suffer bitterly regret after finding out Tian Guinong was a despicable person.

◆中譯◆ 南蘭發現田歸農是無恥小人後甚為後悔痛苦。

◆解析◆ 錯誤例句中主詞是第三人稱單數現在式，動詞尾要加 s；因為整句是過去時態，所以動詞要用過去式。

 KEY 96

〇 Tian Guinong's kung fu skills were immeasurably poor compared with Hu Yidao and Miao Renfeng.

✗ Tian Guinong's kung fu skills was immeasurably poor compared with Hu Yidao and Miao Renfeng.

◆中譯◆ 田歸農的功夫與胡一刀和苗人鳳根本無法相比。

◆解析◆ 主詞 skills 是複數，動詞也應當用複數。

武俠人物 39 - Miao Ruolan (苗若蘭)

MP3
39

Miao Ruolan (苗若蘭) is Miao Renfeng's only daughter, a beautiful girl with gentle character. Although she is well protected by her father, Miao Ruolan is independent and kindhearted. Her intelligence and rationality also impress people. Miao Renfeng did not teach her any martial arts skills. He believed kung fu will be misused as a weapon that brings about disastrous consequences.

　　苗若蘭是苗人鳳的獨生女，一位溫柔美麗的姑娘。雖然被父親保護的很好，苗若蘭仍然善良獨立。她的智慧和理性令人印象深刻。苗人鳳沒有傳授給她任何武藝，因為他相信被濫用的功夫會成為武器並導致災難。

Miao Ruolan grows up with a single parent; therefore, the father-daughter bond between she and Miao Renfeng is stronger than that from any normal family. She understands her father and always stays beside him. They were both abandoned by the mother and coped the hardship in life together. Miao Ruolan is a considerate girl. When Miao Renfeng was poisoned and temporarily lost eyesight, she was just a little girl but made her effort to comfort her father. This gentle girl also holds chivalrous characters; she is very persistent and always keeps her promises. Miao Renfeng hides the precious map in her headwear as he knows his daughter is quite reliable.

　　苗若蘭成長於單親家庭，因為他們父女間的情感紐帶比來自一般家庭的父女更強。她理解自己的父親，經常陪伴在他身邊。母親的離去讓他們共同面對生活中的困難，苗若蘭是一個體貼的女孩。苗人鳳中毒暫時失明時，苗若蘭雖是一個小孩，也盡自己所能讓父親安心。這個善良的女生也具有俠義精神，她做事堅持不懈並信守承諾。苗人鳳深知自己女兒可靠，他把藏寶地圖藏在苗若蘭的頭飾裏。

When Monk Baoshu narrated the story about Hu Yidao's death, he falsified some details as Baoshu also played an evil role inside. Miao Ruolan pointed out those alternations and corrected them into the truth. Later Hu Fei came to the manor of Jade Brush Peak; everyone fled away just Ruolan was left to deal with Hu Fei. They developed romantic feelings after a brief talk. Ruolan was waiting for Hu Fei at the end of the story.

　　當寶樹和尚講到胡一刀之死，他篡改了一些細節，因為他自己也在其中扮演了不光彩的角色。苗若蘭指出了這些不實之處，並將真相告訴大家。之後胡斐來到玉筆山莊，每個人都驚懼逃跑，只有苗若蘭留下來應對胡斐。她和胡斐談話後互生好感，在小說結尾，苗若蘭靜靜等候胡斐歸來。

文法解析

KEY 97

○ Her intelligent and rationality also impress people.

✕ Her intelligent and rationality also impresses people.

◆中譯◆ 她的智慧和理性令人印象深刻。

◆解析◆ 主詞是智慧和理性,並非單數,動詞無須加 es。

KEY 98

○ Miao Ruolan grows up with a single parent; therefore, the father-daughter bond between she and Miao Renfeng is stronger than that from normal family.

✕ Miao Ruolan grow up with a single parent; therefore, the father -daughter bond between she and Miao Renfeng is stronger than that from normal family.

◆中譯◆ 苗若蘭成長於單親家庭,因而他們父女間的情感紐帶比來自一般家庭的父女更強。

◆解析◆ 主詞苗若蘭是第三人稱單數,句子是現在式,因而動詞要詞尾加 s。

天龍八部

鹿鼎記

笑傲江湖

雪山飛狐

神鵰俠侶

射鵰英雄傳

連城訣
碧血劍

書劍恩仇錄

武俠人物 40 - Monk Baoshu (寶樹和尚)

Monk Baoshu (寶樹和尚) used to be a doctor named Yan Ji (閻基). After he was defeated by Miao Renfeng, Tian Guinong found Yan Ji. Miao broke Tian's sword as a warning to restrain him form doing evil. However, <u>Tian Guinong was deeply humiliated and sworn to revenge.</u> He paid Yan Ji to kill Miao Renfeng. Yan Ji utilised his medical skills to smear Miao Renfeng's weapons with poison before his duel, indirectly causing Hu Yidao's death.

　　寶樹和尚曾是一名醫生，俗名叫做閻基。田歸農被苗人鳳打敗後找到了他。苗人鳳打斷了田歸農的兵器以警告他不要繼續作惡。田歸農深受侮辱並發誓報仇。他收買了閻基在苗人鳳的武器上下毒，間接導致了胡一刀之死。

As an avaricious and contemptible person, Yan Ji hid in the darkness awaiting for Hu Yidao's death because he coveted Hu's personal belongings. After Hu Yidao's wife committed suicide, Yan Ji rushed into their room to steal their parcels. He was hit by Hu's servant Ping A'si from the back and fainted. At that crucial moment, Ping A'si did not seize back two pages of the Manuel of Hu's Swordplay from Yan Ji, as his priority was to protect infant Hu Fei. Yan ji practiced Hu's swordplay since then; and used his kung fu in robbery.

閻基貪婪可鄙，他藏在暗處等待胡一刀死後可以偷他財物。胡夫人自刎後，閻基衝到他們房間搶包裹，被胡家僕人平阿四從背後打暈。因為救胡斐是第一要務，平阿四沒有奪回閻基手中緊握著的胡家刀譜。閻基練習了胡家刀法，把功夫用在打劫中。

Yan Ji was later captured as a bandit. <u>He was forced to become a monk and correct his behaviors.</u> However, as Monk Baoshu, his wicked nature intensified. In the manor of Jade Brush Peak, all the pugilists were quarrelling for a bigger share of the treasure. The most vicious Monk Baoshu united the pugilists to search for the treasure together. Since he harboured ill intention against Hu Fei, Miao Ruolan was immobilized as a trap. Miao Renfeng, thus, has been misled into believing that Hu Fei molested his daughter.Yan Ji with other greedy people were finally locked up with the treasure forever.

閻基後來作為綠林大盜被抓，他被迫削髮為僧改惡從善。但是作為寶樹和尚的他邪惡本性變本加厲。在玉筆山莊，所有武者都吵著想要分更多財寶。最壞的寶樹整合了這些人一起去尋寶。因為他對胡斐心懷歹意，就將苗若蘭點穴使她無法活動，誤導了苗人鳳以為胡斐對苗若蘭行為輕薄。閻基和其他貪財的拳師們被永遠困在了寶藏洞內。

天龍八部

鹿鼎記

笑傲江湖

雪山飛狐

神鵰俠侶

射鵰英雄傳

連城訣碧血劍

書劍恩仇錄

文法解析

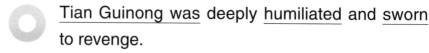 **KEY 99**

○ Tian Guinong was deeply <u>humiliated</u> and <u>sworn</u> to revenge.

✗ Tian Guinong was deeply <u>humiliated</u> and <u>swear</u> to revenge.

✦中譯✦ 田歸農深受侮辱並發誓報仇。

✦解析✦ 整個句子都是過去式,句子中兩個並列的動詞都應該用過去式。

 KEY 100

○ He was <u>forced to become</u> a monk <u>and correct</u> his behaviors.

✗ He was <u>forced to become</u> a monk <u>and corrected</u> his behaviors.

✦中譯✦ 他被迫削髮為僧改惡從善。

✦解析✦ become 和 correct 這兩個動詞都是 forced to 後的動詞,都應用動詞原形。

Glossary 字彙一覽表

benevolence *n.* 仁慈，善行	avaricious *adj.* 貪婪的
covet *vt.* 垂涎,覬覦	contemptible *adj.* 可鄙的
disastrous *adj.* 慘重的	descendant *n.* 後裔
elope *vt.* 私奔	effeminate *adj.* 柔弱的
evildoer *n.* 作惡的人，為惡者	enmity *n.* 敵意
feud *n.* 世仇	falsify *vt.vi.* 偽造，竄改，撒謊
furious *adj.* 狂怒的，激烈的	flashbacks *n.* 倒敘
gregarious *adj.* 群居的，愛交際的	immobilise *vt.* 使不動，使固定
immeasurably *adv.* 無限地，不可測量地	odourless *adj.* 無味的
incompetent **adj.** 無能的，不適任的	pharmaceutic *adj.* 製藥的
molest *vt.* 騷擾	prequel *n.* 前傳
persistent *adj.* 持久的，堅持的	pugilist *n.* 拳師
poisonousness *n.* 毒性	taciturn *adj.* 沈默寡言的
prominent *adj.* 突出的	unintentionally *adv.* 無意地
remorseful *adj.* 懊悔的	unscrupulously *adv.* 不擇手段地
smear *vt.* 塗抹	virulent *adj.* 劇毒的，惡性的
ultimate *n.adj.* 終極,最終的	volant *adj.* 展翅的，飛行的
unprivileged *adj.* 無特權的	

天龍八部

鹿鼎記

笑傲江湖

雪山飛狐

神鵰俠侶

射鵰英雄傳

碧血劍

青劍恩仇錄

《Unit 5》

分詞
《神鵰俠侶》

文法主題介紹－分詞

分詞 (Participles)

分詞是由動詞變化而來的，可分成現在分詞（Ving)和過去分詞（Vpp)，功能為形容詞，作為修飾名詞，或是作補語使用。所修飾的名詞若是具主動去做的能力，則搭配現在分詞修飾；若動作是被加諸在這名詞上，則使用過去分詞修飾。

1. 分詞的功能

當形容詞：可放名詞前面或後面修飾或是當補語修飾主詞或是受詞。

當副詞（分詞構句）：來修飾主要動詞發生的時間、因果、條件、讓步……等關係。

有時會和某些附屬連接詞（如：after/before/since/when/while/once/unless...）一起出現

2. 現在分詞 (Ving）進行 / 主動；過去分詞 (Vpp) 完成 / 被動
3. 情緒動詞的分詞

過去分詞：由情緒動詞所衍生出的過去分詞是用來描述修飾者/物的自身感受		現在分詞：描述修飾者/物所帶給外界的感受。	
satisfied	(對…感到滿意的)	satisfying	(令人感到滿意的)
amused	(對…感到好笑的)	amusing	(令人感到好笑、好玩的)
pleased	(對…感到喜悅)	pleasing	
interested	(對…感到有興趣的)	interesting	(令人感到喜悅的)
excited	(對…感到興奮的)	exciting	(令人感到有趣的)
fascinated/	(對…感到著迷的)	fascinating/	(令人感到刺激的)
enchanted	(對…感到感動的)	enchanting	(令人著迷的)
touched	(受到…感到鼓勵的)	touching	(令人感動的)
encouraged		encouraging	(令人感到鼓勵的)
embarrassed	(對…感到尷尬的)	embarrassing	(令人尷尬的)
bored	(對…感到無聊的)	boring	(令人感到無聊的)
confused/	(對…感到困惑的)	confusing/	(令人困惑的)
puzzled		puzzling	
perplexed		perplexing	
worried	(對…擔憂的)	worrying	(令人擔憂的)
frightened /	(對…感到驚嚇/的)	frightening	(令人恐懼的)
scared	(對…感到厭煩的)	tiring	(令人疲倦的)
tired	(對…感到失望的)	disappointing	(令人感到失望的)
disappointed	(對…感到惱怒的)	annoying	(令人惱怒的)
annoyed	(對…感到噁心的)	disgusting	(令人作嘔的)
disgusted	(對…感到沮喪的)	frustrating	(令人沮喪的)
frustrated	(對…感到沮喪的)	upsetting/	(令人沮喪的)
upset/	(對…感到恐慌/擔憂的)	depressing	(令人恐慌/擔憂的)
depressed		alarming	
alarmed			
stunned	(對…感到訝異的)	stunning	(令人震驚的)
surprised/	(對…感到驚訝的)	surprising/	(令人驚訝的)
shocked		shocking	
amazed/		amazing/	
astonished		astonishing	

4. 慣用搭配語

demanding jobs/supervisors (吃力的工作/要求高的主管)	experienced/ dedicated workers/ employees (有經驗的/勤勞的 員工)
challenging/ overwhelming tasks/projects (有挑戰的/過重的 任務/方案)	qualified applicants (有資格的申請者)
existing equipment/system (現存的設備/系統)	written documents/consent (書面檔案/同意)
the opposing viewpoints/ voices (相反的 觀點/聲音)	designated area (指定區域)
opening/closing remark (開幕/閉幕 致詞)	required inspections/ training (必需的 檢查/訓練)
missing luggage (遺失的行李)	detailed information (細部資訊)
mounting workload (增加的工作量)	confirmed reservation (已確定的預約)
a letter inviting... (邀請...的信件)	items unclaimed (無人認領的物品)

5.「分詞片語」由形容詞子句（即關係子句）簡化而來的形容詞片語，放在名詞之後修飾該名詞。

🗡 主動含意：N + 現在分詞 Ving 片語（N 為動作的主事者）

🗡 被動含意：N + 過去分詞 Vpp 片語（N 為動作的接受者）

6.「分詞構句」是由副詞子句 / 對等子句簡化而來，放在句子前或後修飾該句。

- 主動含意： 現在分詞 Ving 構句, S + V
- 被動含意： 過去分詞 Vpp 構句, S + V

進階觀念

- 完成式分詞構句→Having +Vpp：已經 ~（表時間相對較早之事件）
- 否定分詞構句 → Not +Ving/Vpp；Not having+ Vpp / Having not + Vpp
- 附屬連接詞 + S + BE 動詞 + 形容詞 → 可省略「S + BE 動詞」
- BE 動詞 + 形容詞分詞構句 → (being) + 形容詞

 武俠人物 41 - Yang Guo (楊過) *MP3* *41*

Yang Guo (楊過) is the protagonist in the Returns of the Condor Heroes (神鵰俠侶). His father Yang Kang was the antagonist in prequel the Legend of Condor Heroes. He was named by Guo Jing in the hope that he would correct his father's mistakes. Yang Guo was rebellious as well as faithful; he had complex character with a mixture of his father's mercurial nature and his mother's kind-hearted personality. A series of challenges and adventures had made Yang Guo a highly respected national hero.

　　楊過是《神鵰俠侶》中的主角。他的父親楊康是前作《射鵰英雄

傳》的大反派，郭靖為他命名，希望他能夠改正他父親的錯誤，楊過個性反叛又很忠誠，他的複雜性格融合了他父親的反覆無常和母親的柔和善良。一連串的冒險和挑戰令楊過成為一位受到尊敬的民族英雄。

Yang Guo became an orphan at the age of eleven. He developed a sneaky and cynical personality from the life as a beggar, thief, and unwelcome apprentice in Quanzhen Sect (全真教). Guo Jing used to adopt him, but Huang Rong was suspicious of Yang Guo because she noticed his resemblance with Yang Kang. Huang Rong took precautions against Yang Guo by only teaching him literacy instead of martial arts. Yang Guo was once provoked by Guo Jing's disciple; he injured his opponent critically with the Toad Stance (蛤蟆功) that he learnt from Ouyang Feng years ago. Guo Jing had to took him to the Quanzhen Sect for a better moral training.

　　楊過在十一歲時變成了孤兒，他做過乞丐、小賊，又在全真教被排斥，這些經歷讓他變得有些陰險和憤世嫉俗。郭靖曾經撫養楊過，黃蓉感覺他很像楊康，一直對楊過有所提防，她只教楊過書上經典而不傳授武功。楊過曾被郭靖的弟子激怒，使出了很久前從歐陽鋒那裏學到的蛤蟆功把對方打成重傷，郭靖不得不把他帶去全真教接受正統的德行教育。

Forced to stay in Quanzhen Sect, Yang Guo developed a terrible relationship with his fellow apprentices and was bullied all the time. His master Zhao Zhijing (趙志敬) also only taught him theoretical rather than practical martial arts skills. <u>Yang Guo was disappointed with the prejudice he suffered in the Sect and fled away to avoid further punishment.</u> He made his way to the Ancient Tomb Sect (古墓派) and met Xiaolongnü (小龍女) there.

　　由於被迫待在全真教，楊過與師兄弟關係很壞並且一直被霸凌，他的師父趙志敬仍然只肯教他武學理論，全無功夫教學，楊過對自己受歧視感到失望，為了逃避懲罰逃出了全真教，他去了古墓派並在那裏認識了小龍女。

 文法解析

 KEY 101

○ A series of challenges and adventures had made Yang Guo a highly respected national hero.

✗ A series of challenges and adventures had made Yang Guo a highly respecting national hero.

✦中譯✦　一連串的冒險和挑戰令楊過成為一位受到尊敬的民族英雄。

✦解析✦　受到尊敬是被動態，要用過去分詞 respected。

 KEY 102

○ Forced to stay in Quanzhen Sect, Yang Guo developed a terrible relationship with his fellow apprentices and was bullied all the time.

Forcing to stay in Quanzhen Sect, Yang Guo developed a terrible relationship with his fellow apprentices and was bullied all the time.

✦中譯✦ 由於被迫待在全真教，楊過與師兄弟關係很壞並且一直被霸凌。

✦解析✦ 過去分詞做表示原因的副詞，並且含有被動的意思。

KEY 103

○ Yang Guo was disappointed with the prejudice he suffered in the Sect and fled away to avoid further punishment.

✕ Yang Guo was disappointing with the prejudice he suffered in the Sect and fled away to avoid further punishment.

✦中譯✦ 楊過對自己受歧視感到失望，為了逃避懲罰逃出了全真教。

✦解析✦ 用過去分詞 disappointed 表示楊過的自身感受，對……感到失望。而現在分詞表示某事物帶給外界的感受。

 武俠人物 42 - Yang Guo (楊過) *MP3* *42*

Yang Guo (楊過) used to be impulsive and rebellious; he had attempted to assassinate Guo Jing to avenge his father. However, he gradually learnt Guo Jing was a real hero and all he did to Yang Guo was because of love. He also found out the true nature of his father. <u>Yang Guo then became very faithful to Guo Jing</u> despite <u>the fact that he was always disliked by Huang Rong and he lost one arm from Guo Fu (郭芙)</u>. Yang Guo saved Guo Jing's family from danger multiple times, and he protected baby Guo Xiang (郭襄) from abduction.

楊過原本叛逆又衝動,他曾試圖暗殺郭靖為父親報仇,然而楊過漸漸明白了郭靖是真正的英雄,他對自己所作的一切也都是出於愛心,在了解到自己父親的本性後,楊過對郭靖變得非常忠誠,即使他一直不被黃蓉喜歡,甚至被郭芙砍斷了一隻手臂,楊過幾次搭救郭靖全家,還保護了被綁架的小嬰兒郭襄。

<u>Leaving the Quanzhen Sect, Yang Guo became the disciple of Xiaolongnü in the Ancient Tomb Sect.</u> Apart from the relationship of master and apprentice, they also developed romance, which was a taboo in the conservative society. <u>Their love was not blessed; Guo Jing strongly opposed the idea that Yang Guo would marry his teacher and Yang Guo's maverick character worsened the situation.</u> Both Yang Guo and Xiaolongnü suffered from tremendous pressure for maintaining their relationship. The couple was separated for sixteen years before they finally reunited.

楊過離開全真教後成為了古墓派小龍女的弟子,除了師徒關係,他們也成為一對戀人。這卻是保守社會中的禁忌,他們的戀情沒有受到祝福,郭靖強烈地反對楊過和小龍女結婚,而楊過離經叛道的個性讓他們的處境更加艱難,為了維持這段感情,楊過和小龍女都承受很大的壓

天龍八部

鹿鼎記

笑傲江湖

雪山飛狐

神鵰俠侶

射鵰英雄傳

連城訣 碧血劍

書劍恩仇錄

力，他們忍受了十六年的分別才最終走到一起。

During the time waiting for his beloved Xiaolongnü, Yang Guo turned into a mature hero. He had devised the Divine Melancholic Palms (黯然銷魂掌). It was composed by Yang Guo's lifetime martial arts skills that he learnt from several elite kung fu masters. Huang Yoshi praised Yang Guo's for his genius and creativity; the Palms technique was used to conquer the formidable antagonist Golden Wheel Lama (金輪國師).

在等待心愛的小龍女的漫長時間，楊過變成了一個成熟的英雄，他融合學自各路高手的絕招，自創了武功黯然銷魂掌。黃藥師稱讚過楊過的天份和創造力，這套掌法曾被用來打敗了武功高強的反派人物金輪國師。

 文法解析

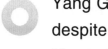 KEY 104

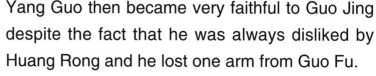

Yang Guo then became very faithful to Guo Jing despite the fact that he was always disliked by Huang Rong and he lost one arm from Guo Fu.

Yang Guo then became very faithful to Guo Jing despite that he was always disliking by Huang Rong and he lost one arm from Guo Fu.

✦中譯✦ 楊過對郭靖變得非常忠誠，即使他一直不被黃蓉喜歡，甚至被郭芙砍斷了一隻手臂。

✦解析✦ Dislike 不是主詞楊過發出的動作，是被人不喜歡。表示被動用過去分詞且句中須用 despite the fact 連接而非 despite that。

 KEY 105

○ Leaving the Quanzhen Sect, Yang Guo became the disciple of Xiaolongnü in the Ancient Tomb Sect.

✗ Left the Quanzhen Sect, Yang Guo became the disciple of Xiaolongnü in the Ancient Tomb Sect.

✦中譯✦ 楊過離開全真教後成為了古墓派小龍女的弟子。

✦解析✦ 分詞構句修飾後面的主句。因為是主動含義，所以用現在分詞。

 KEY 106

○ Their love was not blessed; Guo Jing strongly opposed the idea that Yang Guo would marry his teacher and Yang Guo's maverick character worsened the situation.

✗ Their love was not blessing; Guo Jing strongly opposed the idea that Yang Guo would marry his teacher and Yang Guo's maverick character worsened the situation.

天龍八部

鹿鼎記

笑傲江湖

雪山飛狐

神鵰俠侶

射鵰英雄傳

連城訣

碧血劍

書劍恩仇錄

◆中譯◆ 他們的戀情沒有受到祝福，郭靖強烈地反對楊過和小龍女結婚，而楊過離經叛道的個性讓他們的處境更加艱難。

◆解析◆ 過去分詞表示被動，主詞 their love 並沒有發出動作。

武俠人物 43 - The condor (神鵰)

The condor (神鵰) is a special character in the Return of Condor heroes. The condor's previous companion was the invincible swordsman Dugu Qiubai (獨孤求敗), who wandered around the martial arts world for years and found out no rival in the Wulin. Dugu Qiubai lived as a hermit until he was deceased.

神鵰是《神鵰俠侶》中的一個特別角色，神鵰之前曾陪伴無敵劍客獨孤求敗，獨孤求敗曾行走武林多年而未曾遇見武功相當的對手，他後來退隱江湖一直到去世。

When the Mongolian army beleaguered Xiangyang City, Yang Guo assisted Guo Jing to defend against invasion and became a national hero. However, due to misunderstandings, the already injured Yang Guo was attacked by Guo Fu and lost his right arm. Yang Guo staggered away and fainted because of excessive bleeding. The legendary condor rescued Yang Guo and helped him to recover. The condor provided Yang Guo with the sword and techniques from Dugu Qiubai. The encounter with the condor had made Yang Guo a greater swordsman.

蒙古大軍圍困襄陽城時，楊過幫助郭靖抵禦入侵而成為了民族英雄，可是由於誤會，已經重傷的楊過被郭芙攻擊失去了右臂，楊過蹣跚著離開並因失血昏倒，傳奇的神鵰救了楊過，還幫助他恢復，後來神鵰交給楊過獨孤求敗的劍和劍譜，與神鵰的相遇讓楊過變成了武功更高的劍俠。

Yang Guo practiced excessively using Dugu Qiubai's Heavy Iron Sword (玄鐵重劍) with only one arm. He accomplished the top level of swordplay and ventured out with the condor to search for Xiaolongnü. Meeting Xiaolongnü again, Yang Guo found out she was heavily injured and unable to recover. She jumped into an abyss with a promise of reuniting with Yang Guo in sixteen years.

獨臂楊過用獨孤求敗的玄鐵重劍努力練習，他達到了劍術的至高水準，與神鵰相伴去找小龍女，楊過再遇到小龍女時，她已經身受重傷且無望恢復，她向楊過承諾十六年後相見就跳下深淵。

After leaving Xiaolongnu, Yang Guo had further improved his martial arts skills. He still behaved chivalrously around the world and earned a nickname the Condor Swordsman (神鵰俠); since he was always accompanied by the condor. When the couple finally reunited after sixteen years, they showed up together with the condor in Xiangyang and saved the city once more from the conqueror of the Mongolian troops.

離開小龍女後，楊過的武功更加精進。他依然行俠仗義，因為時常伴著神鵰而得到了「神鵰俠」的綽號。十六年後楊過和小龍女重聚，他

天龍八部

鹿鼎記

笑傲江湖

雪山飛狐

神鵰俠侶

射鵰英雄傳

連城訣碧血劍

書劍恩仇錄

167

們和神鵰又一次將襄陽從蒙古大軍進攻中解救下來。

 文法解析

KEY 107

⭕ The already injured Yang Guo was attacked by Guo Fu and lost his right arm.

❌ The already injuring Yang Guo was attacked by Guo Fu and lost his right arm.

✦中譯✦ 已經重傷的楊過被郭芙攻擊失去了右臂。

✦解析✦ 過去分詞 injured 當形容詞修飾名詞，受傷有完成／被動含義，所以是過去分詞。

KEY 108

⭕ Meeting Xiaolongnu again, Yang Guo found out she was heavily injured and without much chance to recover.

❌ Met Xiaolongnu again, Yang Guo found out she was heavily injured and without much chance to recover.

✦中譯✦ 楊過再遇到小龍女時，她已經身受重傷且無望恢復。

✦解析✦ 分詞構句修飾後面的主句，Meet 是主詞楊過發出的動作。因為是主動含義，所以用現在分詞。

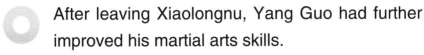

KEY 109

⭕ After leaving Xiaolongnu, Yang Guo had further improved his martial arts skills.

❌ After leave Xiaolongnu, Yang Guo had further improved his martial arts skills.

✦中譯✦ 離開小龍女後，楊過的武功更加精進。

✦解析✦ 介系詞後面應當加現在分詞／動名詞，加動詞則要與主句時態一致。

 武俠人物 44 - Xiaolongnu (小龍女)

MP3
44

Xiaolongnu (小龍女), the Little Dragon Maiden, was the chief of the Ancient Tomb Sect. The Ancient Tomb Sect was founded by Lin Chaoying (林朝英), the lover as well as rival of Wang Chongyang (王重陽) who had established the Quanzhen Sect. Lin hated Wang Chongyang for his ignorance of her love; she created the Jade Maiden Heart Sutra (玉女心經) which was the contrary to the Quanzhen martial arts techniques. Lin's maid became her apprentice. Xiaolongnü and Li Mochou (李莫愁) were her grand students. However, Li Mochou became into a notorious killer; making Xiaolongnu the operator of the Sect.

　小龍女是古墓派掌門人。創辦古墓派的林朝英是全真教開創者王重陽的情人兼對手，林朝英痛恨王重陽忽略她的感情，於是創造了《玉女心經》，與全真教的武功完全相剋。林朝英的僕人後來成為她的弟子，

小龍女和李莫愁則是再傳弟子，但是李莫愁變成了聲名狼籍的殺手，令小龍女成為門派繼承人。

Xiaolongnu was a beautiful maiden; she was described as white as snow and her elegant temperament was beyond convention. She appeared to be cold and never showed her real emotions. When Yang Guo was bullied and arrived at the Ancient Tomb Sect, she once refused him to stay. It was not until her maid, granny Sun got killed by Quanzhen apprentice that she agreed his stay. After that Yang Guo became the first male disciple in the Ancient Tomb Sect, and they cooperated to practice the Jade Maiden Heart Sutra.

小龍女是美麗的少女，她被描寫成肌膚勝雪、超凡脫俗的仙子，她個性冷淡，情緒從不外露，當楊過難耐全真教的欺凌來到古墓派時，小龍女曾拒絕收留他，直到她的僕人孫婆婆被全真弟子所殺後，她才同意楊過留下來，小龍女一直練習《玉女心經》，她收楊過為古墓派的第一個男弟子後，他們就合作一起練習。

Living together in the tomb for several years, love was naturally nourished between them even if their relationship was challenged by the conservative value of the era. After leaving the tomb, they experienced numerous tests and separated for several times. Even after getting married, they were still apart, living in isolation but faithful to each other for sixteen years until they eventually reunited.

在古墓一起生活多年令兩人漸生情愫，儘管他們的感情為當時保守的價值觀所不容。離開古墓後，他們經過了無數歷練，又多次分開，就算結婚之後，他們也仍然分離，楊過和小龍女抱著對彼此的忠誠，獨自生活了十六年才終於重逢。

 文法解析

 KEY 110

○ However, Li Mochou changed into a notorious killer; <u>making</u> Xiaolongnu the inheritor of the Sect.

✗ However, Li Mochou changed into a notorious killer; <u>make</u> Xiaolongnu the inheritor of the Sect.

✦中譯✦ 但是李莫愁變成了聲名狼籍的殺手，令小龍女成為門派繼承人。

✦解析✦ 對等子句改為分詞構句，主詞是李莫愁，故而用現在分詞構句。改為並列子句時，動詞應當都為過去式。

 KEY 111

○ Living together in the tomb for several years, love was naturally nourished between them.

✗ Lived together in the tomb for several years, love was naturally nourished between them.

✦中譯✦ 在古墓一起生活多年令兩人漸生情愫。

天龍八部

鹿鼎記

笑傲江湖

雪山飛狐

神鵰俠侶

射鵰英雄傳

連城訣碧血劍

書劍恩仇錄

◆解析◆ 由於是主動含義，live 的動作由 them 發出，所以用現在分詞。

武俠人物 45 - Xiaolongnu (小龍女)

Similar to Yang Guo, Xiaolongnu was also an orphan. She was abandoned as an infant and picked up by a Quanzhen apprentice. Since the Quanzhen Sect did not accept female disciples, Granny Sun from the Ancient Tomb Sect took her away.

　　像楊過一樣，小龍女也是孤兒，她在嬰兒時候被遺棄，由全真弟子撿到，因為全真教不收女弟子，她就被隔壁古墓派的孫婆婆帶走。

Trained all the martial arts skills from the Ancient Tomb Sect, Xiaolongnu became a fairly powerful kung fu master from a very young age. Xiaolongnu inherited the leadership of the sect after her senior apprentice Li Mochou was expelled. Li held jealousy towards Xiaolongnu and spread rumors on her. Many young men believed the rumour and gathered outside the tomb in the hope of marrying Xiaolongnu. Xiaolongnu utilized her typical martial arts skills to drive them away. She played an ancient instrument to instruct her jade bees to sting enemies and used her flexible weapon the Long Sash of Golden Bells (金鈴索) to attack the opponents.

　　小龍女被訓練了所有古墓派絕技，在很年輕時候就成為功夫高手，

在師姐李莫愁被逐出門派之後，小龍女繼承了古墓派掌門。李莫愁由於嫉妒，四處散播小龍女的謠言，很多年輕男子都相信了傳言，聚集在古墓前以期能和小龍女結婚，小龍女用她的高超武藝趕走了這些人。她擅長演奏古琴引導玉蜂叮咬敵人，伸縮自如的金鈴索被她用作武器來攻擊對手。

Xiaolongnu and Yang Guo found out the Nine Yin Manual in the tomb inscribed by Wang Chongyang; their martial arts skills improved significantly after practicing the Manual. She assisted Yang Guo to defeat the Golden Wheel Lama and supported Guo Jing to hold the position of martial arts world's leader. However, the orthodox swordsmen could not tolerate Xiaolongnu having a love affair with her student, so she had to leave Yang Guo to protect him. She even accepted the proposal from the villain Gongsun Zhi (公孫止). Luckily, Yang Guo's persistence had earned her back. Xiaolongnu was finally able to bear the pressure from the social stigma and enjoyed the true love with Yang Guo.

　　小龍女和楊過在古墓找到了王重陽刻錄的《九陰真經》，他們練習之後武功大增，她幫助楊過擊敗了金輪國師，也協助郭靖守住了中原武林盟主的位置。正派劍俠無法容忍小龍女與徒弟戀愛，她只得為了保護楊過而離開他，她甚至接受了惡人公孫止的求婚，幸運的是，楊過的堅持打動了她，小龍女終於可以抵禦社會壓力的影響，和楊過幸福地生活在一起。

天龍八部
鹿鼎記
笑傲江湖
雪山飛狐
神鵰俠侶
射鵰英雄傳
連城訣 碧血劍
書劍恩仇錄

文法解析

KEY 112

○ <u>Trained all the martial arts skills</u> from the Ancient Tomb Sect, Xiaolongnu became a fairly powerful kung fu master from very young age.

✗ <u>Training all the martial arts skills</u> from the Ancient Tomb Sect, Xiaolongnu became a fairly powerful kung fu master from very young age.

✦中譯✦ 小龍女被訓練了所有古墓派絕技，在很年輕時候就成為功夫高手。

✦解析✦ 原本句子為 Xiaolongnu was trained all the skills，語態是被動態。所以是過去分詞構句。

KEY 113

○ Xiaolongnu and Yang Guo found out the Nine Yin Manual in the tomb inscribed by Wang Chongyang.

✗ Xiaolongnu and Yang Guo found out the Nine Yin Manual in the tomb inscribing by Wang Chongyang.

✦中譯✦ 小龍女和楊過在古墓找到了王重陽刻錄的《九陰真經》。

✦解析✦ 《九陰真經》是被刻 inscribed，此處應當是過去分詞修飾名詞。

KEY 114

○ The orthodox swordsmen could not tolerate Xiaolongnu having love affair with her student.

✗ The orthodox swordsmen could not tolerate Xiaolongnu had love affair with her student.

✦中譯✦ 正派劍俠無法容忍小龍女與她徒弟戀愛。

✦解析✦ 分詞當形容詞，做受詞補語。小龍女是發出動作的主體，所以用現在分詞。

 ## 武俠人物 46 - Li Mochou (李莫愁)

MP3
46

Li Mochou (李莫愁) was nicknamed the Red Fairy (赤練仙子). She was infamous for her ferocious and merciless conduct. Li Mochou fell in love with Lu Zhanyuan (陸展元) when she was young; because of this, she was expelled from the Ancient Tomb Sect. Lu shattered her dream by marrying another girl; Li Mochou became a Taoist nun and sworn vengeance.

　　李莫愁綽號赤練仙子，她由於兇殘無情而臭名昭著。李莫愁年輕時曾愛上陸展元，還因此被古墓派驅逐。陸展元和其他人結婚令李莫愁夢想破滅，她做了道姑並發誓復仇。

Li Mochou's failure in her relationship made her disdainful to love. She became a vicious killer and sent her vengeance to Lu Zhanyuan's family members. Her concealed weapon was

天龍八部

鹿鼎記

笑傲江湖

雪山飛狐

神鵰俠侶

射鵰英雄傳

連城訣 碧血劍

書劍恩仇錄

the Silver Needles of Freezing Soul (冰魄銀針) which was the typical Ancient Tomb Sect style dart, but needles Li used were poisonous. She also used the Taoist Fly Whisk to attack people, and the techniques of using flexible weapons were also trained in the Ancient Tomb Sect.

感情失敗令李莫愁對愛情不屑，她變成了兇惡的殺手，向陸展元的家人洩憤。她的暗器是典型古墓派風格的冰魄銀針，但李莫愁用的是毒針。她也用拂塵攻擊人，使用柔韌武器的技法也是來自古墓派的訓練。

She was depressed that her teacher was in favor of Xiaolongnu and could not suppress her desire for the Jade Maiden Heart Sutra. She constantly chased after Xiaolongnu attempting to seize the Sutra. However, due to the meticulous protection from Xiaolongnu and Yang Guo, her dream of taking back the Sutra failed to materialize.

她對自己師傅偏愛小龍女感到沮喪，無法抑制對《玉女心經》的渴望，她不停追著小龍女試圖搶奪經書，但楊過和小龍女的細心保護令她從未得逞。

Li Mochou's conscience also made her a motherly figure for baby Guo Xiang whom she had kidnapped. She nurtured little Guo Xiang until she was taken back to her parents. Li Mochou died in the Passionless Valley (絕情谷). She was stabbed by the virulent Passion Flower and became delirious. Seeing her old lover Lu Zhanyuan due to a delusion, Li Mochou walked into fire.

　　李莫愁良心未泯，她搶走郭襄後曾像母親一樣照顧她，直到她回到父母身邊。李莫愁後來死於絕情谷，被劇毒的情花刺中而變得神智不清，透過模糊的意識看到了舊情人陸展元，李莫愁走入火中。

 文法解析

 KEY 115

⭕ Her concealed weapon was the Silver Needles of Freezing Soul.

❌ Her concealing weapon was the Silver Needles of Freezing Soul.

✦中譯✦ 她的暗器是冰魄銀針。

✦解析✦ 過去分詞當形容詞修飾名詞。**Concealed weapon** 是固定用法。

 KEY 116

⭕ She was depressed that her teacher was in favor of Xiaolongnü and could not suppress her desire for the Jade Maiden Heart Sutra.

❌ She was depressing that her teacher was in favor of Xiaolongnü and could not suppress her desire for the Jade Maiden Heart Sutra.

天龍八部
鹿鼎記
笑傲江湖
雪山飛狐
神鵰俠侶
射鵰英雄傳
連城訣碧血劍
書劍恩仇錄

✦中譯✦ 她對自己師傅偏愛小龍女感到沮喪，無法抑制對《玉女心經》的渴望。

✦解析✦ 過去分詞 depressed 修飾主詞自身的感受，意思是對……感到沮喪；現在分詞表示主詞帶給外界的感受，意思是……是令人沮喪的。此處應當是過去分詞。

KEY 117

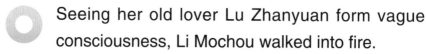 Seeing her old lover Lu Zhanyuan form vague consciousness, Li Mochou walked into fire.

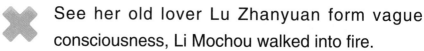 See her old lover Lu Zhanyuan form vague consciousness, Li Mochou walked into fire.

✦中譯✦ 透過模糊的意識看到了舊情人陸展元，李莫愁走入火中。

✦解析✦ 由主動語態轉化為現在分詞構句。將分詞變為動詞原型是錯誤用法。

 ## 武俠人物 47 - Guo Fu (郭芙) MP3 47

Guo Fu (郭芙) is the oldest daughter of Guo Jing and Huang Rong. Although she was beautiful and attractive; Guo Fu had inherited the capricious and impulsive quality from Huang Rong but not the intelligence. Guo Fu was accustomed to be spoiled and praised which made her naive but ignorant. She was insolent to Yang Guo since very young and harmed him several times.

　　郭芙是郭靖和黃蓉的大女兒，儘管她美麗動人，卻遺傳到黃蓉的任性衝動而非高智，郭芙習慣被寵溺誇獎，這令她的個性天真傲慢，她從小就對楊過粗魯無禮並幾次傷害他。

Guo Fu's bully made Yang Guo live a tough life in Guo Jing's family. Guo Fu at first despised Yang Guo and opposed Guo Jing's idea of marrying him. However, years later when they reunited, she became infatuated with him. When Guo Jing mentioned their engagement again, Yang Guo refused unhesitatingly since he was deeply in love with his teacher Xiaolongnu. Guo Fu felt offended for Yang Guo's refusal.

　　郭芙的欺凌讓楊過在郭靖家的生活非常辛苦，郭芙本來鄙視楊過，反對郭靖要把他們撮合在一起。然而多年以後當她再次見到楊過，卻被他深深吸引，當郭靖再次提及要為兩人訂婚，楊過馬上回絕了這提議，因為他已經深愛小龍女。楊過的拒絕令郭芙深受冒犯。

Guo Fu misunderstood that Xiaolongnu traded her infant sister Guo Xiang (郭襄) for the antidote to save Yang Guo. She scolded Yang Guo and their quarrel went up in flames. She mentioned Xiaolongnu's rape incident in fury; Yang Guo could not bear the insult and slapped her on the face. Guo Fu has never been humiliated like this; she attacked him with her sword. Yang Guo had no strength to defend since he was already severely injured; then his right arm was severed by Guo Fu.

　　郭芙誤會了小龍女搶走郭襄是為楊過換解藥，她怒斥楊過，兩人激烈爭吵，郭芙在盛怒下提到小龍女被玷污的事情，令楊過難忍侮辱打了她一耳光，郭芙從來沒有被如此對待過，她舉劍攻擊楊過，楊過已經身受重傷無力反擊，因此被郭芙砍掉右臂。

She later married Jeh Lv Qi (耶律齊), a descendant from Liao's royal family. Yang Guo rescued Yelv Qi from the siege of the Mongolian army, which made Guo Fu felt remorseful for her wrong deeds to Yang Guo. Guo Fu finally became mature and wise enough to reach reconciliation with Yang Guo.

　　她後來嫁給了遼國皇室後裔耶律齊，楊過從蒙古大軍包圍中救過耶律齊，令郭芙對自己曾經對楊過的所作所為深感懊悔。她終於變得成熟明智並與楊過和解。

文法解析

 KEY 118

 However, years later when they reunited, she became infatuated with him.

 However, years later when they reunited, she became infatuating with him.

✦中譯✦　然而多年以後當她再次見到楊過，卻被他深深吸引。

✦解析✦　吸引不是郭芙發出的動作，而是加諸於她的狀態，所以用過去分詞。

KEY 119

◯ Guo Fu felt offended for Yang Guo's refusal.

✕ Guo Fu felt offending for Yang Guo's refusal.

✦中譯✦ 楊過的拒絕令郭芙深受冒犯。

✦解析✦ 過去分詞表示被冒犯 offended；而現在分詞表示冒犯的，違法的。

 ## 武俠人物 48 - Guo Xiang (郭襄) *MP3* *48*

Guo Xiang (郭襄) was the younger daughter of Guo Jing and Huang Rong. She was named after the city of Xiangyang, the front line where her parents defended the Mongolian armies' invasion. When Guo Xiang was an infant, Li Mochou mistakenly thought she was Xiaolongnu's daughter and kidnapped her. Yang Guo seized her back and protected her from the enemies. Yang Guo was very fond of Guo Xiang.

When Guo Xiang became a teenager, she was deeply enchanted by Yang Guo. Yang Guo thought of her as his beloved younger sister; he promised to complete three of her wishes. Guo Xiang used the first request to see Yang Guo's face; the second one to invite him to attend her sixteenth birthday celebration; and the third wish to prevent Yang Guo from attempting suicide when he believed his wife was dead.

　　郭襄是郭靖和黃蓉的小女兒，她的名字取自襄陽城，是她的父母抵禦蒙古軍隊入侵的前線。郭襄還是嬰兒時，李莫愁誤以為她是小龍女的女兒將她劫走，楊過把她搶回，又保護她不被敵人攻擊，楊過非常喜歡郭襄。而當郭襄成為少女時，她非常喜歡楊過，楊過把她當作珍愛的小妹妹，答應完成她的三個願望，郭襄用了第一個願望看到了楊過的真容；用第二個願望邀請楊過為她慶祝十六歲生日；第三個願望阻止了認定小龍女已死的楊過自殺。

During an attack to Xiangyang City, the Mongolians tied up Guo Xiang as a hostage. The Golden Wheel Lama threatened to burn her to force Guo Jing to surrender. Guo Xiang was not frightened, and she was determined to die for the nation. Yang Guo couple came with the condor and halted the invasion. Guo Xiang was saved again; she got Yang Guo's Heavy Iron Sword as a gift. Unable to deal with her feelings of the loss of Yang Guo, she inadvertently practiced the Nine Yang Manual (九陽真經) and became one of the finest martial arts masters. Years later, the city of Xiangyang was finally conquered by the Mongolian troop and Guo Xiang's family members all died in the battle. Guo Xiang became the founder of the E'mei Sect (峨嵋派), continued her family's missions to defend her people.

　　在蒙古軍對襄陽的一次進攻中，郭襄被當作人質綁了起來，金輪國師威脅要燒死郭襄，以威脅郭靖投降，郭襄毫不畏懼，決定為民族而死。楊過伉儷和神鵰的到來阻止了這次入侵，郭襄再次被救，她得到了楊過的玄鐵重劍作為禮物。楊過離開後，郭襄無法排遣失落感，她無意

中練習了《九陽真經》變成了頂尖高手。幾年後，襄陽城最終被蒙古攻下，郭襄的家人都死於抵抗入侵的戰鬥中，郭襄後來創建了峨嵋派，繼續著她家人保護平民的使命。

文法解析

KEY 120

When Guo Xiang became a teenager; she was deeply enchanted by Yang Guo.

When Guo Xiang became a teenager; she was deeply enchanting by Yang Guo.

✦中譯✦ 郭襄成為少女時，她非常喜歡楊過。

✦解析✦ Enchanted 表示主詞對……感到著迷；enchanting 表示主詞令人著迷。

KEY 121

Guo Xiang was not frightened and she determined to die for the nation.

Guo Xiang was not frightening and she determined to die for the nation.

✦中譯✦ 郭襄毫不畏懼，決定為民族而死。

✦解析✦ 過去分詞 frightened 表示對……驚懼害怕；現在分詞 frightening 意思是令人恐懼的。郭襄不畏懼應當是過去分詞。

武俠人物 **49** - Jinlun Guoshi (金輪國師) *MP3* **49**

Jinlun Guoshi (金輪國師), the Golden Wheel Lama is one of the antagonists in the novel. He was originally from Tibet and became the Imperial Advisor for the Mongol Empire. The Golden Wheel Lama was sent by the Mongolian Khan to challenge the Han Chinese martial arts world. His weapon were five wheels made by gold, silver, copper, iron, and lead respectively. He also practiced advanced inner power skills, the Dragon Elephant Prajna Techniques (龍象般若功).

金輪國師是小說中的一個反派角色。他來自西藏又做了蒙古帝國的國師，金輪國師被蒙古可汗派遣挑戰中原武林，他的武器是分別由金、銀、銅、鐵、鉛製造的五種輪子，他也練習極高深的內功龍象般若功。

Jinlun Guoshi attended the kung fu contest in which heroes from the whole country compete for the leader of martial arts world. He defeated a group of swordsmen until Guo Jing showed up and repelled him by the Dragon Strike Palms. Jinlun Guoshi was unwilling to accept the failure; he kidnapped Guo Fu as a hostage to prepare for the revenge. Yang Guo and Xiaolongnü made a joint effort to save Guo Fu back.

金輪國師參加了天下英雄雲集的武林盟主大會，他擊敗了很多功夫高手，只有敗給郭靖的降龍十八掌，金輪國師不願接受失敗，他綁架了郭芙做人質準備報仇，楊過和小龍女聯手救回郭芙。

天龍八部

鹿鼎記

笑傲江湖

雪山飛狐

神鵰俠侶

射鵰英雄傳

連城訣碧血劍

書劍恩仇錄

Jinlun Guoshi returned to Mongolia and practiced relentlessly; he later came back to the central land as a more powerful swordsman. He abducted Guo Xiang to hamper Guo Jing, whereas he gradually appreciated Guo Xiang's wisdom and courage. Jinlun Guoshi used to have three apprentices. The most talented one died young, and the other two were not his ideal disciple. He planned to cultivate Guo Xiang as his successor, so he persuaded her several times to become his student. During the battle of attacking Xiangyang, Jinlun Guoshi stroke away a firing pillar to protect Guo Xiang and died from exhausting. Yang Guo and Huang Rong saluted for him for his chivalrous deed.

金輪國師回到蒙古刻苦練習武藝，之後他回到中原時已擁有更強大的功夫，他綁走郭襄以妨害郭靖，但卻漸漸被郭襄的智慧和勇氣打動，金輪國師曾有三位弟子，資質最優的徒弟英年早逝，其餘兩位都不為他所喜歡，他打算培養郭襄繼承他的武學，幾次三番勸她拜師。在攻打襄陽一役中，金輪國師為了保護郭襄擊開了著火的柱子，精疲力盡而死，楊過和黃蓉都為他的仗義之舉致敬。

文法解析

KEY 122

His weapon were five wheels made by gold, silver, copper, iron, and lead respectively.

❌ His weapon were five wheels making by gold, silver, copper, iron, and lead respectively.

✦中譯✦ 他的武器是分別由金、銀、銅、鐵、鉛製造的五種輪子。

✦解析✦ 過去分詞表示被動,武器由……製作應當用 **made**。

 KEY 123

⭕ During the battle of attacking Xiangyang, Jinlun Guoshi stroke away a firing pillar to protect Guo Xiang and died from exhausting.

❌ During the battle of attacking Xiangyang, Jinlun Guoshi stroke away a fired pillar to protect Guo Xiang and died from exhausting.

✦中譯✦ 在攻打襄陽一役中,金輪國師為了保護郭襄擊開了著火的柱子,精疲力盡而死。

✦解析✦ 現在分詞有進行時,主動的意思。著火的柱子應當是現在分詞 **firing**。

 武俠人物 50 - Gongsun Zhi (公孫止) MP3 **50**

Gongsun Zhi (公孫止) was the wicked master of the Passionless Valley (絕情谷). His noble manner and gentlemanly conduct deceived people from finding out that he was actually cold-blooded and ruthless. Gongsun Zhi was a lecherous hypocrite; he used to have an illicit relationship with his maid. After his <u>domineering</u> wife Qui Qianchi (裘千尺) <u>forced the maid to die, he made a plot and casted his wife's into an underground pit</u>, where she was supposed to die inside.

公孫止是絕情谷的邪惡主人，他的高貴舉止和紳士風度蒙蔽了人們去察覺他冷血無情的真面目，公孫止是個好色的偽君子，他曾和家裡女僕有私情，在他專橫的妻子裘千尺逼死女僕後，公孫止設計將她妻子關在了地底深坑中，打算讓她死在那裡。

Gongsun Zhi was handsome and skilled in martial arts. His weapons were a toothed golden saber and a black sword. He fought by both hands with the combat style of combining flexibility and rigidness. Gongsun Zhi saved Xiaolongnu by chance; then forced her to marry him. On the wedding day, Yang Guo searched Xiaolongnu to the Passionless Valley and prohibited this <u>absurd</u> wedding from happening. At the same time, Gongsun Zhi's wife reappeared; she managed to operate her inner energy to maintain life during the time underground. Qui Qianchi blinded her husband's one eye with date pit as revenge; meanwhile, Gongsun Zhi showed his real personality after seeing her. He fought Yang Guo three times and failed all of them; so he poisoned Yang Guo with the passionless flower and locked him in the dungeon.

公孫止相貌英俊武藝高強，他的武器是鋸齒金刀和黑劍，他雙手同

天龍八部

鹿鼎記

笑傲江湖

雪山飛狐

神鵰俠侶

射鵰英雄傳

連城訣碧血劍

書劍恩仇錄

時進攻，武功剛柔並濟。公孫止無意中救了小龍女後就強迫她嫁給自己，婚禮當天，楊過尋找小龍女來到了絕情谷，阻止了這場荒謬的婚禮，同時公孫止的妻子又出現了，她在深坑裡運用內功續命才得以存活，作為報復，裘千尺用棗核射瞎了公孫止的一隻眼睛，公孫止也在看到妻子後展現出自己的陰險本性，他和楊過大戰三場，每次都敗給楊過，於是他用劇毒的情花毒害楊過，並把楊過也關進地牢。

Having defeated by Xiaolongnu, Gongsun Zhi could not help but give Yang Guo the antidote. Their daughter the compassionate Gongsun Lu'e (公孫綠萼) also sacrificed her life to help Yang Guo. Gongsun Zhi died from Qui Qianchi's plot, but he managed to perish together with her.

公孫止被小龍女打敗，不得不向楊過交出了解藥，他善良的女兒公孫綠萼也為了救楊過犧牲性命。公孫止最後被裘千尺害死，但他還是做到了與她同歸於盡。

 文法解析

 KEY 124

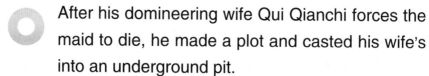

After his domineering wife Qui Qianchi forces the maid to die, he made a plot and casted his wife's into an underground pit.

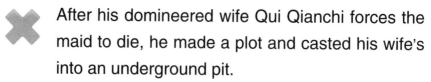

After his domineered wife Qui Qianchi forces the maid to die, he made a plot and casted his wife's into an underground pit.

✦中譯✦ 在他專橫的妻子裘千尺逼死女僕後，公孫止設計將她妻子關
在了地底深坑中。

zuanh

✦解析✦ 現在分詞 **domineering** 由動詞 **domineer**（擅權）變化而
成。功能為形容詞，表示專橫的、作威作福的，修飾名詞
wife。

KEY 125

○ Having defeated by Xiaolongnu, Gongsun Zhi
had to give Yang Guo the antidote.

✗ Defeating by Xiaolongnu, Gongsun Zhi had to
give Yang Guo the antidote.

✦中譯✦ 公孫止被小龍女打敗，不得不向楊過交出了解藥。

✦解析✦ 完成式分詞構句的主詞是公孫止，由於是被擊敗，要用過去
分詞而非現在分詞。

Glossary 字彙一覽表

abduct *vt.* 誘拐，綁架，劫持	absurd *adj.* 荒唐的，不合理的
abyss *n.* 深淵	
accustomed *adj.* 習慣的，通常的	avenge *vt.* 為……報仇
beleaguer *vt.* 圍攻	capricious *adj.* 任性的
celebration *n.* 慶典	compassionate *adj.* 富於同情心的

天龍八部

鹿鼎記

笑傲江湖

雪山飛狐

神鵰俠侶

射鵰英雄傳

連城訣碧血劍

書劍恩仇錄

conquer *vt.* 征服	conscience *n.* 良心
conservative *adj.* 保守的	contrary *n.adj.* 相反；相反的，對立的
convention *n.* 公約	delirious *adj.* 發狂的，精神錯亂的
despise *vt.* 鄙視，看不起	despite *prep.* 儘管，任憑
disdainful *adj.* 蔑視的，輕蔑的	domineering *adj.* 盛氣凌人的
era *n.* 時代	excessively *adv.* 過分地
exhaust *n.vt.vi.* 抽乾；排出氣體；排出	ferocious *adj.* 兇猛的
hamper *vt.n.* 阻礙；障礙物	illicit *adj.* 非法的
impulsive *adj.* 容易衝動的	inadvertently *adv.* 不經意間，不慎地
infamous *adj.* 臭名昭著的	infatuate *vt.* 吸引住，使著迷
inscribe *vt.* 題，刻，雕	isolation *n.* 隔離，孤立
jade *n.* 玉	lecherous *adj.* 好色的
melancholic *n.adj.* 憂鬱；憂鬱的	mercurial *adj.* 易變的，敏捷的
passionless *adj.* 不熱情的，冷靜的	perish *vi.vt.* 消滅，枯萎；使死去
Prajna *n.* 般若	prejudice *n.* 偏見
proposal *n.* 建議，提議，求婚	repel *vt.* 擊退，驅除，排斥，抵制

resemblance *n.* 相似	scold *vt.* 罵
severe *adj.* 嚴重的，劇烈的	sneaky *adj.* 偷偷摸摸的，暗中的
stagger *n.vt.vi.* 搖晃，蹣跚；使搖晃，使猶豫；蹣跚而行	stance *n.* 姿態,立場
stigma *n.* 恥辱，汙名	unwilling *adj.* 不甘心的，不情願的
venture *n.* 冒險	

筆記欄

天龍八部

鹿鼎記

笑傲江湖

雪山飛狐

神鵰俠侶

射鵰英雄傳

碧血劍連城訣

書劍恩仇錄

Unit 6

不定詞與動名詞

《射鵰英雄傳》

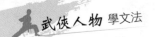

 ## 文法主題介紹－不定詞與動名詞

不定詞與動名詞 (Infinitives & Gerund)

不定詞（to V）具有名詞、形容詞與副詞的功能，在句中扮演非動詞的角色，但仍具有動詞的特徵，可以帶有受詞、補語或副詞，也可以用否定、進行式、完成式，甚至被動式，是個多方位的角色。

1. 將不定詞作為受詞的動詞：即 S + V + to V

Ask, expect, intend, mean, plan, offer, propose, tend, promise, seem, appear, decide, afford, manage, desire, aim, agree, wish, prefer, fail, refuse, pretend.

2. 將不定詞作為受詞補語的動詞：即 S + V + O + to V

Ask, expect, encourage, allow, advise, convince, enable, invite, force, prompt, remind, require, permit, persuade, forbid, warn, tell, order.

3. 後面常搭配不定詞的名詞：即 N + to V

Ability, capacity, authority, effort, opportunity, plan, decision, way right, claim.

4. 後面常搭配不定詞的形容詞：即 Adj + to V

Able, unable, eligible, liable, likely, unlikely, ready, willing, unwilling, reluctant, eager, anxious.

5. 以 it 當虛主詞或虛受詞代替不定詞的用法：

🗡 It 當虛主詞時：It 開頭的句子，真主詞（to + V)放在後面

It is/was + adj + for 人 to V

It is/was + adj + of 人 to V ＝人 + be + adj + to V (此類形容詞多表示人的性格與能力)

🗡 It 當虛受詞時：放動詞之後，代替後面出現的真受詞（to + V)。

S + V + it + Adj + to V

S + V + it + N + to V

6. 表示「結果」的句型：

🗡 如此……以至於...... S + V＋so + adj/adv + as to + V   S + V＋ adj/adv + enough + to V

🗡 太.....而不能...... S + V＋too + adj/adv + (for someone) + to V

動名詞（Ving）是由動詞轉變而來，但具有名詞功能的性質。與不定詞相同，是可以有受詞、補語、副詞修飾語，及完成時態、被動語態的用法，與真正名詞還是不同。

7. 將動名詞作為受詞的動詞：即 S + V + Ving

Enjoy, mind, imagine, suggest, recommend, avoid, admit, consider, postpone, practice, deny, quit, discuss.

8. 動名詞慣用語：

be capable of Ving

be aware of

be worth Ving

天龍八部

鹿鼎記

笑傲江湖

雪山飛狐

神鵰俠侶

射鵰英雄傳

連城訣

碧血劍

書劍恩仇錄

be busy Ving

There is no Ving

It is no use Ving

can't help Ving

spend money/time Ving

go Ving

do a lot of / a little Ving

feel like Ving

look forward to Ving

object to = be opposed to

get used/accustomed to Ving

have difficulty/trouble/a problem Ving

be devoted/committed/dedicated to Ving

9. 動名詞與名詞的不同：

名詞：前面可加 a 或 the；前面可加「形容詞」修飾；後面不可接受詞

動名詞：前面可加 the，但不可以加 a；前面可加「副詞」或是「所有格」修飾；後面可接受詞

武俠人物 51 - Guo Jing (郭靖)　 *MP3* *51*

Guo Jing (郭靖) is the protagonist in The Legend of the Condor Heroes (射鵰英雄傳). The story is set in the late Southern Song Dynasty when the nation was under the threat of the nomadic ethnics in the north, such as the Jurchen and the Mongolian. Born in Mongolia, Guo Jing was a posthumous child, and his mother took him to join Genghis Khan's tribe. He became sworn brother with Khan's forth son Tolui (托雷) and demonstrated loyalty to the tribe. Genghis Khan even betrothed his daughter to Guo Jing.

《射雕英雄傳》主角為郭靖，小說背景設定在南宋晚期，當時南宋受到女真族、蒙古族等北方遊牧民族的威脅。郭靖是個遺腹子，出生在蒙古，他的媽媽帶著他加入了成吉思汗的部落，郭靖和成吉思汗的兒子托雷結拜為兄弟，他忠誠於蒙古部落，成吉思汗還把女兒許配給他。

Guo Jing's first martial arts teachers were the Seven Freaks of Jiangnan (江南七怪). They obeyed the promise made with taoist priest Qui Chuji (丘處機) and taught Guo Jing kung fu to prepare him for the contest with Yang Kang (楊康) when he turns eighteen. Guo Jing left Mongolia as a young swordsman, already possessing the inner energy skills form the Quanzhen Sect (全真教) and was good at Mongolian combat techniques.

郭靖最早的武術師傅是江南七怪，他們遵循與丘處機道長的約定教、郭靖武功，為他十八歲時與楊康比武做準備。郭靖離開蒙古時已經是一個年輕的劍俠，他已掌握全真教的內功並精於蒙古搏擊術。

He met a little beggar disguised by Huang Rong (黃蓉), who became Guo Jing's life-long partner in the future, and they went on adventures together. Guo Jing then encountered the leader of the Beggars' Sect Hong Qigong (洪七公); Huang

天龍八部

鹿鼎記

笑傲江湖

雪山飛狐

神鵰俠侶

射鵰英雄傳

碧血劍

書劍恩仇錄

Rong incited Hong Qigong to teach Guo Jing his powerful skill: the Dragon-strike Palms (降龍十八掌). Guo Jing then went to the Peach Blossom Island (桃花島) to meet Huang Rong's father; he came across the Old Imp Zhou Botong (老頑童周伯通) and made him his sworn brother. Zhou taught Guo Jing the Seventy-two Vacant Fists (七十二路空明拳) and the Ambidexterity (雙手互搏). The slow-learning Guo Jing gradually became stronger as he matured.

他遇見了打扮成小叫化子的黃蓉兩人一起行走江湖，黃蓉後來成了他一生的伴侶。郭靖又偶遇丐幫幫主洪七公，黃蓉鼓動洪七公教郭靖絕技降龍十八掌。郭靖後來去桃花島與黃蓉的父親相見，在島上認識了老頑童周伯通還與他結義。周伯通教給郭靖七十二路空明拳和雙手互搏的技術後，笨腦筋的郭靖武功變得越來越強。

 文法解析

 KEY 126

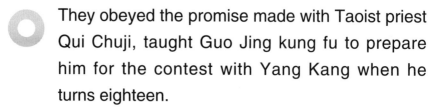

They obeyed the promise made with Taoist priest Qui Chuji, taught Guo Jing kung fu to prepare him for the contest with Yang Kang when he turns eighteen.

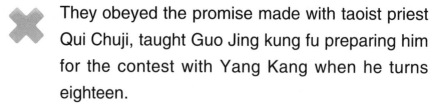

They obeyed the promise made with taoist priest Qui Chuji, taught Guo Jing kung fu preparing him for the contest with Yang Kang when he turns eighteen.

◆中譯◆ 他們遵循與丘處機道長的約定教郭靖武功，為他十八歲時與
楊康比武做準備。

◆解析◆ 這裏不定詞用作副詞，表示原因或目的。而動名詞常表示性
質或狀態。

 KEY 127

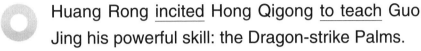

⭘ Huang Rong <u>incited</u> Hong Qigong <u>to teach</u> Guo
Jing his powerful skill: the Dragon-strike Palms.

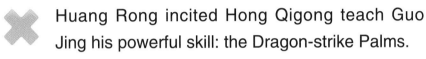

✖ Huang Rong incited Hong Qigong teach Guo
Jing his powerful skill: the Dragon-strike Palms.

◆中譯◆ 黃蓉鼓動洪七公教郭靖絕技降龍十八掌。

◆解析◆ incite 是將不定詞作為受詞補語的動詞 incite sb to do
sth。to 不能省略。

 KEY 128

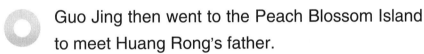

⭘ Guo Jing then went to the Peach Blossom Island
to meet Huang Rong's father.

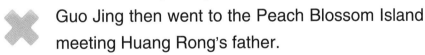

✖ Guo Jing then went to the Peach Blossom Island
meeting Huang Rong's father.

◆中譯◆ 郭靖後來去桃花島與黃蓉的父親相見。

◆解析◆ 不定詞片語修飾動詞 went to，表示去桃花島的目的，不能
替換為動名詞。

天龍八部

鹿鼎記

笑傲江湖

雪山飛狐

神鵰俠侶

射鵰英雄傳

連城訣碧血劍

書劍恩仇錄

武俠人物 52 - Guo Jing (郭靖) MP3 52

Guo Jing (郭靖) got the Nine Yin Manual (九陰真經) from Zhou Botong; he learnt the incredible techniques inside and cultivated extraordinary inner energy skills. He also found out the Book of Wumu (武穆遺書) on Iron Palm Peak (鐵掌峰); it was a military strategy classic which made Guo Jing a military tactician.

　　郭靖從周伯通那裏得到了《九陰真經》，他從中習得了高深的武藝和驚人內功，他還在鐵掌峰上得到了《武穆遺書》，這部軍事經典讓郭靖成為了戰略家。

Huang Rong was wounded by Qui Qianren's (裘千仞) 'iron palm' and Guo Jing took her to find Reverend Yideng (一燈大師) for cure. When they came back to the Peach Blossom Island, five of the Seven Freaks of Jiangnan were killed. Guo Jing misunderstood Huang Rong's father as the murderer, but they were actually killed by Ouyang Feng (歐陽鋒) and Yang Kang (楊康). Guo Jing went back for revenge and lost contact with Huang Rong for half a year.

　　黃蓉被裘千仞的鐵掌擊傷後，郭靖帶她去找一燈大師療傷，他們回到桃花島才發現江南七怪中的五個人已經被殺，郭靖誤以為黃蓉的父親是兇手，但實際上他們是被歐陽鋒和楊康害死的。郭靖回到中原復仇，和黃蓉失去聯繫半年之久。

Guo Jing served in Genghis Khan's army and returned in triumph. Finding out that Khan's next target was Song Empire had shocked Guo Jing, he renounced loyalty to Mongolia and settled in Xiangyang to protect his motherland. Guo Jing went to the contest in Huashan and was beaten by Ouyang Feng; however, under the witness of Hong Qigong, he engaged to Huang Rong.

郭靖在成吉思汗大軍中立下戰功凱旋歸來。發現成吉思汗的下一個目標是宋，這令郭靖感到震驚，他放棄了效忠蒙古，轉而回到襄陽城保衛母國，之後郭靖參加華山論劍敗給歐陽鋒，但在洪七公的見證下他與黃蓉訂婚。

Guo Jing is inarticulate and low-witted; moral rectitude and patriotism are his outstanding traits. Huang Rong cherishes his precious qualities even Guo Jing's intelligence is much inferior to her. Guo Jing encountered a series of adventures and transformed into a great hero. At last, his martial arts skills reached the level of the Five Greats.

郭靖不善言辭，也沒有靈敏的反應能力，正直和愛國心是他的優異品質。黃蓉雖比郭靖聰明很多，卻很看重郭靖身上的可貴之處。郭靖歷經磨煉成為偉大的英雄，他的武功也達到了五大高手的水準。

天龍八部

鹿鼎記

笑傲江湖

雪山飛狐

神鵰俠侶

射鵰英雄傳

連城訣 碧血劍

書劍恩仇錄

文法解析

KEY 129

⭕ Guo Jing took her to find Reverend Yideng for cure.

❌ Guo Jing took her to finding Reverend Yideng for cure.

✦中譯✦ 郭靖帶她去找一燈大師療傷。

✦解析✦ 不定詞做受詞補語。不定詞結構為 to＋動詞原型，to＋Ving 是錯誤用法。

 ### KEY 130

⭕ Finding out that Khan's next target was Song Empire had shocked Guo Jing, he renounced loyalty to Mongolia and settled in Xiangyang to protect his motherland.

❌ To find out that Khan's next target was Song Empire had shocked Guo Jing, he renounced loyalty to Mongolia and settled in Xiangyang to protect his motherland.

✦中譯✦ 發現成吉思汗的下一個目標是宋，這令郭靖感到震驚，他宣布放棄了效忠蒙古，轉而回到襄陽城保衛母國。

✦解析✦ 動名詞表達的是已經發生，不定詞常表示將要發生，此處應當為動名詞。

武俠人物 53 - Huang Rong (黃蓉) *MP3* **53**

Huang Rong (黃蓉) was Huang Yaoshi's (黃藥師) only daughter growing up on Peach Blossom Island where Huang Yaoshi imparted her with miscellaneous knowledge and kung fu skills. Huang Rong was extremely intelligent and quick-witted; being over-spoiled made her a bit capricious. Like her father, She was versatile, specialized in many fields, in addition to martial arts. As a quick learner, Huang Rong's kung fu skill was not as powerful as Guo Jing due to her lack of patience and consistence.

黃蓉是黃藥師的獨生女，在桃花島長大。黃藥師傳授給她各種知識和武功，黃蓉極為聰明機敏，被溺愛讓她有些任性，黃蓉像她的父親一樣多才多藝，除武術之外精通許多其他領域。因為學什麼都很快，所以她缺乏耐心和堅持，這讓黃蓉的功夫反而不及郭靖。

Huang Rong ran away from home after quarrelling with her father and she dressed up as a beggar to wander around. She met Guo Jing in a restaurant where she ordered lots of fine cuisine and Guo Jing paid the bill. The single-minded Guo Jing pitied this poor beggar; he gave Huang Rong his clothes and horse. Huang Rong found Guo Jing honest, kind-hearted, and innocent; she secretly protected him from lots of dangers.

黃蓉和父親吵架之後離家出走，扮成小乞丐四處流浪，她和郭靖在

餐館相遇，黃蓉點了許多美食讓郭靖付帳，單線條的郭靖憐憫這個小乞丐，送給黃蓉自己的衣服和寶馬，黃蓉發現他誠實、善良又單純，便暗中保護郭靖。

She confessed her true identity to Guo Jing and they embarked on adventures together. Guo Jing's teachers the Seven Freaks of Jiangnan disliked Huang Rong as they believed Guo Jing's ideal partner should be the Mongolian princess. Huang Rong treated them reverently, wishing that they would change their impression towards her. She cooked for Hong Qigong; in exchange, Hong Qigong taught Guo Jing his Dragon-strike Palms. Hong Qi Gong lost his inner energy after being bitten by Ouyang Feng's venomous serpent; he accepted Huang Rong as his disciple. Huang Rong learnt the Dog Beating Stick Technigues and became the chief of the Beggars' Sect.

後來她向像郭靖坦承了自己真實身分，兩人便一起行動，郭靖的師傅江南七怪不喜歡黃蓉，他們覺得郭靖的伴侶應該是蒙古公主，黃蓉對待七怪非常恭敬，希望改善他們對她的印象，黃蓉為洪七公煮飯，作為交換，洪七公教給郭靖降龍十八掌。後來洪七公被歐陽鋒的毒蛇咬傷失去內力，他收黃蓉為徒，傳授她打狗棒法讓她接任了丐幫幫主。

文法解析

 **KEY 131**

○ Huang Rong was Huang Yaoshi's only daughter growing up on Peach Blossom Island.

✗ Huang Rong was Huang Yaoshi's only daughter to grow up on Peach Blossom Island.

✦中譯✦ 黃蓉是黃藥師的獨生女，在桃花島長大。

✦解析✦ 動名詞做受詞補語表示狀態，此處不可換作不定詞。

 KEY 132

○ Huang Rong was extremely intelligent and quick-witted; being over-spoiled made her a bit capricious.

✗ Huang Rong was extremely intelligent and quick-witted; to be over-spoiled made her a bit capricious.

✦中譯✦ 黃蓉極為聰明機敏，被溺愛讓她有些任性。

✦解析✦ 被溺愛是既成事實而非將要發生，所以此處用動名詞。

 KEY 133

○ Huang Rong treated them reverently to change their impression towards her.

Huang Rong treated them reverently changing their impression towards her.

━━━━━━━━━━━━━━━━━━━━━━━━━━━━━━━━━━━━━

✦中譯✦ 黃蓉對待七怪非常恭敬,希望改善他們對她的印象。

✦解析✦ 不定詞作副詞表目的,不可換作動名詞。

武俠人物 54 - Huang Rong (黃蓉)

At first, Hang Rong's martial arts skills were more sophisticated than Guo Jing's. She made every effort to assist Guo Jing to become a great swordsman. During their adventure, Huang Rong's wisdom helped them getting through obstacles and challenges. She saved Hong Qigong from Ouyang Feng's attack. During the way of finding Reverend Yideng, she solved puzzles set by his four disciples and found the master successfully. Huang Rong cleared Guo Jing's misunderstanding of his teachers' death and found out the real murderers. She assisted Guo Jing to succeed in military actions when he served in the Mongolian army, and they cooperated to capture Ouyang Feng several times.

　　一開始,黃蓉的武功比郭靖更高,她盡全力幫助郭靖成為大俠。在郭靖和黃蓉的歷險過程中,黃蓉總是用聰慧戰勝困難和挑戰,她從歐陽鋒手裏救下洪七公,在尋找一燈大師的路上,黃蓉解開了大師四位弟子設置的難題,成功見到了一燈大師。黃蓉幫郭靖找出了殺死他師傅們的真兇,解除了郭靖的誤會,她幫助郭靖指揮蒙古軍隊取得勝利,並且兩

人聯手幾次抓住歐陽鋒。

Huang Rong was also associated with Yang Kang's death. Yang Kang made a deadly strike on her to prevent Huang Rong from revealing his criminal behaviours. The spot he hit was Huang Rong's left shoulder where her spike armour was stained with Ouyang Feng's snake venom. Yang Kang was poisoned to death, his son was later educated by Guo Jing and Huang Rong.

楊康的死與黃蓉有關，楊康向黃蓉痛下殺手，以阻止她揭露自己的犯罪行徑，他打在黃蓉軟蝟甲的左肩位置，那裏剛好沾了歐陽鋒的蛇毒，楊康因此被毒死，他的兒子楊過後來受到郭靖和黃蓉的教育。

Huang Rong had a stunning appearance; when Guo Jing first saw her real face, he was astonished by her beauty and became wordless. Everyone she encountered noticed her fair looking. Ouyang Feng's nephew Ouyang Ke was also completely enchanted by Huang Rong. He chased after Huang Rong devotionally even through he was despised and fooled by her every time.

黃蓉有驚人美麗的容貌，郭靖第一次見到她原來的樣貌就吃驚到說不出話來。她遇到的所有人都注意到黃蓉的美貌，歐陽鋒的姪子歐陽克就被黃蓉迷倒，儘管每次都慘遭愚弄，還是癡心追尋黃蓉。

天龍八部

鹿鼎記

笑傲江湖

雪山飛狐

神鵰俠侶

射鵰英雄傳

連城訣碧血劍

書劍恩仇錄

Huang Rong possessed various skills, such as cooking, playing music, and chess. She had profound knowledge on medicine, mathematics, literature, strategy, and so on. She also inherited the near-photographic memory from her mother. She was one of the most perfect figures among all female characters in Jing Yong's martial arts novels.

黃蓉精於烹飪、琴棋等技藝，她對藥學、數學、文學、策略等領域也涉獵很深，她還從母親遺傳到驚人的記憶力，黃蓉是金庸小說中近乎完美的女生形象。

 文法解析

 KEY 134

 She made every effort to assist Guo Jing to become a great swordsman.

 She made every effort assisting Guo Jing to become a great swordsman.

✦中譯✦ 她盡全力幫助郭靖成為大俠。

✦解析✦ Effort 是後面常搭配不定詞的名詞。慣用型為 effort to V。

 KEY 135

 She assisted Guo Jing to succeed in military actions when he served in the Mongolian army, and they cooperated to capture Ouyang Feng several times.

She assisted Guo Jing succeed in military actions when he served in the Mongolian army, and they cooperated to capture Ouyang Feng several times.

✦中譯✦ 她幫助郭靖指揮蒙古軍隊取得勝利,並且兩人聯手幾次抓住歐陽鋒。

✦解析✦ 去掉 to 則失去不定詞的結構,句子成為有兩個動詞的語病句。

KEY 136

◯ Yang Kang made a deadly strike on her to prevent Huang Rong from revealing his criminal behaviours.

✗ Yang Kang made a deadly strike on her preventing Huang Rong from revealing his criminal behaviours.

✦中譯✦ 楊康向黃蓉痛下殺手,以阻止她揭露自己的犯罪行徑。

✦解析✦ 不定詞做副詞表目的,不可替換為動名詞。

 武俠人物 55 - Yang Kang (楊康) *MP3* *55*

Yang Kang (楊康) and Guo Jing were both named by Qui Chuji to memorize the national calamity of Song Empire. Yang Kang was raised up in Jin Empire since his parents were forced apart during an attack plotted by Jurchen Prince Wanyan Honglie (完顏洪烈). Wanyan Honglie then saved Yang Kang's mother and adopted Yang Kang as his foster son.

楊康和郭靖都是由丘處機命名，以紀念國難。楊康在金國長大，他的爸媽由於完顏洪烈策劃一次攻擊行動被迫離散，完顏洪烈救了楊康的母親並收他做養子。

Yang Kang grew up as a Jurchen noble; he was accustomed to having power and wealth. When his biological father showed up and persuaded him to turn back as a normal Song civilian, Yang Kang refused to acknowledge his original identity. His parents committed suicide in the siege leaded by Wanyan Honglie; however, Yang Kang could not resist the temptation as a royal prince; he still showed loyalty to his foster father Wanyan Honglie.

楊康作為女真皇族長大，習慣於擁有權力和財富，當他的生父出現勸他做回宋國的平民時，楊康拒絕了認同自己本來的身份，儘管楊康的親生父母因為被完顏洪烈圍困一起自殺，他卻難抵做皇子的誘惑，仍然表示效忠養父完顏洪烈。

Yang Kang was sinister and merciless. He sneakily killed Ouyang Ke, replaced him as Ouyang Feng's only apprentice ,and framed Guo Jing as the murderer. He also assisted Ouyang Feng to kill five of the Seven Freaks in Jiangnan; then left Guo Jing to suspect Huang Yaoshi. When Guo Jing tried to persuade him to take the Song Empire's side, he stabbed Guo Jing with a dagger. Yang Kang met Mu Nianci (穆念慈) in a martial arts contest. Although they were fond of each other; Yang Kang's <u>treachery to his ethnicity and his indulgence to power made Mu Nianci give up their relationship.</u> He died bitterly from poisoning. During the last phase of his life, his abandonment by everyone made him realize his mistakes. Guo Jing buried him and Qui Chuji made a tombstone for his treacherous disciple.

楊康的個性陰險無情，他悄悄殺死歐陽克，代替歐陽克做了歐陽鋒唯一的弟子，並嫁禍給郭靖。他也協助歐陽鋒殺了江南七怪中的五人，還讓郭靖懷疑是黃藥師所為。當郭靖勸說楊康站在大宋一邊，他用匕首刺傷了郭靖。楊康在一場比武招親中遇見了穆念慈，他們雖然喜歡彼此，楊康對國族的背叛和醉心於權勢讓穆念慈放棄了他們的感情。楊康因中毒痛苦死去，在生命最後階段被所有人拋棄終於令楊康意識到自己的錯誤，郭靖埋葬了他，楊康的師傅丘處機為這個背叛的徒弟題寫了墓誌銘。

文法解析

 KEY 137

Yang Kang and Guo Jing were both named by Qui Chuji to memorize the national calamity of Song Empire.

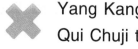

❌ Yang Kang and Guo Jing were both named by Qui Chuji to memorized the national calamity of Song Empire.

✦中譯✦ 楊康和郭靖都是由丘處機命名，以紀念國難。

✦解析✦ 不定詞為 To＋V 原型，to 後面不能接動詞原型外的其他時態。

 ### KEY 138

⭕ When his biological father showed up and persuaded him to turn back as a normal Song civilian; Yang Kang refused to acknowledge his original identity.

❌ When his biological father showed up and persuaded him turning back as a normal Song civilian; Yang Kang refused to acknowledge his original identity.

✦中譯✦ 當他的生父出現勸他做回宋國的平民時，楊康拒絕了認同自己本來的身份。

✦解析✦ Pursuade 是將不定詞作為受詞補語的動詞 S ＋ persuade＋ O ＋ to V。

 ### KEY 139

⭕ Yang Kang's treachery to his ethnicity and his indulgence to power made Mu Nianci give up their relationship.

Yang Kang's treachery to his ethnicity and his to indulgence to power made Mu Nianci give up their relationship.

✦中譯✦ 楊康對國族的背叛和醉心於權勢讓穆念慈放棄了他們的感情。

✦解析✦ 動名詞做名詞，此處表示狀態應當為動名詞。

 武俠人物 56 - Huang Yaoshi (黃藥師) MP3 *56*

Huang Yaoshi (黃藥師) was Huang Rong's father and the master of the Peach Blossom Island. He was nicknamed the Eastern Heretic (東邪) because he held an unorthodox value and was labeled as a maverick in martial arts world. Huang Yaoshi was a formidable kung fu master; he was among the Five Greats of the time. He lived a seclusive life on the island to avoid contacting with social norms. Huang Yaoshi had a compassionate nature, but he tried to cover it up. He deliberately spread out rumors, such as that he poisoned his servants to deaf; in fact, he trained physically challenged people to work for him in order to protect them from discrimination.

　桃花島島主黃藥師是黃蓉的父親，黃藥師非正統的價值觀和在武林中特立獨行的風格令他有「東邪」的綽號。黃藥師武功高強，是當世五大高手之一。他獨居在孤島上以避免接觸社會，黃藥師心地善良，但他

試圖掩蓋這一點。他故意放出謠言是自己毒聾了桃花島上的僕人，事實上是黃藥師訓練殘障人士為他工作，以避免他們在俗世受到歧視。

Huang Yaoshi had various hobbies and was skilled in many other areas apart from martial arts. Huang Rong was well protected and cultivated by the father. Huang Yaoshi was once betrayed by two of his apprentices who stole his precious Nine Yin Manual and fled away. Huang's wife tried to rewrite the manual for him from her memory and died from mental exhaustion soon after giving birth to Huang Rong. Consecutive misfortunes had further made Huang Yaoshi a wield heretic.

　　黃藥師興趣廣泛，武學之外精通很多領域，黃蓉就被父親保護和培養得很好。黃藥師曾被兩位徒弟背叛，偷了《九陰真經》逃走，黃藥師的妻子為幫他重新默寫出經書而耗盡心力，在黃蓉出生後不久就去世。接連的不幸令黃藥師個性更為古怪。

Huang Yaoshi used to set a competition to select an ideal son-in-law. Ouyang Ke and Guo Jing were the contestants, and both were helped by Ouyang Feng and Hong Qigong respectively. Although Guo Jing won the test, Huang Yaoshi considered him a dumb boy and forbad Huang Rong from marrying him. Eventually, it was not until at the summit of Huashan that Huang Yaoshi believed that the true love between Guo Jing and Huang Rong, and gave the couple all his bless.

黃藥師曾經設置比賽來甄選自己如意的女婿，參賽者是歐陽克和郭靖，他們二人又分別得到歐陽鋒和洪七公的協助，雖然郭靖贏得了比賽，黃藥師還是覺得郭靖太過愚笨而沒有應允他與黃蓉結婚，直到華山論劍時，黃藥師被郭靖和黃蓉間的真愛打動，送給他們滿滿的祝福。

 文法解析

 KEY 140

⭕ Huang Yaoshi had a compassionate nature but he tried to cover it up.

❌ Huang Yaoshi had a compassionate nature but he tried cover it up.

◆中譯◆ 黃藥師心地善良，但他試圖掩蓋這一點。

◆解析◆ **Try to do sth** 為不定詞固定搭配，**to** 不應該省略。

 KEY 141

⭕ He trained physically challenged people who work for him in order to protect them from discrimination.

❌ He trained physically challenged people who to work for him in order protecting them from discrimination.

◆中譯◆ 黃藥師訓練殘障人士為他工作，以避免他們在俗世受到歧視。

天龍八部

鹿鼎記

笑傲江湖

雪山飛狐

神鵰俠侶

射鵰英雄傳

連城訣碧血劍

書劍恩仇錄

✦解析✦ **In order to do** 是固定用法，意思是「為了……，以便 ……」，也可以用 **in order that**＋句子。**In order doing** 則 是錯誤用法。

武俠人物 57 - Ouyang Feng (歐陽鋒)

MP3
57

Ouyang Feng (歐陽鋒) the Western Venom (西毒) came from the White Camel Mountain (白駝山) in the west. Ouyang Feng was a master of toxicology; he carried his venomous snakes around and used them during the fight. His typical kung fu the powerful Toad Skill (蛤蟆功) and Divine Serpent Stick Skill (靈蛇杖法) made him one of the Five Greats, but Ouyang Feng aimed to be the best of all. He resorted to all means to seize the Nine Yin Manual which recorded supreme martial arts power.

"西毒" 歐陽鋒來自西方的白駝山，歐陽鋒是毒物專家，他隨身攜帶毒蛇並在打鬥中把它們當作武器。他強大的絕技蛤蟆功和靈蛇杖法令他也成為五大高手之一。不過歐陽鋒志在稱霸武林，他想方設法要取得載有至上武功的經書《九陰真經》。

Ouyang Feng met Guo Jing in the Peach Blossom Island; he found out that Guo Jing had memorized the Nine Yin Manual. After they left the island, Ouyang Feng saved Guo Jing to his ship; he forced Guo Jing to write a copy of the Manual. Under Hong Qigong's suggestion, Guo Jing wrote a version in a reverse manner, resulting in Ouyang Feng's practice based on wrong versions. Ouyang Feng tried to kill Guo Jing after he got the copy; they had a fight which made the ship sink. Guo Jing's life was saved since they all stranded on an island and needed to support each other to survive.

歐陽鋒在桃花島遇見了郭靖，就發現郭靖背下了整部《九陰真經》，他們離開桃花島後，歐陽鋒把郭靖救上了自己的船，他強迫郭靖為自己默寫一本真經，在洪七公的建議下，郭靖把書中口訣倒著寫，使得歐陽鋒後來依照錯誤的版本練習武功。歐陽鋒得到默寫版本後就試圖殺死郭靖，他們在船上打鬥導致船開始下沉，他們擱淺在一個小島上，需要互相幫助來生存，郭靖因此得以保命。

Ouyang Feng practiced the wrong nine Yin Manual obsessively; he had never suspected the genuineness of his copy. He kidnapped Huang Rong to explain the verse in the Manual and was further misled by her fictitious information. Indulging in wrong practice drove Ounyang Feng insane; but his kung fu was still improved significantly. During the contest on the Huashan summit, he became an invincible lunatic.

歐陽鋒瘋狂練習錯誤的《九陰真經》，從未疑心過經書的真實性，他綁架了黃蓉來解釋經書中的詞句，被黃蓉的胡亂解釋更加誤導，沈迷於錯誤的練習令歐陽鋒精神失常，但他的功夫仍然進步顯著。在華山論劍時，他成了一個不可戰勝的瘋子。

天龍八部

鹿鼎記

笑傲江湖

雪山飛狐

神鵰俠侶

射鵰英雄傳

連城訣 碧血劍

書劍恩仇錄

文法解析

 KEY 142

○ He forced Guo Jing to write a copy of the Manual.

✕ He forced Guo Jing writing a copy of the Manual.

✦中譯✦ 他強迫郭靖為自己默寫一本真經。

✦解析✦ Force 是將不定詞作為受詞補語的動詞，後面不能加動名詞。

 KEY 143

○ Indulging in wrong practice drove Ounyang Feng insane.

✕ To indulge in wrong practice drove Ounyang Feng insane.

✦中譯✦ 沈迷於錯誤的練習令歐陽鋒精神失常。

✦解析✦ 動名詞做主詞，表示一個持續的狀態。不可以換作不定詞。

 武俠人物 58 - Hong Qigong (洪七公) MP3 58

Hong Qigong (洪七公), the chief of the Beggars' Sect was known as the Northern Beggar (北丐). He was also among the Five Greats skilled with the Dragon Strike Palm and the Dog

Beating Stick Techniques. Hong Qigong came across as an optimistic beggar who wandered around care-freely; his chivalrous conduct earned him respect from the whole martial arts world. Hong Qigong was a super gastronome that was associated with his other nickname: the Nine Fingered Divine Beggar (九指神丐). He once failed to save another hero due to indulgence in fine cuisine; he severed one of his fingers to remind him not to make the same mistake.

　丐幫幫主洪七公綽號是「北丐」，也是五大高手之一。洪七公的絕技是降龍十八掌和打狗棒，洪七公看起來是個四處雲遊的樂天乞丐，行俠仗義使得他在整個武林威望很高。洪七公是超級美食家，這個習慣還和他的另一個綽號「九指神丐」有關，他曾經因為貪吃美食而錯過了拯救一位英雄，洪七公於是砍掉自己一隻手指以提醒自己不再犯同樣錯誤。

Hong Qigong met Guo Jing and Huang Rong by chance; he was actually attracted by the tasty smell of Huang Rong's cooking. Huang Rong prepared fine cuisine for him every day; in exchange, he imparted Guo Jing the Dragon Strike Palm and taught Huang Rong the Carefree Fist (逍遙遊). Hong Qigong formally accepted Guo Jing and Huang Rong as his apprentices after they cooperated to strike the ruffians.

　洪七公偶然間遇到了郭靖和黃蓉，他是被黃蓉煮飯的香氣吸引過去的，黃蓉每天為洪七公烹調美食，作為交換，他傳授郭靖降龍十八掌且

天龍八部　鹿鼎記　笑傲江湖　雪山飛狐　神鵰俠侶　射鵰英雄傳　碧血劍　書劍恩仇錄

教給黃蓉拳法逍遙遊。後來經歷了聯手除惡後，洪七公正式收郭靖和黃蓉為徒。

Hong Qigong assisted Guo Jing to win the contest on Peach Blossom Island; on their way back, he had a fight with Ouyang Feng. The Western Venom attacked him with a snake and Hong Qigong lost his inner energy by purging the poison out of body. Huang Rong rescued him and inherited the chief of the Beggars' Sect. His kung fu was restored after Guo Jing had a thorough understanding of the Nine Yin Manual and helped his recovery. Hong Qigong was finally died together with Ouyang Feng during a duel; they had both achieved the highest level of kong fu skills. They died with laughter and reconciliation.

洪七公幫助郭靖贏取了桃花島比武的勝利，在回程途中，他和歐陽鋒大戰起來，由於西毒用蛇攻擊，洪七公耗盡了內力清除體內蛇毒，黃蓉救了洪七公並繼承了他的丐幫幫主位置。郭靖徹底掌握《九陰真經》後也幫助洪七公恢復了內力，洪七公最終死於和歐陽鋒的決鬥，那時的兩人已分別到達了功夫的至高境界。他們死時大笑和解。

 文法解析

 KEY 144

 He once failed to save another hero due to indulgence in fine cuisine.

He once failed save another hero due to indulgence in fine cuisine.

✦中譯✦ 他曾經因為貪吃美食而錯過了拯救一位英雄。

✦解析✦ Fail to do 為固定搭配，去掉 to 則成為病句。

KEY 145

⭕ Hong Qigong assisted Guo Jing to win the contest on Peach Blossom Island.

❌ Hong Qigong assisted Guo Jing to winning the contest on Peach Blossom Island.

✦中譯✦ 洪七公幫助郭靖贏取了桃花島比武的勝利。

✦解析✦ Assist sb to do sth 是將不定詞做受詞，另一個習慣用法是 assist sb in doing sth。

 武俠人物 59 - Zhou Botong (周伯通) MP3 *59*

Zhou Botong (周伯通) was famous for his mischievous personality. He constantly sought for surprise and entertainment as if he was a child; therefore, he was nicknamed the Old Imp (老頑童). Unlike his senior Wang Chongyang (王重陽), a rigid swordsman as the founder of Quanzhen Sect (全真教), Zhou Botong disobeyed any rules. He roamed around to detect interesting stuffs; sometimes he initiated a fight just for fun.

天龍八部

鹿鼎記

笑傲江湖

雪山飛狐

神鵰俠侶

射鵰英雄傳

連城訣碧血劍

書劍恩仇錄

周伯通因個性淘氣廣為人知，他像孩童一樣不停找尋驚喜和玩樂，因而得到「老頑童」的暱稱。周伯通的師兄全真教創始人王重陽是個嚴肅的大俠，與之相反，周伯通不服從任何規矩，他只四處漫遊尋找趣事，有時為了樂趣找人打架。

Zhou Botong once inherited the Nine Yin Manual from Wang Chongyang. When he met the Huang Yaoshi couple, he allowed Huang's wife who had eidetic memory to read the latter half of the Manual. She recited it all after reading only one time and told Zhou Botong that the Manual he had was a normal song book that many people knew. Zhou teared the Manual in anger. Later, he realized he was fooled by the couple and went to the Peach Blossom Island for an explanation. By the time he reached the island, Huang Yaoshi had lost his copy stolen by his betrayed students, and his wife died after giving birth to Huang Rong. Huang Yoshi vented his anger to Zhou Botong and sealed off all exits from the island; Zhou Botong was forced to stay on the island for fifteen years.

周伯通曾從王重陽處繼承了《九陰真經》，他遇見黃藥師伉儷後，允許黃藥師過目不忘的妻子閱讀了後半部經。她只讀一遍就全數背誦下來，還騙周伯通說他的經書是眾人皆知的普通歌謠集，於是周伯通憤怒的撕毀了經書，後來他反應過來被騙，跑去桃花島講理，適逢黃藥師的徒弟偷走經書，妻子也在生下黃蓉後去世，黃藥師將憤怒發洩在周伯通身上，他封住桃花島所有出口，周伯通被迫在島上生活了十五年。

Zhou Botong became bored by himself, so he invented the techniques of ambidexterity to self-entertain. When Guo Jing came to the island, he made sworn brother with Zhou Botong and learnt the complete Nine Yin Manual. Zhou Botong also assisted Guo Jing in the contest with Ouyang Ke. He left the island, but the boat sank on the way. Zhou Botong managed to ride a shark back to the mainland.

周伯通一個人在島上無聊，於是創造了左右手互搏的技術自娛。郭靖上島後和周伯通結義，得到了完整的《九陰真經》，周伯通也幫助了郭靖勝過歐陽克。周伯通離開桃花島的船在中途沈沒，他騎著鯊魚返回了大陸。

 文法解析

 KEY 146

 He allowed Huang's wife who had eidetic memory to read the latter half of the Manual.

 He allowed Huang's wife who had eidetic memory reading the latter half of the Manual.

✦中譯✦ 他允許黃藥師過目不忘的妻子閱讀了後半部經書。

✦解析✦ Allow 是將不定詞作為受詞補語的動詞，慣用型為 S+allow+O+to V。

天龍八部

鹿鼎記

笑傲江湖

雪山飛狐

神鵰俠侶

射鵰英雄傳

連城訣碧血劍

書劍恩仇錄

KEY 147

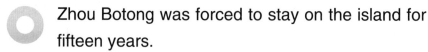

⭕ Zhou Botong was forced to stay on the island for fifteen years.

❌ Zhou Botong was forced stay on the island for fifteen years.

✦中譯✦ 周伯通被迫在島上生活了十五年。

✦解析✦ Force to do 迫使某人做某事，是不定詞慣用型。

武俠人物 60 - Duan Zhixing (段智興) MP3 60

Duan Zhixing (段智興) was also one of the Five Greats with the title of Southern Emperor (南帝). He used to be the king of the Dali Empire in the south and later became a Buddhist monk known as Reverend Yideng. Duan Zhixing's signature martial arts skill was the Yiyang Finger (一陽指) that inherited in the Dali Royal family; the skill concentrates inner energy into one finger tip and emits force towards enemies. As a Buddhist, Reverend Yideng always uses this technique to heal people from internal injury; since Yiyang Finger was useful in purging out venoms. The Southern Emperor saved Huang Rong's life after she was severely injured by Qui Qianren.

　　「南帝」段智興也是五大高手之一，他曾是南方的大理國王，後來出家成為了一燈大師。段智興的絕技是大理皇家家傳的一陽指，一陽指可以將內力集中在指尖上，對敵方施放力道。因為一陽指可以幫助清除

體內毒素，僧人一燈大師常用這種絕技幫人治療內傷，黃蓉被裘千仞打傷後就是被南帝所救。

When Duan Zhixing was still the emperor, his concubine Yinggu (瑛姑) had an affair with Zhou Botong and gave birth to a son. The infant boy lost his life from an deadly attack. Duan Zhixing's refusal to save the boy's life made Yinggu resentful; the emperor also felt ashamed for his remorseless behavior and became a monk. Duan Zhixing's four faithful subordinates followed him to provide him with continuous protection; they disguised themselves as a fisherman, a woodcutter, a farmer, and a scholar to stop suspicious people from contacting Reverend Yideng.

段智興還是皇帝時，他的妃子瑛姑曾和周伯通生下一個兒子，那個男嬰因為被重擊夭折，段智興拒絕救男嬰性命令瑛姑非常憤恨，他自己也愧於自己的殘忍行徑出家為僧，段智興的四個忠誠的下屬追隨他，繼續護衛他的安全，他們分別扮作漁、樵、耕和讀四種職人，阻擋可疑人士接近一燈大師。

She managed to meet Yideng, but encountered four obstacles set by four guards. She eventually received Yideng's treatment. Yideng used tremendous inner energy to heal Huang Rong and almost lost his life from energy deprivation. Guo Jing saved him from Yinggu's assassination. On the summit of Huashan, Reverend Yideng made the villain Qiu

天龍八部

鹿鼎記

笑傲江湖

雪山飛狐

神鵰俠侶

射鵰英雄傳

連城訣 碧血劍

書劍恩仇錄

Qianren to become his Buddhist apprentice.

　　黃蓉設法見一燈大師卻面臨四位護位設下的四道關卡。一燈大師為救黃蓉，幾乎差點耗盡所有內力而喪命，而郭靖保護了南帝免受瑛姑的行刺。在華山論劍時，一燈大師將大惡人裘千仞收做自己的弟子。

 文法解析

 KEY 148

⭕ Reverend Yideng always uses this technique to heal people from internal injury.

❌ Reverend Yideng always uses this technique heal people from internal injury.

✦中譯✦　一燈大師常用這種絕技幫人治療內傷。

✦解析✦　Use sth to do 是慣用法，ing 型常為 use sth for doing。

 KEY 149

⭕ Duan Zhixing's four faithful subordinates followed him to provide him with continuous protection.

❌ Duan Zhixing's four faithful subordinates followed him providing him with continuous protection.

✦中譯✦　段智興的四個忠誠的下屬追隨他，繼續護衛他的安全。

✦解析✦　To provide 為不定詞做副詞修飾整個句子，表示目的。

KEY 150

⭕ She managed to meet Yideng, but encountered four obstacles set by four guards

❌ She managed meeting Yideng, but encountered four obstacles set by four guards

◆中譯◆ 她見到了一燈大師並接受了他的治療。

◆解析◆ Manage 是將不定詞作為受詞的動詞，manage to do sth 是固定用法。

Glossary 字彙一覽表

ambidexterity *n.* 雙手靈巧的本領，懷二心	armour *n.vt.* 裝甲，盔甲；穿上盔甲
betroth *vt.* 把……許配給	biological *adj.* 生物的，生物學的
calamity *n.* 災難，不幸	consecutive *adj.* 連續不斷的，連貫的
contestant *n.* 選手	dagger *n.* 匕首
deliberately *adv.* 故意地，慎重地	devotionally *adv.* 信仰地，虔誠地
discrimination *n.* 區別，辨別，不公平待遇	divine *adj.* 神聖的，非凡的
eidetic *adj.* 異常清晰的，鮮明的	embark *vt.vi.* 使從事；從事

天龍八部

鹿鼎記

笑傲江湖

雪山飛狐

神鵰俠侶

射鵰英雄傳

碧血劍
連城訣

書劍恩仇錄

exhaustion *n.* 虛脫，耗盡，枯竭	extraordinary *adj.* 非凡的
freak *n.* 反常現象，怪異行為	gastronome *n.* 美食家
genuineness *n.* 真誠，真實	heretic *n.* 異教徒，持異端者
imp *n.* 惡魔，頑童	impart *vt.* 傳授，分給
inarticulate *adj.* 口齒不清的，不會說話的	incite *vt.* 煽動，激勵
insane *adj.* 瘋的，精神病的	miscellaneous *n.* 雜項
mischievous *adj.* 調皮的	photographic *adj.* 攝影術的，生動的
posthumous *adj.* 死後的，遺腹的	recite *vt.* 背誦
rectitude *n.* 正直	remorseless *adj.* 無悔意的
renounce *vt.* 聲明放棄	resentful *adj.* 怨恨的，憤恨的
reverently *adv.* 虔誠地	reverse *vt.adj.* 逆轉，顛倒；顛倒的
scent *n.* 香味	sealed *adj.* 密封的
severe *adj.* 嚴重的	siege *n.* 圍城，包圍
sophisticated *adj.* 閱歷豐富的	spike *n.* 穗，釘子，尖釘
strand *n.* 縷，股	strike *vi.vt.* 打擊，攻擊
stunning *adj.* 令人驚嘆的	subordinate *n.* 下屬
suspicious *adj.* 可疑的	tactician *n.* 戰術

temptation *n.* 誘惑	toad *n.* 蟾蜍
treachery *adj.* 背信棄義的	unorthodox *adj.* 非正統的
versatile *adj.* 多才多藝的	

筆記欄

天龍八部

鹿鼎記

笑傲江湖

雪山飛狐

神鵰俠侶

射鵰英雄傳

碧血劍
連城訣

書劍恩仇錄

❮ *Unit 7* ❯

對等連接詞

《連城訣與碧血劍》

 ## 文法主題介紹－對等連接詞

對等連接詞（**Coordinating & Correlative Conjunctions**）

1. 對等連接詞（**Coordinating conjunctions**）的功能

連接同詞性的單詞、片語與句子。

「單詞」＋ 對等連接詞（片語）＋「單詞」

「片語」＋ 對等連接詞（片語）＋「片語」

「句子」＋ 對等連接詞（片語）＋「片語」

2. 對等連接詞（片語）的種類

對等連接單詞

and, but, or, nor 可連接單詞、片語與句子

so, for, yet 可連接句子

對等連接片語

both A and B, not only A but also B, either A or B, neither A nor B, not A but B, A as well as B.

3. 轉承詞

「轉承詞」是帶出句子與句子或段落間語意的起承轉合，但本身是副詞，而非連接詞，因此要用轉承詞連接句子時，若不使用句點隔開，則前方必須加上分號，後面搭配逗點。

添加/補充類：

besides, in addition, moreover, furthermore, likewise, also, meanwhile.

對比/相反類：

but, instead, instead of, in spite of, however, nevertheless, on the other hand, on the contrary.

因果類：

because of, due to, therefore, consequently, as a result, thus.

讓步類：

although, though.

 ## 武俠人物 61 - Di Yun (狄雲) MP3
61

Jin Yong's novel A Deadly Secret (連城訣) revolves around the protagonist Di Yun (狄雲), a grass root martial artist who had experienced a series of plots and conspiracies. It is a story of the revenge through which the dark side of human nature revealed.

　　金庸的小說《連城訣》的主角是來自草根的俠客狄雲，他經歷了一連串陰謀和暗算。《連城訣》是一個復仇的故事，展現了人性黑暗的一面。

Di Yun was a straightforward country boy who grew up with his martial arts teacher Qi Zhangfa (戚長發). Qi Zhangfa's beautiful daughter Qi Fang (戚芳) was Di Yun's fellow apprentice as well as his girlfriend. Di Yun's simple life changed after his teacher took him to attend the birthday banquet of Wan Zhenshan (萬震山). Di Yun was imprisoned after the Wan family accused him of his larceny and sexual harassment.

狄雲原是率直的鄉下男孩，由師傅戚長發養大，戚長發的美麗女兒戚芳是狄雲的師妹兼女友，狄雲的單純生活在隨老師參加萬震山的壽宴後改變，狄雲被萬家指控盜竊和性騷擾而入獄。

Di Yun desperately needed his master's help, but Qi Zhangfa disappeared mysteriously. Di Yun was further framed by Wan Gui (萬圭), who managed to intensify Di Yun's sentence and won Qi Fang's affection. In the prison, Di Yun was bullied by another prisoner Ding Dian (丁典). Ding Dian suspected Di Yun was a spy inmate sent from his enemy. Until Di Yun attempted suicide after hearing Qi Fang married Wan Gui; Ding Dian saved Di Yun, and they became close friends.

狄雲極為需要他師傅的幫助，但戚長發神秘失蹤，狄雲更被萬圭陷害，萬圭令狄雲刑責加重，還搶走了戚芳的青睞。狄雲在獄中一直被另一個犯人丁典折磨，丁典懷疑同屋狄雲是仇家派來的間諜，直到狄雲聽到戚芳嫁給萬圭的消息憤而自殺，丁典救活了狄雲而兩人成為好友。

Di Yun heard the story of "Lian Cheng Swordplay Manual", a martial arts manual with secrets, of hidden treasure, form Ding Dian. It was given to Ding Dian from master Mei Nian Sheng (梅念笙). Many pugilists casted their greedy eyes on this "Lian Cheng Swordplay Manual" since it is an invaluable treasure. Because of the manual, Mei Nian Sheng lost his life from his

own disciples including Qi Zhangfa. Di Yun leant the powerful
skill in the Manuel from Ding Dian.

　　狄雲從丁典口中得知了《連城訣》，是武術大師梅念笙送給丁典的
劍譜兼寶藏秘密，許多練武人都覬覦《連城訣》，梅念笙就是因為這本
劍譜被包括戚長發在內的幾個徒弟所殺。狄雲向丁典學習了《連城訣》
中記載的武學技藝。

文法解析

KEY 151

○ Qi Zhangfa's beautiful daughter Qi Fang was Di
Yun's fellow apprentice as well as his girlfriend.

✕ Qi Zhangfa's beautiful daughter Qi Fang was Di
Yun's fellow apprentice as well as his girlfriend.

✦中譯✦ 戚長發的美麗女兒戚芳是狄雲的師妹兼女友。

✦解析✦ 對等連接詞前後要連接相同詞性的單字或片語或句子。

KEY 152

○ Di Yun desperately needed his master's help, but
Qi Zhangfa disappeared mysteriously.

✕ Di Yun desperately needed his master's help, but
Qi Zhangfa disappeared mysteriously.

✦中譯✦ 狄雲極為需要他師傅的幫助，但戚長發神秘失蹤。

天龍八部

鹿鼎記

笑傲江湖

雪山飛狐

神鵰俠侶

射鵰英雄傳

連城訣碧血劍

書劍恩仇錄

235

✦解析✦ 對等連接詞 but 前面需要加上逗號，原因是後面要接完整的
句子。一般不用 but 做句子的開頭。

 KEY 153

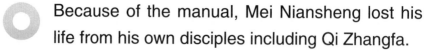
○ Because of the manual, Mei Niansheng lost his life from his own disciples including Qi Zhangfa.

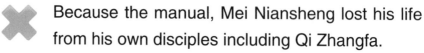
✕ Because the manual, Mei Niansheng lost his life from his own disciples including Qi Zhangfa.

✦中譯✦ 梅念笙就是因為這本劍譜被包括戚長發在內的幾個徒弟所
殺。

✦解析✦ Because of 後面加名詞；because 後面加子句。

武俠人物 62 - Di Yun (狄雲) MP3 62

Ding Dian was poisoned to death soon after his prison break with Di Yun. Di Yun went to Qi Fang's place and found out her little daughter had Di Yun's childhood nickname.

　　丁典在和狄雲越獄後不久就被人毒死，狄雲獨自找到了戚芳的住所，發現她的小女兒也用了自己兒時的暱稱。

Di Yun later encountered a cannibalistic monk Baoxiang (寶象). If Baoxiang had not drunk the poisoned mouse soup, he would have eaten Di Yun. Baoxiang's teacher the Blood Saber Grandmaster (血刀老祖) mistakenly considered Di Yun his grand-apperentice since Di Yun wore the robes from Baoxiang. Di Yun was protected by Grandmaster from the orthodox attackers.

狄雲後來遇見了吃人的和尚寶象，寶象喝了有毒的老鼠湯被毒死，否則狄雲也會被他吃掉，因為狄雲穿著寶象的僧袍，令寶象的師傅血刀老祖誤以為狄雲是他的徒孫，出手保護狄雲免遭江湖正派人士攻擊。

To escape form pursuers, Di Yun and the Grandmaster fled to the Snowy Valley but encountered an avalanche. After realizing Di Yun was not his peer, the Grandmaster tried to kill Di Yun but unintentionally helped Di Yun to complete his inner force practice. The following experience made Di Yun more disappointed with human nature. His fellow survivor Hua Tiegan (花鐵幹), a reputable swordsman, fed on the dead bodies of his companions to survive. After they left the Valley, Hua Tiegan blamed Di Yun for immorality.

為逃避追緝者，狄雲和血刀老祖逃進大雪山但他們遇到雪崩，血刀老祖發現狄雲不是自己同夥後本想殺死狄雲，卻意外幫助狄雲練成神功。後來的遭遇令狄雲對人性更加失望，圍困雪山的另一倖存者花鐵幹本是德高望重的俠客，他為求生不惜吃下同伴的遺體，離開雪山後，花鐵幹率先指控狄雲不道德。

Di Yun investigated the story behind his incarceration and found out his teacher Qi Zhangfa was a real villain.

天龍八部

鹿鼎記

笑傲江湖

雪山飛狐

神鵰俠侶

射鵰英雄傳

連城訣碧血劍

書劍恩仇錄

Furthermore, his beloved Qi Fang was killed by her husband Wan Gui. At last, the Lian Cheng Swordplay Manual was deciphered and all the antagonists went insane after touching the venom-smeared jewels. Di Yun returned to reclusive life back to the Snowy Valley with Qi Fang's daughter, where a kind-hearted girl was waiting for him.

　　狄雲調查了自己被關的真相，發現他的師傅戚長發是個大惡人，此外，他所愛的戚芳也被萬圭殺害。最後《連城訣》被解密，所有反派都因觸碰塗了毒藥的珍寶而發瘋，狄雲帶著戚芳的女兒回到雪山隱居，那裡有個善良的女生等著他。

 文法解析

 KEY 154

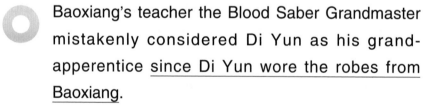
○ Baoxiang's teacher the Blood Saber Grandmaster mistakenly considered Di Yun as his grand-apperentice since Di Yun wore the robes from Baoxiang.

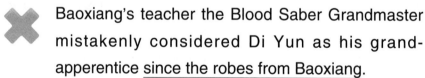
✗ Baoxiang's teacher the Blood Saber Grandmaster mistakenly considered Di Yun as his grand-apperentice since the robes from Baoxiang.

✦中譯✦ 因為狄雲穿著寶象的僧袍，令寶象的師傅血刀老祖誤以為狄雲是他的徒孫。

✦解析✦ Since 後接句子時是連接詞，表示原因；後接名詞時是介系

詞，表示自從某時間點。

 KEY 155

○ To escape form pursuers, Di Yun and the Grandmaster fled to the Snowy Valley but encountered an avalanche.

✕ To escape form pursuers, Di Yun and the Grandmaster fled to the Snowy Valley but encountered an avalanche.

✦中譯✦ 為逃避追緝者，狄雲和血刀老祖逃進大雪山但他們遇到雪崩。

✦解析✦ 對等連接詞 But 連接的兩端必須對等，**fled to the Snowy Valley** 和 **caught an avalanche** 是兩個片語。不可以用片語＋but＋單字。

 KEY 156

○ Di Yun investigated the story behind his incarceration and found out his teacher Qi Zhangfa was a real villain. Furthermore, his beloved Qi Fang was killed by her husband Wan Gui.

 ✕ Di Yun investigated the story behind his incarceration and found out his teacher Qi Zhangfa was a real villain. And furthermore, his beloved Qi Fang was killed by her husband Wan Gui.

天龍八部

鹿鼎記

笑傲江湖

雪山飛狐

神鵰俠侶

射鵰英雄傳

連城訣碧血劍

書劍恩仇錄

✦中譯✦　狄雲調查了自己被關的真相，發現他的師傅戚長發是個大惡
人。此外，他所愛的戚芳也被萬圭殺害。

✦解析✦　Furthermore 作為加強語氣的副詞可以放在句子開頭，也可
以放在句中。用 and furthermore 是放在句中的狀況。

武俠人物 63 - Ding Dian (丁典)

MP3
63

Ding Dian (丁典) was an upright swordsman. He used to save Mei Niansheng when his three disciples hunted down Mei. Touched by the noble character of Ding Dian, <u>Mei Niansheng imparted him with the Lian Cheng Swordplay Manual, a martial art classic with clues of finding tremendous treasure, and Divine Shinning Skills (神照功), a top-level inner energy skill.</u> After Qi Zhangfa and his fellow apprentices murdered Mei, Ding became the target of many martial artists since he was the only person who obtained the Lian Cheng Swordplay Manual.

　　丁典是個正派的大俠，他救下被三個徒弟追殺的梅念笙，由於被丁典的高尚品格打動，梅念笙傳授給他劍術和寶藏秘笈《連城訣》及內功經典《神照功》。梅念笙被戚長發等弟子殺害後，丁典成為了許多習武人的目標，因為他已是當世唯一知道《連城訣》秘密的人。

Ding Dian fell in love with a talented and versatile girl Ling Shuanghua (凌霜華) whose father was a cold-blooded magistrate Ling Tuisi (凌退思). Ling Tuisi poisoned Ding Dian to demand the secret of Lian Cheng Swordplay Manual. <u>In spite of terrible torture, Ding Dian refused his request.</u> Ling Shuanghua also disfigured herself to reject the marriage arranged by her father.

丁典愛上了聰慧的才女凌霜華，她的父親是冷血知府凌退思，凌退思毒倒丁典以求得到《連城訣》的秘密，丁典儘管遭受酷刑，仍然拒絕了他的要求，凌霜華也毀容明志，拒絕了父親安排婚姻。

After Di Yun was framed into the prison, he was locked in the same cell with Ding Dian. Ding suspected Di Yun was a spy sent by Ling Tuisi. Ding Dian beat Di Yun constantly until his suicidal attempt. They convinced each other as trustworthy friends and managed to break out from the prison together.

狄雲被陷害入獄後與丁典被關在同一間牢房，丁典懷疑狄雲是凌退思派來的奸細，不停的打他直到狄雲自殺未遂，他們變成互信的友人，後來一起越獄逃走。

When Ding Dian saw Ling Shuanghua again, she had already been buried alive by her father. <u>Ding Dian touched the coffin smeared with venom and was poisoned to death.</u> Di Yun practiced Ding Dian's last word; he buried Ding Dian together with Ling Shuanghua and planted lots of chrysanthemum around their grave.

天龍八部

鹿鼎記

笑傲江湖

雪山飛狐

神鵰俠侶

射鵰英雄傳

連城訣 碧血劍

書劍恩仇錄

丁典再一次見到凌霜華時，她已被自己父親活埋，丁典撫摸了塗抹了劇毒的棺木也被毒死，狄雲遵循丁典的遺言，把他和凌霜華葬在一起，並在他們的墓地種植了許多菊花。

 文法解析

 KEY 157

○ Mei Niansheng imparted him with <u>the Lian Cheng Swordplay Manual</u>, a martial art classic with clues of finding tremendous treasure, <u>and Divine Shinning Skills</u>, a top-level inner energy skill.

✗ Mei Niansheng imparted him with the <u>Lian Cheng Swordplay Manual</u>, a martial art classic with clues of finding tremendous treasure, <u>and a top-level inner energy</u> skill Divine Shinning Skills.

✦中譯✦ 梅念笙傳授給他劍術和寶藏秘笈《連城訣》及內功經典《神照功》。

✦解析✦ 對等連接詞 and 前後應當有平衡的結構，and 前接名詞＋同位語，後面應當也是名詞＋同位語。

 KEY 158

○ <u>In spite of</u> terrible torture, Ding Dian refused his request.

✗ <u>Although</u> terrible torture, Ding Dian refused his request.

天龍八部

鹿鼎記

笑傲江湖

雪山飛狐

神鵰俠侶

射鵰英雄傳

連城訣 碧血劍

書劍恩仇錄

✦中譯✦ 丁典儘管遭受酷刑，仍然拒絕了他的要求。

✦解析✦ In spite of 或 despite 是介係詞，後面接名詞；although 是連接詞，後面接子句。

 KEY 159

○ Ding Dian touched the coffin smeared with venom and was poisoned to death.

✕ Ding Dian touched the coffin smeared with venom and dead.

✦中譯✦ 丁典撫摸了塗抹了劇毒的棺木也被毒死。

✦解析✦ 對等連接詞 and 前面是一個句子，後面不能只是一個單字。

 武俠人物 64 - Maiden Shui Sheng (水笙) *MP3 64*

Maiden Shui Sheng (水笙) and her cousin Wang Xiaofeng (汪嘯風) had a joint name the Bell Sword Duet (鈴劍雙俠). They were famous for their chivalric and brave conduct.

少女水笙和她表哥汪嘯風合稱鈴劍雙俠，二人因勇敢仗義知名。

When Shui Sheng first met Di Yun, he was wearing Monk Baoxiang's robe. Shui Sheng and her cousin misunderstood Di Yun as an evil monk from the Blood Saber Sect (血刀門), so they beat him vigorously and broke his leg. The Blood Saber Grandmaster also believed Di Yun were his fellow apprentince;

he saved Di Yun from attack and captured Shui Sheng as a hostage while fleeing away with Di Yun.

水笙第一次遇見狄雲的時候，他正穿著寶象和尚的袈裟，水笙和表哥誤以為狄雲是血刀門的惡僧，所以痛毆狄雲並將他的腿打斷，血刀老祖也相信狄雲是自己門人，他保護狄雲逃走還綁架了水笙做人質。

Being trapped by an avalanche in the Snowy Valley, The Blood Saber Grandmaster killed three orthodox sects pursuers, including Shui Sheng's father. Luckily, Di Yun managed to eliminate the Grandmaster after he had possessed the ultimate inner energy power. The only survivor of the chasers Hua Tiegan intended to kill Di Yun and Shui Sheng since they witnessed the manslaughter he did to his sworn brother. Shui Sheng had no choice but to collaborate with Di Yun even though she still considered him a cannibalistic lubricious monk. As time went by, she found out Di Yun was a decent and honorable man. Di Yun protected Shui Sheng's safety under the threat of Grandmaster. He also hunted eagles in the Valley to provide her with food and guarded Shui Sheng's father's body from being eaten by Hua Tiegan.

後來因雪崩被困在雪山時，血刀老祖殺了三名追擊他們的江湖正派人士，其中包括水笙的父親。幸運的是，狄雲取得最強內功後除掉了血刀老祖，追來人之中的唯一倖存者花鐵幹打算殺掉狄雲和水笙，因為他

們目擊了他誤殺結義兄弟，這讓水笙不得不和狄雲合作，儘管她仍然誤以為狄雲是個吃人的淫僧，隨著時間流逝，水笙漸漸發現狄雲是個正派又值得尊敬的人，狄雲保護水笙不被血刀老祖傷害，他還獵殺雪山中的鷹做她的食物；又護衛了水笙父親的遺體不被花鐵幹吃掉。

Going out of the Snowy Valley, Di Yun left Shui Sheng for vengeance. He then became totally disillusioned with human nature and went back. To his surprise, Shui Sheng had been faithfully waiting for his return.

離開雪山後，狄雲離開水笙去復仇，之後他徹底失去對人性的信心回到了雪山，出乎狄雲意料，水笙已在那裡忠誠地等他歸來。

文法解析

KEY 160

 Shui Sheng and her cousin misunderstood Di Yun as a evil monk from the Blood Saber Sect, so they beat him vigorously and broke his leg.

 Because Shui Sheng and her cousin misunderstood Di Yun as a evil monk from the Blood Saber Sect, so they beat him vigorously and broke his leg.

✦ 中譯 ✦ 水笙和表哥誤以為狄雲是血刀門的惡僧，所以痛毆狄雲並將他的腿打斷。

✦解析✦ 表因果關係的連接詞 because 和 so 在一個句子中不能同時
出現。

 KEY 161

○ The only survivor of the chasers Hua Tiegan
intended to kill Di Yun and Shui Sheng since they
witnessed the manslaughter he did to his sworn
brother.

✗ The only survivor of the chasers Hua Tiegan
intended to kill Di Yun and Shui Sheng because
of they witnessed the manslaughter he did to his
sworn brother.

✦中譯✦ 追來人之中的唯一倖存者花鐵幹打算殺掉狄雲和水笙,因為
他們目擊了他誤殺結義兄弟。

✦解析✦ Since 在這裡是表示原因的連接詞,而 because of 是介係
詞後面不能加完整的句子。

 KEY 162

○ He also hunted eagles in the Valley to provide
her with food and guarded Shui Sheng's father's
body from being eaten by Hua Tiegan.

✗ He also hunted eagles in the Valley to provide
her with food moreover guarded Shui Sheng's
father's body from being eaten by Hua Tiegan.

◆中譯◆ 狄雲不僅保護水笙不被血刀老祖傷害；而且還獵殺雪山中的
鷹做她的食物；又護衛了她父親的遺體不被花鐵幹吃掉。

◆解析◆ Moreover 是轉承詞。連接句子時應前方加上分號，後面搭
配逗點如；moreover。

 ## 武俠人物 65 - Hua Tiegan (花鐵幹) *MP3* **65**

Hua Tiegan (花鐵幹) ranked number two in the four sworn
swordsmen 'Luohua Liushui' (落花流水). All of them were form
orthodox martial arts sects. Shui Dai (水岱) the youngest one
among the four was Shui Sheng's father. The four swordsmen
chased down the Blood Saber Grandmaster and Di Yun to the
Snowy Valley to rescue Shui Sheng, who had been kidnapped
as a hostage in a previous fight.

花鐵幹是「落花流水」結義兄弟中的二哥，四人都來自名門正派，
水笙的父親水岱是最小的一個，四個劍俠為了救被綁作人質的水笙，追
逐血刀老祖和狄雲進了雪山。

During the fight with the Blood Saber Grandmaster, the oldest
sworn brother was decapitated by the formidable Grandmaster,
Shui Dai's feet were chopped off, and Hua Tiegan unintentionally
killed the third sworn brother. The landslide failure of the 'Luo
Hua Liu Shui' collapsed Hua Tiegan's fighting will. As a result,
he kneeled down to Grandmaster begging for mercy. The critical
moment in Hua Tiegan's life had transformed him from a

respectable swordsman to a treacherous villian.

在和血刀老祖的打鬥中，年紀最大的義兄被強大的血刀老祖斬首，水岱被砍去雙足，花鐵幹失手殺死排行第三的兄弟，「落花流水」的徹底失敗瓦解了花鐵幹的鬥志，因而他雙膝下跪向血刀老祖求饒，花鐵幹的人生在這時突然轉變，他從一個倍受尊敬的大俠變成一個陰險的惡人。

After Di Yun killed the Blood Saber Grandmaster, Hua Tiegan did not feel repentant for his cowardly behavior; on the contrary, his negative quality bursted out. Since they were still trapped in the Valley, he tried to eat the flesh of the other three to survive. He also intended to kill Di Yun and Shui Sheng for fear that they might tarnish him by revealing what happened in the valley. In front of Shui Sheng's fiancé, he accused Shui Sheng of her infidelity and ruined her relationship. Hua Tiegan died together with other greedy pugilists from poisoning after touching the cursed jewels.

狄雲殺死血刀老祖後，花鐵幹並未懊悔於自己的懦弱行為，相反他的邪惡一面徹底爆發出來，由於被困在谷中，他為了活命要吃掉結義兄弟的遺體，又害怕狄雲和水笙將他在被困期間的所作所為說出去，打算殺掉他們，在水笙未婚夫面前，花鐵幹指控水笙行為不忠，毀了他們的婚約。最後花鐵幹和其他貪婪的拳師們都因摸到有毒珠寶而死。

文法解析

KEY 163

The oldest sworn brother was decapitated by the formidable Grandmaster, Shui Dai's feet were chopped off, and Hua Tiegan unintentionally killed the third sworn brother.

The oldest sworn brother was decapitated by the formidable Grandmaster, Shui Dai's feet were chopped off, furthermore Hua Tiegan unintentionally killed the third sworn brother.

✦中譯✦ 年紀最大的義兄被強大的血刀老祖斬首；水岱被砍去雙足；花鐵幹失手殺死排行第三的兄弟。

✦解析✦ 連接詞 And 換作副詞 furthermore 時，furthermore 應當前方加上分號，後面搭配逗點。

KEY 164

The landslide failure of the 'Luo Hua Liu Shui' collapsed Hua Tiegan's fighting will. As a result, he kneeled down to Grandmaster begging for mercy.

The landslide failure of the 'Luo Hua Liu Shui' collapsed Hua Tiegan's fighting will. As a result of he kneeled down to Grandmaster begging for mercy.

◆中譯◆ 「落花流水」的徹底失敗瓦解了花鐵幹的鬥志，因而他雙膝
下跪向血刀老祖求饒。

◆解析◆ As a result of 後面加單字，as a result 後面接子句。

KEY 165

◯ Hua Tiegan did not feel repentant for his cowardly behavior; on the contrary, his negative quality bursted out.

✗ Hua Tiegan did not feel repentant for his cowardly behavior; consequently, his negative quality bursted out.

◆中譯◆ 花鐵幹並未懊悔於自己的懦弱行為，相反他的邪惡一面徹底
爆發出來。

◆解析◆ 這裡的轉承詞連接的子句是轉折關係而非因果關係。

武俠人物 66 - Yuan Chengzhi (袁承志) MP3 66

The story of Sword Stained with Royal Blood (碧血劍)
happened in the late Ming Dynasty. Yuan Chengzhi (袁承志),
the orphaned son of the national hero Yuan Chonghuan (袁崇
煥) was the protagonist in this novel. Ming's emperor has been
misled by rumour spread by Manchus leader; as a
consequence, the patriotic general Yuan Chonghuan was
accused of treason and was sentenced to death. Yuan
Chengzhi became an orphan since he was very young. He

was tutored by kung fu master Mu Renqing (穆人清) in Huashan (華山) for ten years and turned into a young swordsman.

《碧血劍》故事發生在明代晚期，民族英雄袁崇煥的兒子袁承志是本書主角，明朝皇帝被滿州人製造的謠言誤導，結果愛國將軍袁崇煥以叛國罪被處決，袁承志很小就成為了孤兒，他在華山追隨武功高手穆人清習武十年，變成一位年輕的劍客。

Yuan Chengzhi learned martial arts skills form different sects. He left Huanshan to seek for adventures as well as opportunities to revenge for his father. In an unexpected occasion, Yuan Chengzhi discovered the precious Golden Snake Sword (金蛇劍) and its manual.

袁承志學到了各門派的武功，他離開華山闖蕩江湖，並尋找為父報仇的機會，一次偶然經歷讓袁承志發現了金蛇劍和劍譜。

The sword and the manual was once belonged to the mysterious swordsman Xia Xueyi (夏雪宜), nicknamed the Golden Snake Gentleman (金蛇郎君). The Sword's tip was split apart resembling the tongue of a snake; opponent's weapon could be captured during the fight. Yuan Chengzhi practiced the Golden Snake Sword in accordance with the manual and improved his skills to a legendary level.

天龍八部

鹿鼎記

笑傲江湖

雪山飛狐

神鵰俠侶

射鵰英雄傳

連城訣碧血劍

書劍恩仇錄

劍和劍譜過去的主人是神秘劍俠「金蛇郎君」夏雪宜。金蛇劍尖端分叉，如同蛇的舌頭，可以在打鬥中奪取對手的武器，袁承志依照劍譜練習金蛇劍，武功更加精湛超群。

The bond between Yuan Chengzhi and Xia Xueyi continued since Yuan later met a beautiful young maiden We Qingqing (溫青青), who was actually the daughter of the Golden Snake Gentleman. She was as rebellious as her father. Wen Qingqing followed Yuan Chengzhi around the land after she was expelled from her family.

袁承志繼續了與夏雪宜的緣分，他遇到了「金蛇郎君」的女兒溫青青，她像父親一樣叛逆，在被逐出家門後追隨袁承志行走江湖。

文法解析

KEY 166

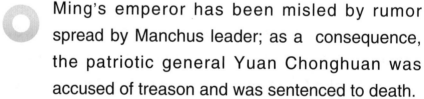

○ Ming's emperor has been misled by rumor spread by Manchus leader; as a consequence, the patriotic general Yuan Chonghuan was accused of treason and was sentenced to death.

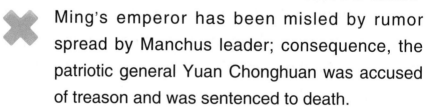

✗ Ming's emperor has been misled by rumor spread by Manchus leader; consequence, the patriotic general Yuan Chonghuan was accused of treason and was sentenced to death.

✦中譯✦ 明朝皇帝被滿州人製造的謠言誤導，結果愛國將軍袁崇煥以叛國罪被處決。

✦解析✦ Consequence 是名詞不能用作轉承詞，as a consequence 可以用副詞 consequently 取代。

 KEY 167

 He left Huanshan to seek for adventures as well as opportunities to revenge for his father.

 He left Huanshan to seek for adventures as well as find opportunities to revenge for his father.

✦中譯✦ 他離開華山闖蕩江湖，並尋找為父報仇的機會。

✦解析✦ 對等連接片語 as well as 前面是名詞 adventures，後面應當也是名詞。

 武俠人物 67 - Yuan Chengzhi (袁承志) *MP3* *67*

Yuan Chengzhi (袁承志) was one of the greatest martial artists at his time. He earned respect for his honesty and heroism. During his adventures, Yuan Chengzhi reconciled many disputes among different sects; he was; therefore, pledged as the leader of the martial arts world. He gathered several martial artists and carried out the same mission like his father: preventing and defending invasion from the Manchus. Yuan chengzhi used to infiltrated into the Manchu capital to assassinate Huangtaiji (皇太極), but his mission was failed.

　　袁承志是當時的絕世高手之一，他因誠摯待人和英雄氣質深得尊敬。在他的冒險途中，袁承志調解了數起門派糾紛，因而被擁戴為武林盟主，他聚集了幾個武林群豪繼續著父親的使命：防範和抵禦滿州人入侵。袁承志曾潛入滿州都城刺殺皇太極，但計畫並未成功。

To seek revenge for his father, Yuan Chengzhi joined Li Zicheng's (李自成) army fighting against the Ming Empire. The rebel army swept through the whole country; it broke through every defensive line of the government troops. Yuan Chengzhi assisted the rebels financially; a treasure he discovered in Nanjing was donated to Li's army. He also destroyed the cannons in the government troops that reduced casualties in the rebels.

　　為了給父親報仇，袁承志加入了李自成的軍隊反抗明朝，李自成的軍隊席捲全國，勢如破竹地擊潰官兵的防線，袁承志幫助叛軍籌資，他將自己在南京發現的寶藏全數捐給李的軍隊，還摧毀官軍的大砲，減少了叛軍傷亡。

After the rebel army occupied the capital city Beijing, Li Zicheng and his followers looted and slaughtered civilians, wrecking the capital devastated. Yuan Chengzhi was deeply disappointed with Li Zicheng and decided to leave the chaos. In Beijing, Yuan Chengzhi saved the Emperor Chongzhen from a coup even through he hated the Emperor's fatuous behavior which caused Yuan Chonghuan's death. Li Zicheng's rebel army was unable to function a normal country; Ming Empire was finally fallen to the Manchus. Yuan Chengzhi heard the news and left his motherland with his companions for good.

　　叛軍佔領北京後，李自成和他的部屬開始搶劫屠殺平民，將首都徹底摧毀，袁承志對李自成極為失望，決定從混亂中離開，儘管袁承志痛恨崇禎皇帝的昏庸行徑導致父親枉死，他還是在一次政變中協助了皇帝。李自成的叛軍無力運行一個正常國家，明帝國最終被陷落於滿人之手，得到消息的袁承志和他的夥伴永遠離開了中原。

 文法解析

 KEY 168

○　Yuan Chengzhi reconciled many disputes among different sects; he was; therefore, pledged as the leader of the martial arts world.

✗　Yuan Chengzhi reconciled many disputes among different sects; he was so pledged as the leader of the martial arts world.

 中譯 袁承志調解了數起門派糾紛，因而被擁戴為武林盟主。

 解析 So 和 therefore 都可以做副詞表示因此、所以，但 therefore 可以緊接在名詞或動詞後，so 則不可以。

KEY 169

⭕ He gathered several martial artists and carried out the same activities like his father: preventing and defending the invasion from the Manchus.

❌ He gathered several martial artists and carried out the same activities like his father: preventing and to defend the invasion from the Manchus.

✦中譯✦ 他聚集了武林群豪繼續著父親的使命：防範和抵禦滿人入侵。

✦解析✦ 對等連接詞 and 前後連接的詞類應當一致，Ving＋and＋to V 是錯誤用法。

 武俠人物 68 - Xia Xueyi (夏雪宜)
MP3
68

Xia Xueyi (夏雪宜) was also one of the main protagonists in the Sword Stained with Royal Blood. In the novel's time frame, Xia Xueyi was a long-dead character; therefore, all his stories were narrated by others.

夏雪宜也是《碧血劍》的主角之一，他在小説中是一個已經過世的人，因此所有他的故事都是由別人敘述的。

The Golden Snake Gentleman featured both heroic and rebellious qualities. He was a cold-blooded vile creature in Wen families' eyes; while his lover Wen Yi (溫儀) infatuated him for his tenderness and chivalry. There was a feud between Xia and Wen family. Xia Xueyi was the only survivor in his clan from a massacre carried out by Wen Yi's uncle, so he sworn to revenge. He practiced formidable martial arts skills and started to kill people from Wen family. Xia Xueyi slaughtered thirty persons brutally until he looted Wen Yi.

金蛇郎君揉合了英勇與反叛的個性，他在仇人溫家人眼中是個邪惡冷血的人，但愛他的溫儀卻深陷於他的溫柔和俠義。夏家和溫家有世仇，溫儀的叔叔屠殺了夏家，夏雪宜是家族唯一的倖存者，他發誓為死去的家人復仇，努力習得強大的武功後，開始屠殺溫家人，夏雪宜綁架溫儀之前已經殘忍屠殺了溫家三十個人。

<u>Instead of killing her, Xia Xueyi and Wen Yi were attracted to each other regardless of the vendettas behind them.</u> They fell in love and had a daughter Wen Qingqing. After Xia Xueyi was not as vigilant as he used to be, he was paralysed by the poison used by Wen's uncle; his kung fu then was totally destroyed as Wen's cut his tendons in his limbs.

夏雪宜沒有殺掉溫儀，相反地他們不顧世仇被彼此所吸引，他們生下了女兒溫青青。夏雪宜放鬆警惕後被溫儀的叔叔投毒變癱，他四肢筋絡被挑斷武功全廢。

Although he was saved by one of his admirers He Hong Yao (何紅藥); Xia Xueyi was further tortured by her since his love to

Wen Yi triggered her jealousy. He Hong Yao broke his legs, left Xia Xueyi dying in a cave. Yuan Chengzhi found out his body and sword years later. Yuan Chengzhi inherited his sword and skills and became his spiritual successor.

雖然夏雪宜被自己的愛慕者何紅藥所救，但他對溫儀的愛引發了何紅藥的嫉妒，何紅藥打斷了夏雪宜雙腿，令他在洞窟中淒慘死去。很多年後，他的遺體和金蛇劍被袁承志發現，袁承志繼承了他的劍和劍術，做了夏雪宜精神上的後繼者。

 文法解析

 KEY 170

○ The Golden Snake Gentleman featured both heroic and rebellious qualities.

✗ The Golden Snake Gentleman featured both heroic and rebellious quality.

✦中譯✦ 金蛇郎君揉合了英勇與反叛的個性。

✦解析✦ Both A and B 表示兩者都有，quality 應當用複數。

 KEY 171

○ Instead of killing her, Xia Xueyi and Wen Yi were attracted to each other regardless of the vendettas behind them.

Instead of killing her, Xia Xueyi and Wen Yi were attracted to each other regardless the vendettas behind them.

✦中譯✦ 夏雪宜沒有殺掉溫儀，相反他們不顧世仇被彼此所吸引。

✦解析✦ **Regardless** 是副詞，後面接子句；**regardless of** 是介系詞，後面接單字。

武俠人物 69 - He Tieshou (何鐵手)
MP3 **69**

He Tieshou (何鐵手) was the leader of the infamous Five Poisons Cult (五毒教). She wore an iron hook in place of her right hand, which implied her name, the iron hand. Chongzhen Emperor's uncle Prince Hui (惠王) once gathered a group of swordsmen, including He Tieshou, in a coup to overthrow the emperor and seize the throne. Yuan Chengzhi assisted the emperor to foil the plot even though he could not forgive for Chongzhen's decision that is responsible for his father's wrong execution. After defeating Prince Hui's allies, He Tieshou was renamed her He Tishou as Yuan's disciple (何惕守).

　　何鐵手是知名的五毒教教主，她名字來自於右手戴的鐵勾，崇禎皇帝的叔父惠王曾集結了包括何鐵手在內的一群劍客發動政變，希望能推翻崇禎帝奪取皇位，袁承志協助了皇帝平息了叛亂，儘管他無法原諒皇帝的決定令他父親枉死，挫敗惠王一夥後，袁承志收何鐵手為徒，並將她改名為何惕守。

He Tieshou and her aunt He Hongyao both experienced unrequited love. He Hongyao met Xia Xueyi when she was a young girl; she detoxicated him from a snakebite and had a crush on this handsome, mysterious, and dangerous man. To support Xia Xueyi's revenge, He Hongyao stole the Golden Snake Sword from the Five Poisons Cult and gave it to Xia Xueyi. However, the Golden Snake Gentleman took advantage of He Hongyao's affection; he abandoned her soon after receiving the sword. He Hongyao was disfigured by the Cult as punishment. He Hongyao carried her portrait drew by Xia Xueyi for her whole life until she met Wen Qingqing. All her hope shattered, turned into hatred, and even resulted in her miserable death.

何鐵手和她的姑姑何紅藥都經歷了單戀，何紅藥年輕時遇到了夏雪宜，她幫助被蛇咬傷的夏雪宜解毒，就愛上了這個英俊、神秘又有危險氣息的人，為了協助夏雪宜復仇，何紅藥從五毒教偷走了金蛇劍送給夏雪宜，但是金蛇郎君利用了何紅藥的感情，他得到金蛇劍後就離開了何紅藥，而何紅藥被五毒教懲罰慘遭毀容，何紅藥一生都帶著夏雪宜畫給她的肖像，直到遇見溫青青，她所有希望破滅變成仇恨，何紅藥也痛苦的死去。

Similarly, He Tieshou encountered Wen Qingqing who disguised herself as a boy and became obsessed with her. She sealed up her emotion after finding out Qingqing was a female. He Tieshou turned herself into goodness eventually.

　　何鐵手也一樣，她愛上了女扮男裝的溫青青，發現溫青青是女生後，何鐵手封存了自己的情感，何鐵手最終變成了善良的人。

 文法解析

 KEY 172

○ He Tieshou and her aunt He Hongyao both experienced unrequited love.

✗ He Tieshou and her aunt He Hongyao both experiences unrequited love.

✦中譯✦ 何鐵手和她的姑姑何紅藥都經歷了單戀。

✦解析✦ Both 帶兩個主詞，動詞應當為複數。

 KEY 173

○ However, the Golden Snake Gentleman took advantage of He Hongyao's amore; he abandoned her soon after receiving the sword.

✗ But, the Golden Snake Gentleman took advantage of He Hongyao's amore; he abandoned her soon after receiving the sword.

✦中譯✦ 但是金蛇郎君利用了何紅藥的感情，他得到金蛇劍後就離開了何紅藥。

✦解析✦ 連接詞 but 一般不放在句首引導一個句子。

天龍八部

鹿鼎記

笑傲江湖

雪山飛狐

神鵰俠侶

射鵰英雄傳

連城訣碧血劍

書劍恩仇錄

武俠人物 70 - Wen Qingqing (溫青青) MP3 70

Wen Qingqing (溫青青) was also named Xia Qingqing (夏青青). She was the heroine in the novel. Wen Qingqing's parents were the Golden Snake Gentleman Xia Xueyi and the lady in the Wen family, Wen Yi. Wen Qingqing learnt martial arts skills from seniors in the Wen Mansion (溫家堡); her unique skill the Thunder Swordsmanship (雷震劍法) had reached a superb level. She developed a romantic relationship with Yuan Chengzhi and accompanied him in his adventures. She played a significant role in assisting Yuan Chengzhi's mission of saving the nation.

溫青青又名夏青青，是小說的女主角。她是「金蛇郎君」夏雪宜和溫家小姐溫儀的女兒，溫青青的武術得到溫家堡長輩的指點，她所擅長的雷震劍法練到了極高的水平，溫青青愛上了袁承志，追隨他四處冒險，她成為袁承志的終生伴侶，輔佐他偉大的救國計畫。

Back home Wen Qingqing was a delicate beauty . When she traveled in the martial arts world by herself, she always wore man's attire and behaved chivalrously. She looked handsome and called herself a boyish name Wen Qing, thereby her figure as a boy attracted the maiden He Tieshou. She first met Yuan Chengzhi during a robbery. Wen Qingqing was a member of brigands which launched a plunder to Li Zicheng's military fund.

　　溫青青在家是個嬌媚的姑娘，而她獨自行走江湖時則常穿男裝且行俠仗義，她扮相英俊並且自稱男孩氣的名字溫青，因此她的男生形象吸引了少女何鐵手。而她第一次與袁承志見面是在一次打劫行動中，溫青青是搶劫闖王軍餉的山賊之一。

Wen Qingqing was a vivacious, frank, and well cooperated with other martial arts heroes. On the other hand, since Wen Qingqing grew up in an incomplete family; her sentimentality resulted in her lack of insecurity. After she acknowledged Yuan Chengzhi was her ideal lover, she chased after him closely and prohibited him from getting closer to other girls. She became his life-long partner and sailed to a distant land with Yuan Chengzhi until his hope of saving the nation vanished.

　　溫青青活潑直爽，與其他劍俠合作愉快，另一方面因為在不完整的家庭長大，溫青青有時會情感脆弱並缺乏安全感，她認定袁承志是自己的一生伴侶後，就緊盯袁承志令他不能和其他女子來往親密，她做了袁承志的終生伴侶，在袁承志服務國族的希望破滅之後，追隨他去了遠方。

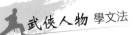

 文法解析

 KEY 174

〇 Back home Wen Qingqing was a delicate beauty, yet when she traveled in the martial arts world by herself, she always wore man's attire and behaved chivalrously.

✕ Back home Wen Qingqing was a delicate beauty, however when she traveled in the martial arts world by herself, she always wore man's attire and behaved chivalrously.

✦中譯✦ 溫青青在家是個嬌媚的姑娘,而她獨自行走江湖時則常穿男裝且行俠仗義。

✦解析✦ Yet 是連接詞可以前面為逗點,後面直接接完整的句子; however 是副詞起轉承作用,應當前面為分號,後面加逗點。

 KEY 175

〇 She looked handsome and called herself a boyish name Wen Qing, thereby her figure as a boy attracted the maiden He Tieshou.

✕ She looked handsome and called herself a boyish name Wen Qing, yet her figure as a boy attracted the maiden He Tieshou.

✦中譯✦ 她扮相英俊並且自稱男孩氣的名字溫青，由此她的男生形象
吸引了少女何鐵手。

✦解析✦ 前後兩個子句是因果而非轉折關係，應當用表示因果關係的
轉承詞／連接詞。

Glossary 字彙一覽表

cannibalistic *adj.* 吃人的	avalanche *n.* 雪崩
chrysanthemum *n.* 菊花	brigand *n.* 土匪，盜賊
cursed *adj.* 被詛咒的	casualty *n.* 受害者
decipher *vt.* 解碼	conspiracy *n.* 陰謀
devastated *adj.* 滿目瘡痍的	decapitate *vt.* 斬首，解僱
heroine *n.* 女英雄	detoxicate *vt.* 解毒
incarceration *n.* 監禁，禁閉	disillusion *n.vt.* 幻滅，覺醒；使幻滅，使覺醒
infiltrate *vt.* 滲透	fatuous *adj.* 昏庸的
insecurity *n.* 不安全，無把握	infidelity *adj.* 不忠的
magistrate *n.* 法官	inmate *n.* 犯人
repentant *adj.* 悔悟的，後悔的	larceny *n.* 盜竊罪
unrequited *adj.* 單相思的	plunder *n.vt.vi.* 掠奪
vigilance *n.* 警覺	reconcile *vt.* 調和，調停，使和解
sentimental *adj.* 感傷的	vigorously *adv.* 活潑地，精神旺盛地

天龍八部

鹿鼎記

笑傲江湖

雪山飛狐

神鵰俠侶

射鵰英雄傳

連城訣碧血劍

書劍恩仇錄

Unit 8

被動語態

《書劍恩仇錄》

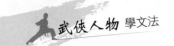

 ## 文法主題介紹－被動語態

被動語態 (Passive Voice)

被動語態的基本形式是 BE +Vpp；根據不同的時態，BE 動詞會有變化。

1. 基本句型：只要有受詞的句型，就可以改寫成被動語態。

S + V + O 變成被動語態：

✎ S + 授與 V + 間接受詞 + 直接受詞或 S + 授與 V +直接受詞 + 介系詞 + 間接受詞

✎ 授與動詞的間接受詞（IO）與直接受詞對調（DO）時，

(1) 接 to 的動詞：award, bring, give, grant, hand, lend, mail, offer, pass, read, send, show, tell , write

(2) 接 for 的動詞：buy, choose, make, order, save, get, leave, find

(3) 接 of 的動詞：ask, demand, beg, inquire, rob

S + V + O + O C 變成被動語態：

✎ 以名詞（片語）為受詞補語的動詞：

appoint, elect, name, label, choose, call, make, consider

✎ 以「(代)名詞 + to V」為受詞補語的動詞：

ask / advise / allow / convince / enable / encourage / expect / forbid / force / invite / need /order / persuade / permit / prompt / remind / require / tell / want / warn...

2. 特殊被動語態的動詞片語

有一類動詞常被定義為「使……」的意思，其用法常用被動語態來使用，以 BE+ Vpp +介系詞呈現，且都有自己獨特的搭配介系詞。

情緒動詞:

✒ 表正面情緒；

be satisfied with, be amused at, be pleased/delighted with, be interested in, be excited about, be fascinated/enchanted with, be touched by, be encouraged by

✒ 表負面情緒：

be worried about, be frightened /scared of, be tired of, be disappointed at sth with sb, be annoyed at sth with sb, be disgusted with sth, be frustrated with, be upset/depressed about sth with sb, be alarmed at/by

✒ 表尷尬、無聊、困惑：

be embarrassed about, be bored with, be confused/puzzled/perplexed about

✒ 表驚訝：

be stunned by, be surprised/shocked/amazed/astonished at

✒ 非情緒動詞：

此類動詞雖然是使用被動語態，但用法不一定全然是被動意味，多是已經為慣用語法。

✒ 與 with 搭配:

be associated with, be faced with, be equipped with,be crowded with, be covered with,be occupied with/in,

🖋 與 to 搭配:

be opposed to, be exposed to, be related to, be devoted/ dedicated to,be committed to, be known to, be based on

🖋 與其他介系詞搭配：

be concerned about, be convinced of, be composed of / be made up of, be engaged in, be absorbed in, be skilled in/at, be involved in

3. 其他

使役動詞 make 的被動態：be made to + V

以下的動詞（片語）不用被動式：

🗡 發生：take place, happen, occur

🗡 連綴動詞：look, feel, smell, taste, remain

🗡 其他：arrive, exist, miss, belong to, consist of, break out

4. 主被動搭配時態

🗡 簡單式被動語態：BE + Vpp

🗡 進行式被動語態：be + being + Vpp.

🗡 完成式被動語態：have + been + Vpp

 ## 武俠人物 71 - Overview (概要) *MP3* *71*

The Book and the Sword (書劍恩仇錄) is Jin Yong's first martial arts novel. The historical background of this story is in the Qing Dynasty during the reign of the Qianlong Emperor (乾隆皇帝). Heroes in the Red Flower Society (紅花會) are protagonists

in this novel. The Red Flower Society is an anti Manchu secret organisation, with an ultimate goal of overthrowing the Qing Dynasty and restoring the Han Chinese rule of the country. An auxiliary story line is the interaction between the Society and the Islamic Tribe in the Northwest.

《書劍恩仇錄》是金庸的第一部武俠小説。這部書的時代背景是清朝乾隆年間，紅花會群雄是小説的主角們。紅花會是反清秘密社團，終極目的是推翻清朝，恢復漢人統治。紅花會和西北回族部落的互動構成了小説的輔線。

The Red Flower Society was led by fifteen swordsmen and Chen Jialuo (陳家洛) was its primary leader. Wen Tailai (文泰), who ranked fourth of the fifteen, knew about the secret of the emperor's true identity. He was attacked and arrested by several kung fu masters sending from the Qianlong Emperor. The Society attempted to rescue Wen Tailai repeatedly and finally managed to save him out from custody.

紅花會由陳家洛為首的十五位劍俠領導。四當家文泰來因為知曉皇帝身世的秘密，而被乾隆派來的一群功夫高手攻擊並抓獲。紅花會的英雄們幾次三番地試圖解救文泰來，最終把他從獄中救了出來。

Wen Tailai told Chen Jialuo that the emperor was also a Han, ethnic and he was actually Chen's elder brother. Heroes from the Society took a chance to make the emperor their hostage.

天龍八部

鹿鼎記

笑傲江湖

雪山飛狐

神鵰俠侶

射鵰英雄傳

連城訣碧血劍

書劍恩仇錄

Chen Jialuo persuaded the emperor to acknowledge his Han identity. He wished the emperor used his political power to expel the Manchu occupiers out of central China. Qianlong reluctantly agreed and pledged to cooperate with the Red Flower Society. <u>However, the promise was breached as soon as the Emperor regained freedom.</u>

文泰來告訴陳家洛乾隆皇帝的秘密，皇帝不但是漢人，而且是陳家洛的哥哥。紅花會群雄曾將皇帝抓為人質，陳家洛勸說乾隆承認自己的漢人身分，並利用皇帝的影響力將佔據中原的滿族人驅除出去。乾隆不情願的接受了勸說，並發誓會與紅花會合作。然而這承諾在皇帝恢復自由之後就立刻被摒棄了。

文法解析

KEY 176

○ The Red Flower Society was led by fifteen swordsmen and Chen Jialuo was its primary leader.

✗ The Red Flower Society was lead by fifteen swordsmen and Chen Jialuo was its primary leader.

◆中譯◆ 紅花會由陳家洛為首的十五位劍俠領導。

◆解析◆ 被動語態的基本句型為 be＋過去分詞，lead 的過去分詞是 led。

KEY 177

 He was attacked and arrested by several kung fu masters sending from the Qianlong Emperor.

He was attacked and arrest by several kung fu masters sending from the Qianlong Emperor.

✦中譯✦ 他被乾隆派來的一群功夫高手攻擊並抓獲。

✦解析✦ Attack 和 arrest 都用作被動式，其中 was arrested 省略了 was。

 **KEY 178**

 However, the promise was breached as soon as the Emperor regained freedom.

 However, the promise breached as soon as the Emperor regained freedom.

✦中譯✦ 然而這承諾在皇帝恢復自由之後就立刻被摒棄了。

✦解析✦ Promise 無法發出動作做主詞，只能被違反，所以要用 be breached。

 武俠人物 72 - Overview (概要) *MP3* *72*

In the title 'the Book and the Sword', the 'Book' refers to the holy book Qur'an from the northwest Islamic tribe; and the 'Sword' used to be belonged to Huo Qingtong (霍青桐), the princess of the tribe. The sword was later given to Chen Jialuo as a gift.

書名《書劍恩仇錄》中，「書」指的是西北回族部落的神聖經典《可蘭經》，「劍」曾經屬於部落首領的女兒霍青桐，「劍」後來被作為禮物送給了陳家洛。

Chen Jialuo first encountered people from the Islamic tribe when they were chasing after the convoy which was escorting the holy book snatched from their tribe. Chen Jialuo helped the tribe to seize back the Qur'an, earning him respect from the Islamic group and Huo Qingtong falling in love with him.

陳家洛第一次遇到回部眾人時，他們正在追逐搶走部落聖書的鏢車。陳家洛協助回部奪回了珍貴的可蘭經，贏得了眾人的尊敬，霍青桐也傾心於他。

The tribe was later invaded by the Qing army. Chen Jialuo traveled northwest to help them again. He met Huo Qingtong's younger sister Kesili(喀絲麗) who had a nickname Princess Fragrance (香香公主). Chen Jialuo and Kesili had romantic feelings but soon she was looted by the Qing army as a tribute to the emperor.

部落後來受到了清軍入侵。陳家洛再次奔赴西北幫助他們。他遇到了霍青桐的妹妹香香公主喀絲麗，陳家洛和喀絲麗互生好感，但不久她被清軍擄走作為禮物獻給了乾隆。

The Qianlong Emperor was amazed by Kesili's beauty and tried to take her as his concubine. Kesili had already determined to be with Chen Jialuo; she resolutely refused Qianlong. At the same time, Chen Jialuo sneaked into the palace to remind the emperor the redemption of his promise. They made a deal again. The emperor pretended that he had the intention to fulfill the words given Chen Jialuo persuading Kesili to become Qianlong's concubine. Chen did so and Kesili was deeply hurt; she committed suicide to show her mind. The Red Flower Society attacked the palace in fury, but they finally realized the emperor would never keep his words. They returned to the west and Chen left a poem at Kasili's tomb.

乾隆皇帝被喀絲麗的美貌折服，想要納她為妃。喀絲麗心屬陳家洛而堅拒乾隆。適逢陳家洛潛入宮中提醒乾隆兌現反清承諾。他們達成另一個協議，皇帝假意應承一旦陳家洛成功勸說喀絲麗做皇妃，他就會實踐曾經的承諾。陳家洛這樣做了，這深深傷害了喀絲麗，她後來自殺表明心跡。憤怒的紅花會眾人攻入皇宮，終於發現皇帝絕不會信守諾言。眾人在回疆引退，陳家洛在喀絲麗墓前留下一首詩。

 文法解析

 KEY 179

 The sword <u>was</u> later <u>given</u> to Chen Jialuo as a gift.

The sword <u>was</u> later <u>gave</u> to Chen Jialuo as a gift.

✦中譯✦ 「劍」後來被作為禮物送給了陳家洛。

✦解析✦ 動詞 give 的過去分詞是 given，過去式是 gave，此處為被動語態 be+Vpp。

KEY 180

Chen Jialuo first encountered people from the tribe when they were chasing after the convoy which was escorting <u>the holy book snatched</u> from their tribe.

Chen Jialuo first encountered people from the tribe when they were chasing after the convoy which was escorting <u>the holy book snatching</u> from their tribe.

✦中譯✦ 陳家洛第一次遇到回部眾人時，他們正在追逐搶走部落聖書的鏢車。

✦解析✦ Snatch 用過去分詞，句子原本是 the holy book (that was) snatched from the tribe.為被動語態的省略形式。而現在分詞沒有被動的意義。

KEY 181

<u>She was looted</u> by the Qing army as a tribute to the emperor.

She was loot by the Qing army as a tribute to the emperor.

✦中譯✦ 她被清軍擄走作為禮物獻給了乾隆。

✦解析✦ Loot 的過去分詞是 looted，她被擄走是被動語態，動詞應當用過去分詞。

 武俠人物 73 - Chen Jialuo (陳家洛) MP3 *73*

Chen Jialuo (陳家洛) was the leader of the Red Flower Society. He was the second son in the Chen family and the Qianlong Emperor was his elder brother. Chen Jialuo grew up in Uygur region in northwest China. He was the apprentice of Yuan Shixiao (袁士霄), the Odd Swordsman of the Heavenly Lake (天池怪俠). Besides, his handsome looking, he also possessed gentle temperament with decent behaviors. Chen Jialuo was expert on kung fu as well as calligraphy and music. He was respected by all the members from the leader of the Red Flower Society regardless of his young age and insufficient experience.

陳家洛是紅花會的首領。他是陳家的次子，乾隆皇帝是他的哥哥。陳家洛在西北維族地方長大，師從天池怪俠袁士霄。他不僅相貌英俊，也個性溫和，舉止文雅。陳家洛精通武藝，書畫和音樂。儘管他年紀輕且資歷淺，陳家洛作為領袖受到紅花會全員的尊敬。

Chen Jialuo's noble and chivalrous conduct earned him high prestige in both the Society and other anti Manchu heroes. At first, Chen Jialuo was reluctant to take the lead; however, he obeyed his foster father Yu Wanting's (於萬亭) last will and accepted the obligation. <u>Chen Jialuo was assigned as the new leader of the Society in the hope that he could use the kinship with Qianlong Emperor to restore the Han Chinese reign.</u>

　　陳家洛氣質高貴和行俠仗義，他在紅花會內部和其他反清英雄中都有很高威望。一開始他並不情願成為紅花會的總舵主，但他遵循義父於萬亭的遺訓接受了這份責任。寄望於陳家洛可以利用與乾隆皇帝的親情，協助漢人恢復統治，他被選擇成為紅花會領頭人。

Members of the Red Flower Society adopted grant etiquette to welcome Chen Jialuo taking up his post. Chen Jialuo led the Society to rescue the sacred book for the Islamic tribe; he also endeavoured and managed to save out Wen Tailai from capture. Chen Jialuo once met up with the Qianlong Emperor who had disguised himself as a business man; a special kind of friendship was formed before knowing each others' identities.

　　紅花會的各位成員用最隆重的禮節迎接新幫主赴任。陳家洛引領眾人幫助回部奪回聖書，也努力救回了被捕的文泰來。陳家洛曾經遇到了扮作商人的乾隆皇帝，他們在互不知曉彼此身分前建立了特別的友情。

文法解析

KEY 182

○ He was respected by all the members from the Red Flower Society as their leader regardless of his young age and insufficient experience.

✗ He was respected from all the members from the Red Flower Society as their leader regardless of his young age and insufficient experience.

◆中譯◆ 儘管他年紀輕且資歷淺，陳家洛作為領袖受到紅花會全員的尊敬。

◆解析◆ Respect 後接 by 時，respect 做動詞；後接 from 時 respect 為名詞，慣用搭配是 win/earn respect from sb。

KEY 183

○ Chen Jialuo was assigned as the new leader of the Society in the hope that he could use the kinship with the Qianlong Emperor to restore the Han Chinese reign.

✗ Chen Jialuo was assigned to the new leader of the Society in the hope that he could use the kinship with the Qianlong Emperor to restore the Han Chinese reign.

天龍八部

鹿鼎記

笑傲江湖

雪山飛狐

神鵰俠侶

射鵰英雄傳

碧血劍 連城訣

書劍恩仇錄

✦中譯✦ 寄望於陳家洛可以利用與乾隆皇帝的親情，協助漢人恢復統治，他被選擇成為紅花會領頭人。

✦解析✦ 此處 assign 後面的介係詞應當是 as。

KEY 184

◯ They built up special friendship before the secret bond between them <u>was revealed</u>.

✗ They built up special friendship before the secret bond between them <u>revealed</u>.

✦中譯✦ 他們在互不知曉彼此身分前建立了特別的友情。

✦解析✦ The secret bond 是句子中的受詞，不能自我披露，應為被動語態 was revealed。

 ## 武俠人物 74 - Chen Jialuo (陳家洛) MP3 *74*

Chen Jialuo (陳家洛) was born of noble origins, behaving elegantly. He is an idealist that is willing to make a sacrifice for the nation. Whenever he captures Zhang Zhazhong, a person who served for the government and cruelly quelled the anti Manchu heroes. Chen Jialuo's tender heart has led to a great loss for the Red Flower Society.

　　陳家洛出身高貴而舉止優雅，他是個為了國族犧牲個人幸福的理想主義者。陳家洛因為心軟，每次抓到張昭重都將他釋放，導致紅花會遭受更大的損失。張昭重為朝廷服務，殘忍的鎮壓反清英雄。

Chen Jialuo's major mission was making alliance with the emperor to revive the Han Chinese Dynasty. He was too naive to trust in Qianlong's verbal commitment. He also over estimated the friendship between him and the emperor would make a significant influence to the nation. Qianlong was much more pragmatic compared with Chen's simplicity. The emperor's promises were made under threat; he could easily abandon the agreements when situations turned advantage on him. Chen was even persuaded to treat his love with political ideals. He made the deal and indirectly caused Kesili's death.

　　陳家洛德主要任務是和皇帝結盟，恢復漢族統治。他太過單純，輕信皇帝的口頭承諾；他也高估了自己和皇帝的私人情感對整個民族的影響力。相較簡單的陳家洛，乾隆皇帝更加務實。皇帝的承諾是在被威脅的情況下做出的，一旦狀況好轉他就會輕易撕毀協定。陳家洛甚至被勸説用他的真愛換取政治理想，陳家洛的決定間接導致喀絲麗死亡。

Chen's bookishness and indecisiveness also led him missed his true love. He first met Huo Qingtong and astonished by her beauty with heroic spirit. Qingtong acknowledged her admiration to Chen Jialuo by giving him a short sword. While he saw Huo Qingtong talked intimately with boyish looking Li Yuanzhi (李沅芷); he misinterpreted Li as Huo's boyfriend without asking her for clarification and gave up the relationship. Soon his emotion to Qingtong was transferred to her younger sister Kesili; he picked snow lotus for her and

天龍八部

鹿鼎記

笑傲江湖

雪山飛狐

神鵰俠侶

射鵰英雄傳

連城訣 碧血劍

書劍恩仇錄

saved her little deer. After Kesili fell in love with Chen, she had to become Qianlong's concubine under Chen Jialuo's request. Chen Jialuo failed in many aspects of his life.

陳家洛德書生氣和優柔寡斷也使得他感情失敗。他先遇到霍青桐，為她的美麗和英氣折服；霍青桐也送劍給陳家洛表明她對陳的仰慕。當陳家洛看到霍青桐和著男裝的李沅芷親密交談，他未加求證就誤認李沅芷是霍青桐男友，自動放棄了這段感情。後來他對霍青桐的感情被轉移到她的妹妹喀絲麗身上，為喀絲麗摘雪蓮、救小鹿。當喀絲麗也情陷於他，卻不得不聽從陳家洛的勸說做了乾隆的妃子。陳家洛在很多方面是一個失敗的人。

 文法解析

 KEY 185

⭕ The emperor's <u>promises were made</u> under threat; he could easily abandon the agreements when situations turned advantage on him.

❌ The emperor's <u>promises made</u> under threat; he could easily abandon the agreements when situations turned advantage on him.

✦中譯✦ 皇帝的承諾是在被威脅的情況下做出的，一旦狀況好轉他就會輕易撕毀協定。

✦解析✦ 主詞＋be＋Vpp，被動語態中不可缺少 be 動詞。

KEY 186

 Chen was even <u>persuaded to</u> treat his love with political ideals.

 Chen was even <u>persuaded</u> treat his love with political ideals.

✦中譯✦ 陳家洛甚至被勸説用他的真愛換取政治理想。

✦解析✦ 此處是特殊被動語態的動詞片語,以 be＋Vpp＋介係詞呈現。

 KEY 187

 Soon <u>his emotion</u> to Qingtong <u>was transferred</u> to her younger sister Kesili.

 Soon <u>his emotion</u> to Qingtong <u>transferred</u> to her younger sister Kesili.

✦中譯✦ 後來他對霍青桐的感情被轉移到她的妹妹喀絲麗身上。

✦解析✦ 感情作為受詞是被轉移而非主動轉移,因而為 be transferrd。

 武俠人物 75 - Huo Qingtong (霍青桐)

MP3
75

Huo Qingtong (霍青桐) was the daughter of Mu Zhuolun (木卓倫), the leader of a Muslim tribe's living near the Mount Heaven. She was a legendary princess with formidable martial arts skills and military talent. <u>Huo Qingtong was highly</u>

respected as the army general in her tribe. Her insightfulness also made her a reliable adviser for other people; her father sought her advice on most matters. Huo Qingtong was graceful and beautiful. Her typical attire were yellow shirts with green feathers. People called her the Worrier in Yellow.

霍青桐是天山回部首領木卓倫的女兒，是一位武藝高強且具有軍事才能的傳奇女子。霍青桐作為回疆軍隊的統領深受尊敬。霍青桐洞察力過人，常為其他人提供意見，她的父親也會在決策前尋求她的建議。霍青桐優雅美麗，時常穿著的「翠羽黃衫」成了她的綽號。

Huo Qingtong was the apprentice of the Twin Eagles of the Mount Heaven (天山雙鷹); she had mastered both the sword and the whip. Huo Qingtong met Chen Jialuo when she led her people chasing after an convoy escorting the precious Qur'an which has been stolen from her tribe. The stealing was plotted by the Qing government, aiming to manipulate the desert tribes. This made the islam people natural ally with the Red Flower Society. The two groups retrieved the book under joint effort. Meanwhile, the relationship between Huo Qingtong and Chen Jialuo became flourished.

霍青桐是天山雙鷹的弟子，擅長的武器是劍和鞭。在引領回部眾人追討搶走可蘭經的車隊時，霍青桐結識了陳家洛。盜取行動被清政府所策劃，為的是操控大漠中的部落。因此回疆民眾和紅花會自然而然地結成反清同盟，兩組人馬合作奪回了可蘭經，陳家洛和霍青桐的感情也漸

漸升溫。

With her intelligence and military tactician, Huo Qingtong successfully directed her people and succeeded in preventing the Qing Imperial army in the battle at the Black Water River from invading. Unfortunately, her sister Kesili was involuntarily involved in the relationship between her and Chen Jialuo. Huo Qingtong decided to step back from this triangle and wished the best for Chen Jialuo and Kesili. She devoted all her effort for the sake of the tribe and suppressed her personal feelings.

霍青桐憑藉智慧和軍事謀略成功指揮她的人馬在黑水河戰勝入侵的清軍。可惜的是她妹妹喀絲麗無意中也捲入與陳家洛的戀情。霍青桐從感情的糾葛中退出，祝禱他們兩人幸福。她將自己的心力集中於保衛部落上，抑制了自己的情感。

文法解析

KEY 188

 Huo Qingtong was highly respected as the army general in her tribe.

 Huo Qingtong was highly respected to the army general in her tribe.

✦中譯✦ 霍青桐作為回疆軍隊的統領深受尊敬。

✦解析✦ 依慣用語搭配要用 as。

KEY 189

⭕ Huo Qingtong met Chen Jialuo when she led her people chasing after an convoy escorting the precious Qur'an <u>which has been stolen from</u> her tribe.

❌ Huo Qingtong met Chen Jialuo when she led her people chasing after an convoy escorting the precious Qur'an <u>which has stolen from</u> her tribe.

✦中譯✦ 在引領回部眾人追討搶走可蘭經的車隊時,霍青桐結識了陳家洛。

✦解析✦ 完成式被動語態的型態是 has/have been＋Vpp。

KEY 190

⭕ <u>The stealing was plotted by</u> the Qing government, aiming to manipulate the desert tribes.

❌ <u>The stealing was plot by</u> the Qing government, aiming to manipulate the desert tribes.

✦中譯✦ 盜取行動被清政府所策劃,為的是操控大漠中的部落。

✦解析✦ 被動語態中動詞應當為過去分詞,plot 變成 plotted。

武俠人物 76 - Wen Tailai (文泰來)

Wen Tailai (文泰來) is the fourth leader of the Red Flower Society. He is nicknamed the Thunderbolt Hand (奔雷手) because Wen Tailai practices powerful kung fu that shocks his rivals like encountering the thunderbolt. Wen Tailai's martial arts style is the combination of quick punches with powerful whoops; the movements turn quicker as the fighting progresses. He is one of the best marital arts masters in the Society and he keeps perseverance and integrity all his life.

文泰來是紅花會的四當家，綽號奔雷手。文泰來的功夫可以使對手感到雷電般的威力。他的武功特點是快拳結合猛喝，纏鬥越久身法越快。文泰來是紅花會中的頂尖好手，他一生正直且不屈不撓。

At the start of the novel, Wen Tailai was seriously injured in an ambush. His wife Luo Bing (洛冰) had to fight four pugilists to protect him. Although Wen Tailai later hid in a cellar; more forces were sent by the emperor and managed to capture him. His fellows in the Red Flower Society made repeatable attempts to rescue him before eventually succeeding.

在小說的開始部分，文泰來被圍攻身受重傷。他的妻子洛冰隻身戰四人。雖然文泰來後來藏身在地窖中，他還是被皇帝派來的更多人捉了去。紅花會的兄弟反覆嘗試救出他，最終獲得了成功。

天龍八部
鹿鼎記
笑傲江湖
雪山飛狐
神鵰俠侶
射鵰英雄傳
連城訣
碧血劍
書劍恩仇錄

Wen Tailai used to accompany the previous leader of the Society to investigate the true identity of the Qianlong Emperor; therefore he knew Qianlong was actually from a Han Chinese family. Fearing that Wen Tailai might reveal the secret, the emperor did everything he could to silence him. During the interrogation, even under the threat and bribery made by Qianlong, Wen Tailai strategically remained unshakable. He told the emperor that the secret will be revealed if he is killed. The wisdom helped him from being killed.

文泰來曾經陪同紅花會的前任總舵主調查乾隆皇帝的身分，因而他知曉皇帝其實是漢人後代。皇帝也竭盡所能令文泰來封口。文泰來在審訊中巧妙的躲過乾隆的威逼利誘，他告訴乾隆如果自己被殺一定會使皇帝身世的秘密被世人所知，他藉此保全了性命。

Everyone in the Society risked his life to save Wen Tailai. Wen Tailai's noble personality was reflected through the precious brotherhood in the Society and Luo Bing's persistence in rescuing him.

紅花會的每個人都為了救文泰來不惜自我犧牲。文泰來的高尚品格被紅花會珍貴的結義之情和洛冰的不離不棄反襯出來。

文法解析

 KEY 191

○ Although Wen Tailai later hided in a cellar; <u>more forces were sent by</u> the emperor and managed to capture him.

✗ Although Wen Tailai later hided in a cellar; <u>more forces sent by</u> the emperor and managed to capture him.

✦中譯✦ 雖然文泰來後來藏身在地窖中，他還是被皇帝派來的更多人捉了去。

✦解析✦ 去掉 was 後，more forces sent by the emperor 成為了片語，使句子沒有動詞。

 KEY 192

○ Wen Tailai's <u>noble personality was reflected through</u> the precious brotherhood in the Society and Luo Bing's persistence in rescuing him.

✗ Wen Tailai's <u>noble personality was reflected</u> the precious brotherhood in the Society and Luo Bing's persistence in rescuing him.

✦中譯✦ 文泰來的高尚品格被紅花會珍貴的結義之情和洛冰的不離不棄反襯出來。

✦解析✦ 此處是 be＋Vpp＋介系詞的固定用法。介系詞不可以省略。

武俠人物 77 - Yu Yutong (余魚同)

Yu Yutong (余魚同) ranked the fourteenth leader in the Red Flower Society. He was good at playing flute, earning him a nickname like the Golden Flute Scholar (金笛秀才). Yu Yutong had a bookish temperament and always picked up other's grammatical errors. He called himself a small potato sarcastically while in fact he was quite arrogant. Sometimes Yu Yutong also showed out his conceit to cover the inferiority complex.

余魚同是紅花會的十四當家。因為擅長吹笛子而得到金笛秀才的暱稱。余魚同書卷氣重,時常咬文嚼字。他諷刺地謙稱自己是紅花會中的小角色但實際卻內心清高,有時他也表現的很自負來掩飾自卑情結。

Yu Yutong had an irrational crush on Wen Tailai's wife Luo Bing. To suppress his affection to her, Yu Yutong conducted self-destruction behaviors such as cutting his arms with knife. When Wen Tailai was captured, Yu Yutong tried to support Luo Bing in her vulnerable time; but it turned out to be the confession of his love to her. Luo Bing rejected Yu Yutong, blaming him that it is immoral. Engulfed by guilt and shame, he asked Luo Bing to kill him but the request was refused as well.

余魚同不理智地愛著文泰來的妻子洛冰。他不斷用刀劃傷自己的手

臂以壓制情感。文泰來被捕後，余魚同試著在洛冰脆弱時候支持她，卻變成他向她示愛。他被洛冰拒絕並責罵為不道德。余魚同愧悔交加，求洛冰殺死他，這個要求也被拒絕了。

During the mission of saving Wen Tailai, Yu Yutong almost lost his life. To stop the bomb from being exploded, he was almost disfigured. Yu Yutong was aware that Li Yuanzhi had romantic feelings on him although he treated her coldly. Li Yuanzhi chased after Yu Yutong persistently even though he was not handsome anymore. For fear of hurting Li Yuanzhi even more, Yu became a monk. Eventually, under the persuasion of Luo Bing, Yu Yutong returned to the secular life and accepted Li Yuanzhi's love.

　　在拯救文泰來的行動中，余魚同幾乎喪命。他為了阻止炸彈爆破而容貌被毀。雖然被他冷淡對待，余魚同知道李沅芷情繫於他。而李沅芷並沒有因為余魚同毀容就放棄對他的追求。余魚同後來為避免傷害李沅芷出家為僧，他最後被洛冰勸服，回歸了世俗生活並接受了李沅芷。

 文法解析

 KEY 193

 To stop the bomb from being exploded, he was almost disfigured.

 To stop the bomb from being exploded, he almost disfigured.

天龍八部

鹿鼎記

笑傲江湖

雪山飛狐

神鵰俠侶

射鵰英雄傳

連城訣碧血劍

書劍恩仇錄

✦中譯✦ 他為了阻止炸彈爆破而容貌近毀。

✦解析✦ 在此句中需用被動式，故為 Ddisfigured.

武俠人物 78 - Kesili (喀絲麗) MP3 *78*

Kesili (喀絲麗) was also the Muslim leader Mu Zhuolun's daughter. Her elder sister was the heroic Huo Qingtong. In the novel, Kesili was described as an innocent pure little princess. She diffused a fascinating fragrance that gave her a nickname the Fragrance Princess. Kesili used to walk into the barrack of the Qing troop to deliver a letter; all the soldiers were fascinated with her beauty, some even dropped their weapons.

喀絲麗也是回部首領木卓倫的女兒，她的姊姊是女俠霍青桐。在小說中，喀絲麗被描繪成一個天真的小公主。她身體散發出清香因而被叫做香香公主。喀絲麗曾走入清軍兵營送信，所有士兵都被她的美麗所震驚，有人甚至為她放下了武器。

Before met Chen Jialuo, Kesili lived a simple life as if she was a fairy tale princess. She drank dews on leafs and ate flowers as food. She not only fed wounded little deer, but also pitied hungry wolves. Kesili could talk with animals while her knowledge of the complicated human natures was almost limited. She was well protected and had very limited connection to real life.

在遇到陳家洛之前，喀絲麗過著如童話中的公主般的單純生活。她飲用葉子上的露水，把鮮花當作食物，她為受傷的小鹿餵奶，也同情受傷的狼群。喀絲麗可以和動物對話，但是她對複雜人世的認知幾乎空白。因為她被呵護得很好，與現實生活甚少連結。

Kesili's pureness seemed unreal. She never took precautions against strangers. she was fascinated by Chen Jialuo's pickup of the snow lotus for her and his act of animal-saving. His kindness behaviors captivated Kesili. Chen became her super hero and Kesili dominated Chen Jialuo's mind as a perfect princess who needed his protection.

喀絲麗的純潔看似不切實際。她從不防範陌生人。陳家洛幫助她摘花和救助動物的善良行動令她著迷，成了她的超級英雄。喀絲麗也成了陳家洛要保護的公主。

Kesili was captured by the Qing army during the invasion of her tribe. Qianlong was astonished by Kesili's fairy temperament as well but she refused to be his concubine. Knowing the relationship between Chen Jialuo and Kasili, the Emperor promised Chen to overthrow the Qing Dynasty if he could persuade Kesili to become the Fragrant Concubine. She followed Chen's persuasion but soon committed suicide to warn him that the Emperor would never keep his promise.

清軍入侵回部並擄走了喀絲麗。乾隆皇帝也被她童話般的氣質迷

天龍八部

鹿鼎記

笑傲江湖

雪山飛狐

神鵰俠侶

射鵰英雄傳

連城訣碧血劍

書劍恩仇錄

倒，但喀絲麗拒絕成為乾隆的皇妃。乾隆得知陳家洛和喀絲麗的關係後，以推翻滿清作為條件請求陳家洛勸説喀絲麗做他的香妃。喀絲麗聽從了陳家洛的勸説，但她不久後就用自殺提醒陳家洛皇帝並不會信守諾言。

 文法解析

 KEY 194

○ Kesili was described as an innocent pure little princess.

✗ Kesili was described an innocent pure little princess.

✦中譯✦ 喀絲麗被描繪成一個天真的小公主。

✦解析✦ Be describe as 為固定用法，不可以省略介系詞。

 KEY 195

○ All the soldiers were fascinated with her beauty, some of them even dropped their weapons.

✗ All the soldiers were fascinated by her beauty, some of them even dropped their weapons.

✦中譯✦ 所有士兵都被她的美麗所震驚，有人甚至為她放下了武器。

✦解析✦ Be fascinated with 為表正面情緒的被動語態特殊片語，介系詞 with 與 fascinated 是固定搭配。

武俠人物 79- **Zhang Zhaozhong** (張召重) *MP3*
79

天龍八部

鹿鼎記

笑傲江湖

雪山飛狐

神鵰俠侶

射鵰英雄傳

碧血劍 連城訣

書劍恩仇錄

Zhang Zhaozhong (張召重) was the most ruthless antagonist in the Book and the Sword. He was a disciple from the Wudang Sect (武當派). Together with two senior apprentices Ma Zhen (馬真) and Lu Feiqing (陸菲青), Zhang Zhaozhong was the most talented and diligent Wudang disciple. His kung fu was also the best of the three.

　　張召重是《書劍恩仇錄》中最邪惡的大反派。他曾是武當弟子，馬真和陸菲青的師弟。在武當三弟子中，張召重是最有天份和習武最勤勉的，因而武功最高。

Zhang was ambitious to seize wealth and fame, which made him abandon the life of a martial arts practitioner and served the government. He was a bureaucrat who was merely concerned about money. Motivated by potential promotions, he worked extremely hard. The Qianlong Emperor always treated his objectors cruelly; Zhang was the emperor's most faithful henchman and executed the lord's orders mercilessly. Most anti-government personnels are feared by his ruthless conduct so that Zhang earned the nickname Fiery Hand Judge (火手判官).

　　張召重醉心名利，因而放棄了單純武者身分為政府效力。他是個眼中只有錢的官僚，為了加官晉爵戮力工作。乾隆皇帝向來殘酷對待自己

的反對者，張召重作為皇帝的忠誠僕從毫不留情地執行皇帝的命令。不少反清志士畏懼他出手兇殘，令張召重得到火手判官的綽號。

Zhang Zhaozhong's nature was twisted by his voracity. He taunted Zhou Zhongying's (周仲英) youngest son to unintentionally reveal where Wen Tailai was hidden. Ma Zhen took Zhang back to Wudang in the hope that he might repent and correct his behaviors; however, Zhang murdered Ma and rejoined the Qing forces. Chen Jialuo captured him several times; every time after Chen releasing him, Zhang would bring back more damage to the Red Flower Society. When Zhang Zhaozhong was dragged into a sand castle surrounded by wolves, Lu Feiqing jumped in to give him a hand but he was almost killed by Zhang. This venomous villain was eventually killed by ravenous wolves.

張召重的本性被貪慾所扭曲。他曾奚落周仲英的幼子，誘導他吐露出文泰來的藏身之所；師兄馬真將張召重帶回武當山，期望他能悔過自新，但張召重殺死了馬真回歸清營；陳家洛曾幾次擒住張召重，每次釋放他都為紅花會帶來更大的損失；當張召重被拖入沙城受到群狼包圍，向他伸出援手的陸菲青還幾乎被他害死。這個狼毒的惡人最後死於惡狼之口。

文法解析

 KEY 196

 Zhang Zhaozhong's <u>nature was twisted by</u> his voracity.

 Zhang Zhaozhong's <u>nature was twist by</u> his voracity.

✦中譯✦ 張召重的本性被貪慾所扭曲。

✦解析✦ Twist 應當為過去分詞而非原形。

 KEY 197

When Zhang Zhaozhong <u>was dragged into</u> a sand castle surrounded by wolves, Lu Feiqing jumped in to give him a hand but <u>he was almost killed by</u> Zhang.

 When Zhang Zhaozhong <u>dragged into</u> a sand castle surrounded by wolves, Lu Feiqing jumped in to give him a hand but <u>he almost killed by</u> Zhang.

✦中譯✦ 當張召重被拖入沙城受到群狼包圍，向他伸出援手的陸菲青還幾乎被他害死。

✦解析✦ 被動語態不可缺少 be 動詞。

天龍八部

鹿鼎記

笑傲江湖

雪山飛狐

神鵰俠侶

射鵰英雄傳

碧血劍連城訣

書劍恩仇錄

武俠人物 80 - Zhou Qi (周綺)、Xu Tianhong (徐天宏)

MP3
80

Zhou Qi (周綺) and Xu Tianhong (徐天宏) were a pair of soul mate in the novel. Xu Tianhong ranked the seventh leader in the Red Flower Society and nicknamed Martial Zhuge (武諸葛). People compared his intelligence with Zhuge Kongming (諸葛孔明) who was extremely ingenious and resourceful. Xu Tianhong experienced a horrific tragedy when he was young; all his family members were slaughtered at a sudden. He grew up independently and developed extraordinary wisdom. After joined the Red Flower Society, he developed strategies for all their missions.

　　周綺和徐天宏是小說中的一對靈魂伴侶。徐天宏是天地會的七當家，綽號武諸葛。他的聰明被拿來和足智多謀的諸葛孔明相提並論。徐天宏年輕時曾遭遇悲慘的經歷，他的家人突然全部被殺。獨立生活給了他超常的智慧。加入紅花會後，徐天宏是幫會所有行動的謀士。

Zhou Qi was a light-hearted girl. Her father was a reputable martial artist Zhou Zhongying, the master of the Fearless Manor (鐵膽莊). Zhou Qi was simple minded with a sense of righteousness. She was called the Pretty Li Kui (俏李逵), indicating her bluntness and carelessness. She was originally at odds with Xu Tianhong since their characteristics were quite opposite to each other. They bickered a lot and burst into quarrels easily during conversation. Each time Xu brought out a strategy, Zhou Qi would hold the opposite position as she thought Xu Tianhong was overly crafty and untrustworthy. Xu Tianhong on the other hand, despised her simplicity as foolish.

周綺是一個樂天女孩，她的父親是知名俠客鐵膽莊莊主周仲英。周綺有些單線條，時常伸張正義。她被稱做俏李逵，以示她的直率和粗心。周綺和徐天宏本來互看不順眼，因為彼此的個性南轅北轍時常爭吵不斷。每次徐天宏想到新的策略，周綺都會反對，因為她覺得徐天宏太過狡猾不可信賴。另一方面，徐天宏則把周綺的單純視作愚蠢。

Through the hardships they underwent together, Zhou Qi (周綺) and Xu Tianhong (徐天宏) have developed good feelings towards each other. They were together through thick and thin and forged a close tie. Xu Tianhong realized how precious Zhou Qi's kindness was; and Zhou Qi leant to live with wisdom. They eventually got married and Xu Tianhong became Zhou Zhongying's successor.

他們兩人由於共同經歷危機，漸漸對彼此產生好感。甘苦與共令他們的關係親密起來。徐天宏理解了周綺善良的可貴，周綺則學著變得更智慧。周徐二人後來結婚，徐天宏成了周仲英的繼承人。

天龍八部

鹿鼎記

笑傲江湖

雪山飛狐

神鵰俠侶

射鵰英雄傳

連城訣 碧血劍

書劍恩仇錄

文法解析

KEY 198

○ All his family members <u>were slaughtered</u> at a sudden.

✕ All his family members <u>were slaughter</u> at a sudden.

✦中譯✦ 他的家人突然全部被殺。

✦解析✦ 被動語態中 **be** 動詞後要接過去分詞。

 ### KEY 199

○ <u>She was called</u> the Pretty Li Kui, indicating her bluntness and carelessness.

✕ <u>She called</u> the Pretty Li Kui, indicating her bluntness and carelessness.

✦中譯✦ 她被稱做俏李逵,以示她的直率和粗心。

✦解析✦ 如果去掉 **be** 動詞,句意變為她打電話給俏李逵,不符合整個段落的意思。

Glossary 字彙一覽表

auxiliary *adj.n.* 輔助的，輔助者	barrack *n.* 軍營
bicker *vi.n.* 鬥嘴，閃動	bluntness *n.* 遲鈍，率直
calligraphy *n.* 書法	bureaucrat *n.* 官僚
conceit *adj.* 高傲的	captivated *v.* 迷住，迷惑
convoy *vt.n.* 護航，護航隊	concubine *n.* 妃子
diffuse *vt.* 擴散	ferocious *adj.* 兇猛的
etiquette *n.* 禮儀	ingenious *adj.* 巧妙的
forge *vt.* 偽造	interrogation *n.* 詢問，審問
henchman *n.* 黨羽	objector *n.* 反對者
inferiority *n.* 自卑感	perseverance *n.* 毅力
insightfulness *n.* 洞察力	pragmatic *adj.* 務實的
irrational *adj.* 不合理的	prestige *n.* 威望，聲望
lighthearted *adj.* 輕鬆的	redemption *n.* 贖回，拯救
practitioner *n.* 醫生，執業者	resolutely *adv.* 堅決地
ravenous *adj.* 餓壞了的，貪婪的	tactician *n.* 戰術
reign *n.* 統治	tenderhearted *adj.* 心軟的
sarcastically *adv.* 諷刺地	voracity *n.* 貪婪
taunt *vt.* 嘲諷	thunderbolt *n.* 霹靂

天龍八部

鹿鼎記

笑傲江湖

雪山飛狐

神鵰俠侶

射鵰英雄傳

連城訣 碧血劍

書劍恩仇錄

Learn Smart！051

跟著武俠人物修練英文文法 （MP3） 創新式學習+『199』個關鍵英文文法考點

作　　者　武董
封面構成　高鍾琪
內頁構成　菩薩蠻數位文化有限公司

發 行 人　周瑞德
執行總監　齊心瑀
企劃編輯　陳韋佑
執行編輯　陳欣慧
校　　對　饒美君、魏于婷
印　　製　大亞彩色印刷製版股份有限公司
初　　版　2015 年 10 月
定　　價　新台幣 369 元
出　　版　倍斯特出版事業有限公司
電　　話　(02) 2351-2007
傳　　真　(02) 2351-0887
地　　址　100 台北市中正區福州街 1 號 10 樓之 2
E - m a i l　best.books.service@gmail.com

港澳地區總經銷　泛華發行代理有限公司
地　　　　址　香港新界將軍澳工業邨駿昌街 7 號 2 樓
電　　　　話　(852) 2798-2323
傳　　　　真　(852) 2796-5471

國家圖書館出版品預行編目(CIP)資料

跟著武俠人物修練英文文法：創新式學習+「199」
個關鍵英文文法考點 / 武董著. -- 初版. --
臺北市：倍斯特，2015.10 面；　公分. --
(Learn smart! ; 51)
ISBN 978-986-91915-4-8(平裝附光碟片)
1.英語 2.語法
805.16　　　　　　　　　　104018781